DEFENDING THE HUNTED

J.R. RASK

Johansen Justice
2168 7th Ave. N. #14
Anoka, MN 55303
www.JohansenJustice.com

ISBN-10: 0990704831
ISBN-13: 978-0-9907048-3-6

CHAPTER 1

A roar blasted Susan Combes from her slumber. She felt the bed beside her. Cold. Tugging the blackout shade up to midway, she darted to the window, pushing sandy hair from her face to peer out.

A red sports car gleamed on the driveway behind the third stall.

Susan spun to shove on her blue slippers, and scurried to the bathroom for her robe, as worn as the terrycloth on her feet. She scampered down the stairs, ordering lights on in the living room and then the dining area as she made her way to the kitchen.

The garage door slammed and a broad-shouldered man with glossy black hair entered the kitchen, stopping as he saw Susan. "Tracking my movements again? Waiting up for me? You won't give me space to breathe. I'm working hard and you're waiting at the window for me to come home to find out my whereabouts. Paranoid, as well as pathetic." Jerald Combes closed the space between them and looked down at Susan in disgust.

She forced herself to stop wringing her hands, and raised them as she approached her husband. "No, Jerry, no. I wasn't going to ask anything about it. I wanted to see if you'd like a nightcap before bed. I know you work hard. I figured it might help you relax. That's all."

"Pour me a scotch. At least you're good for something."

"Yes, right away." She whirled, knocking over the vodka bottle, catching it before it could topple toward the floor.

"Clumsy as ever. At least you caught it before it shattered this time. I swear, woman, you break more glass than anyone I've ever met. Should I serve myself, Spilly? Can you not even manage to pour your husband a drink?"

"No, Jerry, I can do it. See, here it is. Two fingers, just how you like it."

"I want three."

"I can fix it."

"No. You'll probably knock over the scotch next. Your little job doesn't even pay enough to replace it. Out of my way, woman."

She skirted to the side. "Yes, Jerry. Would you like anything else? I can make you a sandwich."

"A sandwich." His top lip curled. "Is that the best you can do?"

"No, no. I could make you anything. What are you hungry for?"

"Nothing. Get off my back. Let me enjoy my drink."

She tried a different tact. "That's a wonderful car, Jerry. Are things going well at work?"

"I'm being well compensated for my skills. About fucking time."

"You got a raise?"

"Stop interrogating me. Always with the twenty questions. Here, I got you this." He pulled a long box out of his briefcase and tossed it onto the granite countertop.

Susan picked it up and studied it. "A carving knife? But Jerry, I have perfectly good knives—"

Jerry slammed his highball glass against the slate counter, and coiled his muscles.

She dropped the box.

"I fucking give you a gift, and still you're not happy. You're ungrateful." He pounded a fist.

She jumped at the bang.

"I fucking go out of my way to get it for you and all you do is nag me." He grabbed the box. "Forget it. It's going back. I won't bother to get you anything again. What's the fucking point?"

Susan reached out, ready to retract her hand if he made a sudden move. When he stayed still, she placed it on his arm. "I'm sorry, Jerry. It's wonderful." She took the package back. "Says here it's industrial—"

"Bitch, bitch, bitch. I can never do anything right

around here. I don't even know why I bother to come home at all. Just shut up." He knocked her hand aside as he raised his, and slapped her. Hard. "Now you've done it. You kept nagging until I lost my temper."

Susan spun and scattered her terrycloth slippers in her race to the front door. She opened it and bolted out, hurrying over the lawn, letting her robe and her mussed tawny hair stream behind her. Her staccato panting punctuated the soft serenade of a summer night.

Reaching the neighbor's front door, she pounded. "Deanna, open up! Help! He's coming after me!"

Jerald meandered across the yard, hands in his pockets.

"Hurry! He's almost here! Let me in!"

A curvy brunette opened the door. Her pink silk robe hung open, revealing a matching negligee. Dismissing Susan, Deanna Connelly looked over and called, "Hello, Jer. Out for a stroll?"

"Deanna, he hit me. He's in one of his tempers. I don't know what he's going to do. We have to get inside."

Deanna ignored her and smiled at Jerry.

"Why won't you help me?"

Jerry started whistling. "It's a beautiful night for a stroll in the moonlight. I'd rather be at home having my scotch, but it seems Susan has other plans for me. I'm so sorry to disturb you, Dede." He climbed the steps and eyed Deanna. "You look beautiful. Susan could take some pointers from you. Look at her ratty robe."

Deanna gave Susan a cool look, and shifted her attention back to Jerry.

"Don't mind her," he said. "She's been hysterical since I got home. She doesn't understand I have to work late. I raised my voice to get it through her thick skull and she ran off." He cupped the back of Susan's neck with his left hand and squeezed.

Susan cried out. "Stop, Jerry. You're hurting me."

He kept his focus on Deanna. "You know how fragile she is, of constitution and mind. Not like you, Dede. I gave her a new kitchen knife, and that wasn't good enough. I thought that'd cheer her up. I've tried everything. She's been so depressed. She didn't even make it to work on Monday. Couldn't find her car remote. I'm at my wit's end with her. But my unstable wife is my responsibility."

Deanna nodded in understanding and gave him a bracing smile.

Susan tried to shake her head, but Jerry tightened his grip. She stared at Deanna, wide-eyed.

Jerry looked at Susan like she was a petulant child. "Let's calm you down and get you to bed. Don't worry. I'm going to help you through this difficult time. I'll take care of you."

Deanna let her robe slip down her shoulder. She feathered her fingertips over her cleavage. "You're so sweet, Jer." She eyed Susan with disdain. "You're so lucky to have him. You don't even appreciate what you have right in front of you." Her eyes warmed as she smiled up at Jerald. "My husband could learn a thing or two from you."

"I'm sure he could."

"Good luck with her, Jer."

"Good night, Dede." Jerald winked at Deanna as she closed the door. He tightened his hold on his wife and threw her down the steps. "Pull another stunt like that and it'll be your last. Get up, you stupid bitch, and go clean up your mess. There's glass and scotch everywhere because of you."

"Yes, Jerry. Right away." She made it to her feet, and hurried across the lawn, keeping her back to Jerald as she swiped away tears—gasoline for his fury. *I should've stayed in bed and minded my own business*, she thought. *The sun's not even up, and I've gone and wrecked my own birthday.*

A curtain of ebony hair concealed her face. Skinny arms wrapped around angular knees. She huddled, wedged into a corner.

Ruby Miller stood in the closet doorway, watching small shoulders shake with sobs.

The girl raised her head. Her toffee skin had an unnatural pallor. Amber eyes glimmered. She whispered, "Help me, Ruby. Help me."

Ruby tried to move forward but her legs were locked. She opened her mouth to speak words to comfort, to soothe. No sound emerged. Mute and motionless, she watched red rivulets stream down cheeks still plump from childhood.

Still, Ruby did nothing. Said nothing.

"See what he's done. See!" The girl released her hands and straightened her legs. A knife protruded from her chest, fastening a red Valentine's heart. Be mine, it read. Blood spewed from the wound, turning the girl's white shirt crimson, creeping along the closet floor toward Ruby's conservative raspberry heels. Amber eyes lost focus. The girl toppled back—looking up yet unseeing. Her hair formed a dark halo around her head.

Ruby awoke with a start, face pressed against a file, right arm numb from its awkward position and her head's weight. She shook sensation back into her arm, raked a hand through her choppy hair, and looked down at her wrinkled brown suit pants and cream shirt. Once again, she hadn't made it into sleep gear.

Her portable supercomputer sounded again—the distinguished ringtone she'd selected for her law firm. Though she judged it early morning by the stillness, the black, she never resented the intrusion. Someone needed her help. And she welcomed the call that had tugged her into the present. Shaking her head, she tried to push back her past, an easier feat when she must stand for her clients.

"PSC engage, audio only, record on. Law office, Ruby Miller speaking."

A woman's voice slurred over the connection. "I need to speak to a lawyer." Image blurred by the jail's cheap video connection, the caller struggled to finger-comb her auburn hair while cuffed.

"You're doing so. Call me Ruby. And you are?"

"Veronica Epstein. Vera. Thank God you answered. You're my first choice. The officer gave me a tablet with all these lawyers. You looked the friendliest. And you were the only woman pictured. So I called you."

"Yes, I'm certainly both. We're not allowed much time, Vera."

"I'm rambling. Sorry. It's just that I've never been here before. I have no clue what to do. The officer was telling me about bail this and impound that. You must know this isn't like me at all. I'm head of the PTA for God's sake."

"Vera, you called the right place. How many kids do you have?"

"Two."

"How old are they?"

"Sixteen and fourteen. I dread them finding out that their mother's locked up like a common criminal."

"Let's focus on the present, Vera. Their father?"

"My husband, Carter. We celebrated our twentieth anniversary last weekend. And did we ever throw a festive affair. I'd understand them hauling me off if I'd tried to drive that night. But tonight—"

"Congratulations on your twentieth, Vera. So the officer brought you in for driving under the influence?"

"Yes, I—"

"We'll get to the specifics, Vera. Let me tell you what's going to happen. Once we disconnect, the officer will ask your permission to test your blood-alcohol content by collecting a blood or urine sample."

"What about a breath test? I thought you had to blow into a machine."

"After a decade spent litigating the reliability of various devices they finally wised up and eliminated that option. If you're offered an archaic breath test, any results couldn't be used against you. Make sense?"

"Yes."

"How many drinks did you have, Vera?"

"No more than usual. I didn't get blasted, as the kids say."

"Vera, I'm not asking as your judge. I'm asking as your lawyer. I need all the facts, even the uncomfortable ones."

"Well, I had a star bright before we teed off. And another during play. It's a fruity vodka drink I discovered when we streamed over to Fiji for a second honeymoon last month."

"Two star brights. Anything else?"

"Nothing out of the ordinary. I had my usual martini at dinner, and another to celebrate my personal best round. And there was that lemon twist Roger made me."

"Roger?"

"He's the bartender at the club. You'd adore him. He's so well-mannered, and provides excellent service.

Sometimes I wish my Carter would be more like Roger. I swear that Roger is telepathic. No sooner do I think of a drink than it appears. It's really Roger that landed me in this predicament."

"I predict they won't press charges against Roger. What did you eat during this time?"

"These little canapés. They're quite delightful. And a strawberry endive salad. I'm on the new Tyrone diet. I had to give up the buckwheat bread I'm so fond of. Javier would make it from scratch."

"Javier?"

"The chef at the club. He is all male, and very French. I'm sorry. Alcohol loosens my tongue. I'm usually reserved."

"We have a lot to discuss. And we'll do so during our visit. The timing of that visit will depend upon the blood-alcohol results. Kaye County has the technology to run the sample on site. It'll take about thirty minutes."

"What do you think the results will be?"

"I've input your food and drink consumption into my BAC application. It's imperfect, but it gets us close. It shows point-one-two-one. The legal limit is point-oh-six."

"I thought it was oh-eight."

"Not since the latest national safety push. That threshold is low. Your star bright likely tipped you over. If you do hit point-one-two that's a gross misdemeanor—one step under a felony. We're talking plate impoundment, an automatic thousand-dollar fine, and three days jail."

"I cannot survive in these atrocious conditions for three days."

"Please focus on the present, Vera. That will come later, if at all. If you refuse to test, then they'll charge you with a gross misdemeanor, and the minimums are lower—an automatic five-hundred-dollar fine, one day jail, and no plate impoundment."

"That doesn't make sense."

"My explanation or the law?"

"The law."

"I can't claim the laws are always consistent or logical. But they're what we have to work with. I suspect, but cannot guarantee, you're on the border between a misdemeanor and a gross misdemeanor. A misdemeanor would involve a three-hundred-dollar fine, and no forfeiture. They'd cite and release you to return at a later date for court. If you test at a gross misdemeanor, they'll hold you for the morning bail calendar. I'll check in with Kaye County within the next hour or two to see if you're still there. If you are, I'll arrive at the courthouse early to meet with you before your hearing. Otherwise, I'll call you tomorrow to arrange a meeting. Do you have any questions for me, Vera?"

"What would you do if you were me, Ruby?"

"Vera, I'll do all I can for you. I can't make this decision for you, or influence it by answering that question. This decision is yours. Do I have your permission to contact Carter and others, and discuss your case as I deem necessary to represent you?"

"Yes, of course."

"Do you have anything on your calendar tomorrow?"

"Yes, I have a volunteer commitment. It's not pressing, but I'd feel badly missing it. Carter will know what to do."

Ruby entered data into the stationary supercomputer on her desk. "I see Carter's phone number isn't in the public directory. What is it?"

"It's six-one-three-two-two-two-eleven-sixteen."

"I'll see you soon, Vera. We'll figure this out together."

"Thank you, Ruby. I'm so glad you answered your phone."

"You're very welcome, Vera."

Using her PSC, Ruby disconnected the call and started her coffeemaker. While she waited for her liquid energy to brew, she tapped notes on her client conversation, saved them, and sent an update to her paralegal. She rose, stretched, and made the short walk from her makeshift office to her cramped kitchen to grab a steaming mug.

Wrestling down memories of ebony hair and pleading eyes that threatened to immobilize her, she directed herself to take her own advice. *Focus on the present*, she thought, and gulped black coffee.

Fortified, she grabbed her PSC, and did what came next in the Epstein case.

A groggy male voice answered, visual blocked.

"Hello? Who the hell is calling at midnight?"

"It's well past midnight. My apologies, but this is urgent. I'm Ruby Miller. I must speak with Carter Epstein. Are you Mr. Epstein?"

"Yes, what's this about?"

"I'll get right to it. I'm Vera's lawyer."

"Her what?"

"Vera is safe. Currently, she's held at Kaye County Jail on suspicion of driving under the influence."

"She's where? Christ."

Ruby sipped coffee, and waited for the news to sink in.

"She often comes home late from the club. I figured she stayed to mingle. When I talked to her at eleven everything was fine. Now you're telling me she's in a goddamn jail cell."

"Yes, I know it's a shock. I wish she were at home instead of in jail. But she's there, and she's hired me to handle her case. I want what's best for her. She needs your help. Can Vera count on you, Carter?"

"Yes, absolutely." He cleared his throat. "What do you need?"

"We need to talk about her drinking habits. She had five hard drinks tonight. Where would you say that lands her in terms of her drinking routine?"

"I'd say that's her usual. Sometimes she has a couple more, rarely a couple less."

"How many nights does she drink?"

"Every night."

"Have your teenagers said anything to you about

her drinking?"

"Yeah, they're worried about her."

"Are you worried about her, Carter?"

He sighed. "Yeah, I am, especially now that she's in jail for a DUI. I still can't believe it."

"You're free to call Kaye County and check. They won't let you talk to her or give you specifics about her case, but they'll confirm her presence. Have you talked to her about cutting back on her drinking?"

"I have, but I don't think she has any control over it. I don't know what to do. I've tried hiding alcohol. I've suggested outings to places where they don't serve, but she won't go. She accuses me of wrecking her fun."

"To your knowledge, has anyone directly told her she has a drinking problem?"

"No, I guess I haven't. I don't think anyone else has, either."

"Let me be clear, Carter. I don't think her drinking is anyone's responsibility but her own. I want to do more than just get her through this criminal case. I suspect you do, too. I want to get at the heart of why she landed in jail tonight. Do you want that for her?"

"Yes, of course I do."

"I think there's no day like today to hold an intervention. It would send the message that you support her in regaining control over her drinking. Please include your teenagers in this. It's important that it's a family effort."

"Okay. I'll talk to the kids. What's going to happen

to her?"

"I'm waiting on test results, and that will determine the charge. She'll either be released within the next couple hours, or she'll be held for a bail hearing. Either way, we'll schedule the intervention for five this afternoon. Can you do what it takes to make that happen for Vera?"

"Yes. I have to rearrange my schedule, but I'll make it work."

"Good. And, please, clear Vera's schedule for today. That'll give her time to settle down before our afternoon session. I have a trusted friend who's fantastic at facilitating tough conversations—that's basically what an intervention is. Before our meeting, I'd like you and your kids to think of concrete ways Vera's drinking has impacted your home life. Focus on the act—her drinking. She's a wonderful person engaged in destructive behavior."

"I'll get started right away. Thank you, Ruby. It's good we have you in charge of her case." He paused. "She means a lot to us, me and the kids." Emotion thickened his voice.

"You're very welcome, Carter. It's obvious her family means the world to her. You're an important part of her team. Feel free to call me any time. I'll see you at five."

Ruby signed off, and settled back in her chair, fingers twined behind her head.

"PSC, call Amy Larson, voice only."

A woman formed in the shadows. She turned her

bedside light on. Her sleeping gown shimmered—the stark white a dramatic contrast to her dark curls. "Disturbed by dreams?"

"Yes, but I'm not calling to get my head shrunk. I got a DUI call. My client and her family are coming in at five. I'd like to host an intervention, facilitated by the best. Are you available?"

"You're in luck. I had a cancellation this afternoon. Count me in, on one condition."

"What condition?"

"You'll make time for you."

"My head feels smaller already with this short chat. You're good."

Amy gave a throaty laugh. "I'm not your therapist, dear. You know that's not what I mean."

As she joined in, Ruby felt the tightness in her chest loosen. "Seriously, thanks. Knowing you're there for me—it matters. You know?"

"I do know, Ruby. And I'm always here for you, even at—" Amy glanced at the PSC's clock, "Quarter past one on a Friday."

Ruby winced. "Sorry about the timing. Veronica picked an inconvenient time. Tell me this. How do you look impeccable at this ridiculous hour? I block my visual for a reason."

"Are you wearing a pore-zapping mask?" Amy gave a cheeky grin.

"You know how I pounce on the latest trends," Ruby said wryly. "I certainly don't put on silk to sleep."

"You also sleep alone, despite my efforts to make some very nice matches for you. That neurosurgeon was a wonderful man."

"Wonderfully dull. I have a law firm to run, another client's case to plan, and no time for romance. Though it pains me, I have no time to discuss the latest suitor with you. Thanks—not for relentlessly setting me up, but for everything else. I'll see you this afternoon."

Ruby returned to the silence of her apartment. She contemplated falling back asleep, this time in her lumpy bed. But the images were still too vivid. Opting to jumpstart her day at 1:22 A.M., Ruby stretched and went to her compact shower. She cranked the temperature to high, and turned the jets on full blast. When the creaky pipes delivered an uneven stream, she whacked the shower head to steady the flow.

CHAPTER 2

Susan Combes darted from room to room, frantic. She'd checked all the usual places—decorative bowls, countertops, tables, pockets. Resorting to the unlikely, she opened the fridge, cupboards, and scoured the pantry. Anywhere a car keys would fit. The stove read 6:14 A.M. Sixteen minutes until her hospital rounds began, until her third tardiness in as many weeks. She patted the pockets of her colorful medical scrubs again. Nothing.

Her husband strode into the kitchen, cool and collected. She'd laundered and pressed his khakis and gray dress shirt by hand.

As she scanned his face for signs of anger, she noticed his shirt matched his eyes.

"What are you scurrying about like a little mouse for? Pull yourself together, woman. You have work."

"Yes, yes, I know. I'm looking for my keys. Have you seen them?"

"You're always throwing your things around. I'm not going to enable your carelessness. If you can't find your keys, then you'll be responsible for the consequences."

"But . . . my work is on the way to yours."

"You never listen to me. I said I won't enable you." He crossed the room, and rested his hand on her head. Looking down at her, he said, "You'll have to find another ride. It's for your own good. You're lucky I love you enough to provide you with a car at all. You have no appreciation for anything I do for you." He cupped her chin, and stepped closer to her. Steel eyes met soft hazel. "I'll expect my dinner at five-thirty. You know how angry you make me when you don't respect my schedule. I'm a busy man. We don't all have the luxury of an easy job like yours." He flicked her collar and scoffed. "What a ridiculous outfit."

"The kids on the floor like it."

"How can you expect to be taken seriously wearing butterflies? You'll never advance to triage looking like a clown. You'll stay on the kiddie floor forever."

"I like it there."

"Of course you do. You're content to make nothing while I pay all our bills. You have no concern for the pressure you put me under to provide for your expensive tastes."

"Maybe I should change into something more

serious."

"Good girl." He kissed the top of her head. "Okay, dinner at five-thirty. Make a memo if you must—whatever it takes to not misplace that information in your scattered brain. Put your car keys in the damn bowl next time."

"Dinner will be ready at five-thirty sharp."

"For fuck's sake, stop standing around. You have a real work outfit to select and keys to find. You'd lounge in bed all day without me, or walk around forgetting what you're after."

"I'll go change." Susan disappeared through the dining room.

Jerald walked out the front door. Spotting his neighbor, he smiled and walked over. "Susan is still out of sorts this morning," he told Deanna. "She's agitated and racing around the house. She should lay low today. If she asks you for a ride, it's probably best not to give in to her."

Deanna nodded, and said, "No problem."

"You're a doll, Dede." He reached up and rested his hand on her face. "My sexy doll."

Deanna preened. She cocked her hip, and rested her hand on it. "You know I'd only drive her as a favor to you. I hate her for all she puts you through. I don't understand why you stay with her. She doesn't appreciate you."

"No, she doesn't. Not like you. But she's my wife, my responsibility. That's enough about her. You look beautiful."

"I just threw this on." She pressed her palms down the skirt of her pink dress, bending forward to highlight the v-neck.

"I'll be over later to take it off." He gave her a wolfish grin.

"Same time?"

"Yes. It'll be the highlight of my day."

She waved as he got in his red car and tore out of the driveway.

Ruby charged into her office suite, and steered toward the tall, stylish man behind the front desk.

Colin Lewis crossed his arms, pushed his glasses up his straight nose, and peered over his mustard-yellow frames at Ruby.

"There's my dedicated paralegal. Quarter to seven and already hard at work. Your boss is very impressed. She raves about you constantly. And she brought you your usual." She set a white bakery bag within smelling distance.

"You cannot bribe me into declaring you the victor, Ruby. I already called it."

"Cass beat me?"

Colin snatched the bag, opened it, and inhaled. He reached in, and said, "Yes, she did. You're on the hook for lunch, boss. Thanks for the danish." He held it up in salute, and took a generous bite that oozed cherry jelly out the side.

"I've been working at home since after midnight.

Shouldn't that count?"

"Perhaps, but that doesn't change the current rules. The victory line is the front entrance. That way I can call it. It replaced the rear-on-the-office-chair rule after you and Cass left wreckage in your wake. Remember that spectacular display of professionalism?"

"Of course I do. I won. You know I'll abide by the rules. But I'll still lobby for my rear on my home office chair to count."

"I have a feeling Cass won't agree to that."

"So do I." She brightened. "At least it's my turn to pick the place."

"A solid consolation prize." Colin brushed off his hands and pulled up Ruby's schedule. "I noticed you have an event this afternoon. And you added it at one this morning. Brutal. I don't know how you do it."

Ruby shrugged. "My phone rang. I answered."

"I could sleep through an air strike at one. A file on Ms. Epstein is already on the cloud. I pulled her case info from the court's database, and confirmed she's on the morning bail calendar."

"Thank you. Judge?"

"Mason."

"Good. She's open to an RPR with standard conditions for a first-time DUI. Prosecutor?"

"Avery."

"Tough, and fair. I like him. But what's he doing handling the misdemeanor calendar? He's one of the best in the office."

"Part of the new county attorney's restructuring."

"It boggles my mind. The new assignments are illogical—not at all an efficient or effective use of the talent at that office."

"Agreed. The office has gone to hell since we worked there."

"Since I stole you away with promises of sugary treats and caffeinated drinks?" She gestured to the bakery bag.

"Yes. It wasn't your commitment to cleaning up criminal defense. It was the treats."

She grinned at him. "Glad we understand each other." She accessed her case notes on her PSC. "This afternoon I expect four to six. Possibly two teens in attendance, so have youthful options—what our refined palates would go for."

"Sweet, fizzy, and caffeinated."

"Exactly. And make sure we have that tea Amy likes."

"Junk, and oolong. Noted. Anything else?"

"Yeah. Check when the devil himself transfers to Mardova."

"That was a rough trial. I can't believe it's been four years."

"Me either. It's the one time I missed the prosecutor's office. I would've enjoyed verbally slashing that smirk off his face during cross." She shook her head to clear his image.

"It took the jury no time to convict. That's something."

"It's my day for consolations. It doesn't bring Tara back, but at least her family saw justice done. I'd like to think that she knows what happened to her mattered. Despite his daddy's clout, Longhorn didn't get away with it. Helped him stay in-state and draw out his appeal this long though." She scrubbed her hands over her face. "Maybe once that degenerate is rotting in a mega-max, I can get some rest."

"You're not a robot, Ruby, regardless of what your mother says. Make some time for you."

"Amy tagged you, didn't she?"

"Perhaps."

She held her hands out, palms facing Colin. "I'm fine." Resting her hands on the ledge, she leveled her gaze. "Let's focus on the living, and those not damned to Mardova. What we can do for this new client and her family. I have treatment info ready to go, thanks to you. I think you covered every program on the planet. My read on Veronica is she'll stick close if she goes. She's involved with her family and her community."

"Do you think she'll go?"

"Yeah, I do. She loves her family, and wants to do right by them. The Aurora Foundation would be a good fit for her."

"Rigorous, high success rate. It encourages family participation."

"You never cease to amaze me." She caught his grim look, and forced a broad smile. "You know how I love a new case. It's exactly what the good doctor herself would prescribe."

"Funny. Amy's recommendation had more of a tropical flair—beaches, hammocks, fruity cocktails."

Ruby sniffed. "What's that I smell? An ulterior motive?"

Colin turned to his screen and averted his gaze. "Oh, look here. You have a prospective intern arriving shortly."

"Real smooth. I'll be in my office."

"There's hot coffee waiting on your desk. It's as strong as our coffeemaker would brew. We could really use—"

"An espresso machine? We'll upgrade soon. And you'll get that vacation. It's been a hectic three years."

"A lucrative three years."

"Yes, but you know me."

"Investing before splurging. Yes, yes. I'm not asking for a prime machine."

"And I'm not saying no. I'm simply saying not yet."

"You're the boss," he said to his screen, and sighed.

"Are you in for lunch?"

"Yeah, and I feel like Thai, if that makes any difference to you."

"How about the international buffet on Third? They always have Thai, Mexican, and Indian. I think it's Moroccan week on the rotation."

"I suppose that would work."

"You're the best, Colin. Better than any prime automaton in development," she teased.

"Damn right. You may think that's a big joke, but I follow tech. It's only a matter of time." He gave her a sidelong glance, caught her grin, and lost the battle to keep his dimple hidden.

Satisfied, she strode to her office and tossed her briefcase on her sleek black desk before continuing down the hall. Stopping in front of the engraved plaque reading CASSANDRA S. DAYTON, Ruby gave it a tilt. Knocking on the doorframe as she entered, she said, "I'm interviewing another eager law student today. I have a good feeling about this one."

Cassandra pushed back from her desk, scooped her long copper hair up in one hand, grabbed a clip from a drawer with the other, and twisted it into a bun before securing it. She spun in her chair to give Ruby her full attention as a few tendrils fell free to frame her oval face. "Think it'll go better than your interview yesterday? What was his name? Jason?" Her clever azure eyes danced with humor.

"Jerome. Je-Romeo, more like. A stereotypical defense lawyer in the making." Ruby lowered her voice and wiggled her brows over eyes that flashed bright green. "Direct quote—'A good looking lady such as yourself could use a man like me around.' I asked him if he was after a job or a date. He didn't think it was rhetorical. 'I'm well-qualified for both.'" Ruby imitated his smarmy smile, and had Cassandra clutching her stomach. "I have hope for this one, Cass."

"You are ever the optimist."

"Positive visualization, Cass. Fresh eyes, eager to learn and work hard. What's not to like about an intern? You decide if you're getting one yet?"

"I'll hold off for now." She turned to her screen to hide her smile. "Maybe your intern will take a special interest in family law with the proper encouragement."

"Clever. I do the grunt work, secure an all-star intern, and you snatch up my resource. Give my intern varied experience—that's great. But when I have work, you keep your grubby hands off. Got it?"

"Hey, I object. My hands are lovely. I treated myself to a manicure to celebrate." She turned back to face Ruby, and fluttered her fingers. "Eggplant. Isn't it fabulous?"

"It's purple. I'm surprised you didn't go with your brand color."

"Citrus-orange nails?" Cassandra held her manicured hands to her heart and clucked her tongue. "You seriously know nothing about fashion."

"Guilty as charged."

"Now your brand color, on the other hand, would look truly mag."

"Teal nails?"

"I was thinking a touch more green than blue. Seafoam green rather than turquoise."

"I think I'll stick to this shade." Ruby pretended to study her nails.

"What shade?"

"I believe the fancy French term is *ongles naturel*."

Cassandra rolled her eyes.

"What are you celebrating with your purple-plant nails?" Ruby prompted.

"Eggplant," Cassandra corrected. When Ruby gave her a blank look, Cassandra waved a hand in frustration, and said, "All right, my fashion-clueless friend. Let's stick to the law, shall we? I may have settled the case of the obstinate opposing counsel."

"Details."

"My client had to give a little on visitation where and when, but she ended up with full custody. Both parents wanted what was best for their kid. Ms. Mule got the boot after I played the threats she'd made at our settlement conference. Surprisingly, they weren't sanctioned by her client." She leaned forward for emphasis. "He was horrified, Ruby. I wish I'd snapped his expression, but I was too busy arming myself and ducking under the conference table."

"Ah, so Ms. Mule didn't take her dismissal well. What'd you grab for protection?" Ruby settled into an accent chair and mused that Cassandra would have a fancy term for this combo of orange and gray. Halloween came to mind, but Ruby held back on making this observation aloud. Cassandra was quick to show off her fashion-forward office, as she and Colin called it. Just another place where her horror-movie fascination showed up, Ruby decided, and tuned back into the conversation to hear Cassandra's reply.

"A crystal vase. It had some real weight to it.

Fortunately, I didn't have to use it. Ms. Mule stormed out. When I replaced the vase on its stand, I noticed that it's stunning. Where'd we get it? It's not your usual style."

"It was a launch present from Alfred."

"It's been there three years?"

"In this suite, yes. Colin insisted on giving it 'pride of place on a pedestal.' His exact words. That was a few months back."

"Oh, Ruby. Where did you have it?"

"In the kitchen. In a cupboard."

"You didn't. Not even you."

"What? There were other vases down there."

Cassandra shook her head. "Knowing Alfred, he must have told you the story behind the piece."

"He did."

"Which is?"

Ruby slipped into her best British accent. "It once overflowed with fresh cosmos flowers and graced the mahogany desk of Madeleine Albright, former U.S. Secretary of State and a trailblazer for women worldwide. When she ascended to this distinguished office, she discarded the war décor to create an ambience for peace."

"And then you go and wreck the beautiful legacy of this vase by stuffing it in some dusty cupboard." She swept her hand toward the kitchen.

"Excuse me? You wielded the peace vase as a weapon."

They burst into laughter.

"I can't wait to tell Alfred," Ruby said. "He'll get a kick out of telling his clients about the peace vase's lively new home."

"Yes, without a doubt. You know what's in order?"

"Of course. You must pick how we commemorate the occasion. Add a placard to the former peace vase's pedestal? Blaze an orange-fruit carpet out the front entry? Hire a trumpeter to announce your entrance and departure with 'Boogie Woogie Bugle Boy?'"

"Is that really a song?"

"Yes, by the Andrews Sisters. Alfred had it on last week."

"I was thinking we'd splurge for lunch and go to Chestnut."

"Done. I guess I'll hold those gems in reserve for my next celebration. I wonder how much a custom teal carpet would set me back. Would it qualify as a business expense? Could I find teal velvet robes to set alongside it?"

"You're ridiculous and possibly insane."

"Some say I'm a dreamer."

"Only those who haven't seen you in action."

"Such flattery will get you a fancy lunch. Colin's craving Thai food. I suspect an upgrade to Chestnut won't be a problem. Since you plan to steal my intern, do you want to check out the application for today's prospect?"

"Sounds fair."

"PSC engage, retrieve intern applications and display on Screen Four." Ruby perused the digital folder on Cassandra's wall screen. "Open Jasmine Sinclair's application." She turned to Cassandra. "That name's familiar. I've met her. Do you know her?"

"No."

"Okay, not a mutual acquaintance. Let me place her. Ah, yes, that day I verbally sparred with my colleagues in defense."

"That really narrows it down, Ruby."

"Well, it didn't start out as usual. You know, calling me honey, sweetie, beautiful as they looked me up and down like an entrée."

"What happened?"

"It started out bland enough. One slicked-back hairstyle asked another how court's been. Jim claimed he got him out of this and her off of that. Their usual banter about sweet deals. Then Larry brought up a probation officer. 'She has a lucky bastard of a husband,'" Ruby parroted.

"Did he mean Cynthia? Her husband Mark is a health activist and a professional caregiver."

"I know it. Larry figures that means Mark plays golf all day and coaches little league all night. Mark spearheaded overhauling his district's school-lunch program."

"Did you know his blog is wildly successful?"

"No, but I'm not surprised."

"What happened next?"

"Larry told Jim he should've seen her in that skirt. He appreciated how she felt free to express her femininity. You know—*hubba hubba*, elbow poke in the ribs. They should've bagged a woman like her and played golf. Larry figured she's quite the tigress out of the courtroom."

"Let me guess. You couldn't just sit there."

"Why would I? My client's shifting in her seat. Jenny the court clerk turned beet red. I could tell from across the courtroom. Somebody had to say something. I was polite about it, Cass."

"I'm sure you were."

"I excused myself for interrupting their degrading conversation. Then I, very politely, informed them my client's a lady. If they'd emerge from their makeshift man cave, they'd see there are other ladies present—all could hear them, and none appreciated their debasing banter. Though inappropriate anywhere, it's better suited to a bar than a courtroom. I gestured toward those standing to applaud, said I present Exhibit A, and told them I rested my case."

"What'd they say?"

"They asked me who the hell I thought I was. 'Ruby Miller of Miller Law Office,' I said. They may have seen my teal billboard off the interchange. Women have taken notice. I have a few ideas why they prefer my representation over theirs."

"You have a knack for making friends."

"Sure do. I have no desire to muddy myself by playing in the pigpen. It turned out Larry's client had joined in the ovation. She went in front of the judge and fired her attorney."

"What was her reason?"

"Unprofessional behavior. She approached me after court for my card. And she wasn't the only one."

"What does this have to do with Jasmine Sinclair?"

"Jasmine approached me, too. She told me she appreciated I'd said something. And now here she is coming in to interview for an internship with me."

"You?"

"Us, intern snatcher. You'll like her. PSC, open resume." Ruby scanned the document. "She's well-qualified for the position."

"Geez, does she ever sleep?"

"If not, she'll be a perfect fit for my firm. A bit of an overachiever for yours."

"Hey, who beat you in this morning?"

"Only because the rule is bogus. I've been meaning to talk to you about it."

"No, Ruby. Your ass on your home chair doesn't count."

"You haven't considered my new arguments."

"Buy me sinfully dark chocolate and I'll take them into consideration."

"Deal." Ruby rose. "Don't you have work to do? Or are you going to rest on your laurels? At this rate, it might be a while before your next celebration."

Cassandra tossed a pen at Ruby, who caught it effortlessly. "Damn it, I forgot you played softball."

"Center field, baby. Captain. MVP."

"Yeah, yeah. Enough about your glory days."

"I heard you bragging me up last week before we crushed the Steffen firm at league. Besides, you should be thankful I have catlike reflexes. You could've stabbed my eye with your atrocious aim."

"Who said that would've been a miss?"

"Nice. Be more careful, Cass. I'm trying to make this the new face of criminal defense."

"Thank God you caught it. You saved me from having to hire a scumbag to combat assault charges."

Ruby's PSC chimed twice before Colin's face appeared on-screen. "Ms. Sinclair has arrived."

"Thanks, Colin. I'll meet her in the conference room."

"PSC to standby." The wall image disappeared as Ruby turned to Cassandra. "Would you like to join us?"

"I have to make calls, and finish prep for an OFP at nine. Bring her by if you're going to hire her."

"Now that it comes down to the legwork, she'd be my intern. Well played, Dayton."

"I don't know what you're talking about. I happen to be swimming in work this morning."

"You're swimming in something. Try getting up at midnight. It's amazing what one can accomplish before dawn."

"Yet still cannot manage to beat one's suitemate into the office."

"Savor your small taste of glory. By the way, your name plaque is crooked. You wouldn't want to give your clients the impression you're off kilter."

"Is that the best you can do?"

"No, it's a tiny warm up. It took me an hour to get

those shreds out of my office. You're not getting off that easy, Cass."

"You told me to take care of shredding our discards when you made me go virtual. I was perfectly fine using hemp paper."

"How's the virtual system working out for you?"

"Great," Cassandra acknowledged.

"Wish you would've held off on that little prank?"

"A tad. Although you have to admit it was hilarious. Colin enjoyed it."

"Only because he was out sick, and didn't have to participate in the cleanup."

"Sheer coincidence."

"I don't believe in convenient coincidences." Ruby moved in front of Cassandra's door. "This plaque is sure wonky," she called out.

"It doesn't bother me in the least."

"I'm glad. Maybe the main event won't faze you."

"Not in the least."

CHAPTER 3

Ruby amused herself by tossing and catching her PSC on the way to the conference room.

Cassandra dashed into the hallway and righted her plaque. "Perfect."

Ruby stopped at Colin's desk. "Observations?"

"She's well put together. Unlike Jerome, she didn't dismiss me. She asked what it was like to work with you."

"Conclusion?"

"She wants the gig, but cares about fit. She's sizing you up, Ruby."

"Good for her. Not enough people realize an interview goes both ways. You tell her what a demanding boss I am?"

"The worst. I discovered there aren't enough nasty epithets to capture the horrors of being under your employ. I coined new ones."

"I like your style, Colin. She get your stamp?"

"I approve. Have you seen her resume? She never sleeps. You could hold meetings at midnight."

"Now that's a bright idea. I'll provide the treats. You in?"

"Sure. I might be a tad late—six hours or so."

"Slacker."

"Sadist."

They grinned at each other.

"Is lunch at Chestnut okay?"

"Let's see, fine dining instead of a buffet. I suppose I can stomach it."

"Maybe Cass will buy Thai food next time. I'm going to weaken her with chocolate and argue for the new rule."

"Good luck."

"It's nice to see you're on my side."

"I'll wish her the same."

"Flip flopper."

"I've learned neutrality is paramount with two bosses. Remember the paper-shredding incident? It wouldn't have been humanly possible to resist laughing at that vid, and yet you vowed to include me in your payback prank. I'm certain the passage of time hasn't affected your recall."

Ruby tapped her temple. "Steel trap, my fair-weather friend. Vengeance is most satisfying when served to the unsuspecting. I've already put my plan in motion. You want in?"

"Two bosses, remember?"

"It's too late to play the neutral card. You caused imbalance with your snickering. It's still ringing in my ears. You can play Switzerland after you help me."

"I'm in."

"I'll send you my diagram."

"Seriously?"

"Yes, every successful operation requires at least one diagram. Besides, it gave me a chance to tinker with that new app Flick programmed before turning rascal."

"I wonder what happened to Flick," Colin said. "Have you heard from him?"

"No. I sure appreciate the tech he left behind though. Think these portable supercomputers will hit the market before or after Flick gets himself in federal hot water?"

"My money is on after."

"Thank God we cut him loose in time to keep our house clean. We need to find a new e-guru. Peruse listings, would you? Keep an eye out for talent that cares about a cause."

"Will do. It won't be hard to find someone with better people skills than Flick."

"No, it won't. His e-skills on the other hand will be hard to match. Nearly impossible to surpass."

"Nobody knew how good he was better than Flick." Colin gave a wry smile.

"Yes, not a humble bone in his body."

"You miss him?"

"Like I miss the politics at the prosecutor's office. Our amped up tech is a nice souvenir from his time here."

"Agreed. Are you going to meet with Jasmine?"

"Just giving her time to settle in and review her notes. Interviewing is nerve-wrecking business, especially when you're a striver like Jasmine. We'll have to work on a nickname for her if we take her on."

"There was a Jasmine at my high school. All the guys wanted to date her."

"Except for you."

"Naturally."

"They called her Mine."

"That's not very clever."

"You know high-school antics. They'd surround her and take turns calling it out. 'Mine, Mine, Mine.' Thoroughly annoyed, I said, 'She's mine, damn it.' I put my arm around her and swept her away. We became great friends after that."

"What happened?"

"We pretended to break up when the new cute guy transferred in. She's married now to a doctor in Phoenix. New guy turned into a summer fling." He gave her a serious look. "We can do better than Mine."

"It's not even on the list, Colin."

"Good, keep it that way."

"If I hire her, I'll want her to start right away. Give her a hand with any legal research, coach her on arguments. Tell her Mason's preferences. If she asks for nickname suggestions, defer to someone else. Dear God, anyone else."

"It's a charming story." He sat in a huff.

"Yes, delightful. Amy would love it."

He turned with a wicked glint in his eye. "Ah, yes, she's coming for the intervention—sappy emotion central. Aren't you in for a treat?"

"I'm glad to see you've stopped sulking."

"I feel much better, thanks. Maybe Amy can work her magic with you. She is a delightful matchmaker. Introduced me to Charles, you know."

"Yes, I know. I'm happy that you're happy."

"On second thought, I suppose she's not a miracle worker."

"Thanks, Colin. I'd be offended if I had any interest in settling down in the suburbs."

"It'd be better than your cramped kaleidoscope of an apartment. I'd keep quiet about an espresso machine if it meant you'd do something about your hideous living quarters."

"We can't all have a designer's eye."

"Yes, but it's as if you're blind. It's abrupt and jarring. It's no wonder you can't sleep in that nightmarish place."

"It's bright and energizing."

"My eyes bleed."

"I'll stop inviting you over."

"Please remember that if you hold midnight meetings with Mine."

"Speaking of Jasmine, hold anything unrelated to Epstein while I meet with her."

"Done."

Ruby entered the conference room.

A sturdy woman set aside her phone and moved to rise.

Motioning for Jasmine to stay seated, Ruby strode over and shook hands, noting in approval that Jasmine was not one to limp-fish a handshake, and took her usual seat at the head of the expansive table. "I hope you didn't mind the wait. Colin and I had important matters to discuss."

Jasmine straightened her lapels. Her sleek brown hair ended in a straight edge at her chin. "Yes, I heard," she began. "Pranks and chocolate take precedence." She gave Ruby a cautious smile. "I appreciated the time to settle in, and to review my notes."

Ruby returned her smile, and said, "You have excellent hearing."

"Uh, I wanted to first let you know that I, excuse me." Jasmine sipped from the water glass in front of her and wiped her hands on her slacks. "I thought about what you told me at the hearing, when you asked why I didn't stand up and say something to those guys."

"That you have as much right as anyone to speak?"

"Yeah. It's just that . . . I'm a law student. I was afraid they wouldn't listen to me."

Ruby measured her. "It takes guts to admit when

you're afraid. But you're making the assumption that I spoke for their benefit. I had no delusion my speech would change decades of bad behavior. I spoke for those who wanted to say something but felt they couldn't. You're different than the average person in the galley. The others are afraid to say or do anything to officers of the court that might impact their legal cases. You're entering legal practice. You'll stand for something, for someone. It's time to practice speaking out against injustice."

"I'm just sorry I blew that chance."

"Trust me, you'll have another. That you wanted to say something matters." Ruby gestured to the tray. "Coffee? Colin made it the way I like it—strong enough to singe your insides. Interested?"

"No, thanks. I don't drink coffee."

"Your choice. I'm a firm believer nothing gets the neurons firing like strong brew. But we're not here to talk about my vices. Why do you want to work with me instead of a Larry or a Jim?"

"You want to make a difference. They're willing to get rich at their clients' expense."

"True, good read. Observing people and discerning their motives are necessary skills in this area of practice. I'm selective about my clients. Does that astonish you?"

"You could run the risk of discrimination."

"Very good. Indeed, if I chose certain criteria—gender, race, religion. What do you think is my criteria?"

"Charged offense?"

"A solid criterion, but no. I've accepted clients accused of battering their spouses, kidnapping their own children. Women who sold their bodies. Neophytes to the system who insist they aren't like those people—those common criminals who deserve a heavy whack from the hammer of justice. What do these people have in common?"

"Complex dynamics?"

"Yes, you're getting there. Some cases aren't what they seem. Law enforcement is ill-equipped to detect dynamics when they fall outside standard protocol. And the justice system cannot force people into better chapters of their lives. As their trusted advisor, I'm in the best place to encourage those who want to do so to take their power back and reclaim their lives."

"And those who aren't a fit for your firm?"

"They've given up on themselves and their ability to do better, to be better. I don't want hardened criminals resigned to a bleak cycle of wrongdoing, punishment, freedom to commit more wrongdoing. This area is rife with lawyers who will defend the scourge of the planet for a price. I believe everyone deserves a defense. But I want to do more than defend my clients. I want to grab hold as they're trying to free themselves from the quicksand in their lives, and help them make a clean break. They keep one foot in, and they'll get sucked down again. I can show them how to get out. But they have to do the work. One of the hardest parts of this job is that you cannot do their work for them." Ruby turned her attention to her PSC. "I know you're qualified. Your references overflowed with superlatives. I have three more questions for you."

"What do you want to know?"

"Does my vision for my firm resonate with you?"

"Oh yes, it's what I went to law school for. I want to make a difference in people's lives."

"Good. Do you mind if I call you Jazz?"

"Yes, of course. I have a brother, and Jazz is much better than what he's called me over the years."

Ruby laughed. "Ask Colin what he came up with."

"Was it good?"

"I'll let you decide. Jazz suits the spark you have within you."

"It can't be too bright or I would've spoken up like you did."

"Stick with me, Jazz. We'll stoke it into a roaring blaze in no time."

"What's your third question?"

"Can you start right now?"

"Yes, absolutely. I didn't want to be presumptuous, but I cleared my day. What's on the calendar?"

"A bail hearing at nine for Veronica Epstein. Her nickname is Vera. She's charged with a DUI. I've set an intervention for this afternoon. Her husband will attend, and hopefully their teenage children. Psychologist Amy Larson will facilitate. You'll see the best in action." She led Jasmine from the conference room, and past Colin's empty desk. "You've met Colin. He's off preparing for the day's events. Let me show you the rest of the office."

Jasmine admired the bold gerbera daisies popping against beige walls.

"We'll go all the way down and come back." They curved right. "Here we have the kitchen. We usually order in or go out. Have you handled a bail hearing?"

Jasmine looked up from taking notes. "We've practiced applying the case law and analyzing the applicable factors in Advanced Trial Advocacy."

"What better time than now to put theory into practice?"

"I'll need time to prepare."

"You'll have it. What did you think of Colin?"

"He's great."

"He'll hook you up with a portable supercomputer. A PSC, as we call them. Our last e-man left tech like that behind. It's essentially a smartphone on steroids. Are you tech savvy?"

"Fairly."

"You'll be a pro in no time. Colin will link your PSC to our system, and help you retrieve the Epstein file. He's a whiz at research, at locating forms, and at applying the law. He's full of practical info about court personnel. Don't hesitate to brainstorm with him. I'll be in my office if you need anything. You can work in the conference room, or in here." Ruby skipped a door and opened the next. She motioned to the passed door. "That's where our e-man worked, before his urge to hack overcame his better judgment. He insisted that hackers benefit mankind by serving as the internet's immune system. What do you say to that rationale?"

"I haven't studied computer crimes in depth, but my guess is the law doesn't see it that way."

"Very good. Maybe it's helpful to have someone locating breaches in data security, but he doesn't need to be on my staff when his 'humanitarian work' is discovered. You could make his old office into your own, if you'd like."

"I'll start here."

"Sounds good. Cassandra's office is next door. Need anything before I let you get started?"

"No, I'm good. Thanks, Ruby."

"Welcome to the team, Jazz. If you see Cassandra's door open, drop in. She wants to meet you."

"I'd like to meet her."

"We're having lunch at Chestnut—my treat. You're invited."

"I'd love to." Jasmine took a seat at the round table in the middle of the room.

Ruby hesitated in the doorway. "It's your chance to stand for someone. Don't get too mired down in details. Learn Vera's story. Focus on the big three—public safety, roots, and contributions. The first is the most important to Judge Mason. I'll come back in half an hour. Go for it, Jazz."

CHAPTER 4

"Sometimes I swear she's a cutting-edge droid in disguise," Cassandra said. "The way her mind works is more computer than human. But her heart is liquid gold, eliminating any real concerns about a Ruby-Robot going rogue among us. And never call her that. Her mother does so in the most insulting way. It's a sore subject."

"Which subject?" Jasmine asked. "The nickname or her mother?"

"Both."

Ruby breezed into Cassandra's office. "Good, you've met. Cass, are you junking up our intern's impressionable mind?"

Thinking fast, Cassandra said, "I was telling her about the latest hit. Horror genre."

"Naturally." Ruby turned to Jasmine, and said, "She watches nothing else."

"It's true," Cassandra confirmed. "Give me a good scare over a rom-com. You never know who is who nowadays if you can believe the technology used in 'Sinister Switch.' This psycho kidnaps and puts women in an induced coma, and then swaps everything—their faces, prints, even their DNA. Then he releases and stalks them. They go to their family and friends for help, but nobody believes them. Meanwhile, this wacko is after them, and—"

"Let me guess, Cass. It ends in a gruesome slaughter. You think he's dead, but Wacko revives in the last scene to allow for a sequel."

"Thanks, spoiler. Still, it's worth the admission. Popcorn flew, screams filled the theater. A pixie of a teen left bawling. I couldn't sleep for a week."

"Cass isn't all there, Jazz." Ruby tapped her temple. "Want me to predict the sequel?"

"Don't wreck another sequel for me, Ruby."

"Jazz?"

"I want to hear," Jasmine said.

Cassandra sighed, waved her hand, and said, "Go ahead."

"See enough in real-life and you get pretty good at predicting dramatized Hollywood horror. They use new combinations to achieve the same end. The identity swapping was a hit. In the sequel, the murderer will swap identities. His victims will have no idea who to watch out for. He could be lurking in the shadows, or any guy in broad daylight that looks at them sideways."

"I hope you're wrong. I'm sick of picking up the movie tab. We'll have to take Jasmine next time. You wouldn't believe the gaping hole in her horror-film education."

"A travesty, Cass. We have a hearing in thirty. Mind if I take off with Jazz? You can give her gore lessons later."

"We can pick this up at lunch."

"Real appetizing, Cass. Not all of us have iron stomachs."

"Do you, Jazz?"

"Usually. Not at the moment."

"Sorry, was it the gore?"

Jasmine shook her head.

"Her rite of passage is today if you want to drop in. It's her first bail hearing as first chair."

"I'll be in chambers at the Family Justice Center. You'll have to tell me all about it at lunch."

"Good thing we're eating after," Jasmine said. "I don't think I could keep anything down right now."

"There's nothing wrong with nerves, Jazz. They're your body's way of getting you ready for fight, flight, or freeze. We fight for our clients, Jazz. And I'll be right there next to you as second chair."

"Thanks."

Ruby guided Jasmine to the back exit and ushered her intern out first. "Do you want to be second chair today? You can take first next time," she said as she fell into step beside Jasmine.

"No, I'll take first."

"That's the spirit."

Jasmine gave a weak smile, and followed Ruby into the elevator.

Ruby pressed the button for underground parking. "It's already quarter to. We're driving. Have you observed a bail hearing at Kaye County?"

"No."

When the doors slid open, Jasmine hurried to keep up with Ruby. Sliding into the driver's seat, Ruby turned and tossed her briefcase in the backseat, and motioned for Jasmine to do the same. Ruby roared the engine to life, floored it in reverse, gunned the engine, and zipped through the underground maze until they emerged on the street. She weaved through traffic.

"Were you a race car driver?"

"I've learned how to go places fast. It comes in handy. Time is not on our side. It's a good thing you have that iron stomach."

"Yes, it's banging around my insides like a pinball." Jasmine kept her eyes trained ahead.

"We're here, and it's our lucky day. A prime parking spot. These are harder to find than a straight-talking politician."

"Maybe I have beginner's luck."

They entered the atrium and Ruby directed Jasmine to stay left, toward the court-side tower.

"You do have the Midas touch today," Ruby said. "I rarely see the security line this short."

Jasmine and Ruby moved quickly through the

queue. When their turn came, they placed their briefcases on the belt and moved alongside through the metal detector.

Cleared, Ruby and Jasmine joined the crowd at the elevator bank. Suits, briefcases, and neutral colors set the legal professionals apart from the colorfully dressed accused. They followed a woman with spiked purple hair and studded boots into the packed box.

"Floor?" she asked around a wad of gum.

"We're twenty-two, thanks," Ruby said.

"You lawyers?"

"I am, and she's well on her way."

"I don't see enough girl lawyers around here."

"Neither do I," Ruby said.

They walked out of the elevator and onto a catwalk bridge. "The courtrooms wrap around this middle atrium," Ruby said. "You'll find one through fifteen on the left, sixteen through thirty on the right."

Ruby motioned for Jasmine to take the lead. Ruby followed, and said, "Kaye is similar to other courts. Some judges start on time while others don't. This one doesn't. Judge Mason allocates the first thirty minutes for prosecutors to meet with pro se defendants, for those represented by counsel to meet with their attorneys, and for the defense and the state to negotiate. It's a bit like the Wild West."

"Organized chaos."

"I suppose it has its own semblance of order."

They reached the other side and Jasmine steered

right. As they approached courtroom twenty-two, Ruby motioned for Jasmine to stop.

"Catch your breath, Jazz. Any questions before we enter the fray?"

"What's your strategy?"

"Convey what makes Vera different, human. She's not another DUI defendant. She's Veronica Epstein. Make that mean something to the state, and to the judge."

"How does it work to meet with our client?"

"I'll take the lead during our client interview. Colin e-filed the Certificate of Representation. You'll check us in, and then we'll head past the divider and through the labyrinth to holding. We'll meet with Veronica, and return to the courtroom."

"What if I miss something and it results in her being held for the duration of her case?"

"I'll be right next to you at counsel table. Do your best, Jazz, but remember that this is my case. The responsibility rests on my shoulders, not yours. Anything else?"

"No." Jasmine took a deep breath and released it. "I'm ready."

"Go ahead, first chair."

Jasmine squared her shoulders, and walked into court holding her head high. She glanced around, noting the defense lawyers settling in, the empty prosecutor's table, and the galley starting to fill with apprehension. She located the court clerk and headed over. "Good morning," she said. "I'm Jasmine Sinclair from Miller Law Office."

"Hello, Jasmine. I'm Penny Johnson. It's nice to see a new face. What's your attorney ID number?"

"I'm a student attorney, certified under the Minnesota Rules of Practice. Ruby Miller is attorney of record. She's present in court today, as required under the Student Practice Rule." Jasmine checked her notes. "Ms. Miller's ID is three-three-seven-nine-two-five."

Penny removed her magenta reading glasses and scanned the galley, where Ruby sat chatting with a teenager and her mother, whose arm was wrapped protectively around her daughter's shoulders. "Hi there, Ruby," Penny said. "I see you finally hired that intern."

"Good morning, Penny. I see you finally caved and bought readers. They suit you."

"Thank you." Penny put them back on her face and smiled as she turned to focus on Jasmine. "Are you familiar with Judge Mason?"

"Not really."

"She's been very concerned with public safety." Penny sent Jasmine a meaningful glance. "You might want to take that into account."

"I certainly will. Thanks, Penny. It's nice to meet you."

"Likewise." Penny lowered her voice. "First bail hearing?"

"Yes. Is it that obvious?"

"So far so good. You're a natural. Show those guys

how it's done." Penny's eyes twinkled as she winked, and turned back to her computer screen. "You're all checked in, Ms. Sinclair. Head back whenever you're ready."

Ruby excused herself and fell into step alongside Jasmine. They approached a barrel-chested man in uniform. "Hey, Rich," Ruby said. "How are your parenting preparations coming along?"

"I don't think I'll ever feel ready, Ruby. Who's your sidekick?"

"Jasmine Sinclair. She's my new intern. Jazz, meet Rich. He and his wife are expecting their first child in a couple months."

"Congratulations."

"Same to you. Let me take you on back."

They filed through the narrow hallway.

"Which one's yours?" he asked.

"Veronica Epstein."

"Nice lady. Wish they were all like her. It'd make my job a lot easier."

"Want to go in front of the judge as a character reference?" Ruby joked.

"I would if I could with this one."

They reached the heavy door and Rich knocked. His partner opened it. "Marian will take over from here. See you back in the courtroom." He waved, and turned back down the hall.

Marian's face broke into a grin. "Here comes trouble."

"Marian, meet Jazz, my new intern."

"Hi Jazz. First time back in holding?"

"Yeah."

"You have nothing to worry about."

"As long as you stay on Marian's good side," Ruby added. "Don't let this lady's smile fool you. She's a fortress. Cass has been after her for her skin secrets. Turns out they're passed down from her great-granny and she's not telling. Cass is convinced she hasn't found the right bribe."

"She might be right," Marian said.

"And you can't twist her arm," Ruby continued. "I've seen Marian take down a guy twice her size, maybe triple—small for a giant, huge for a man."

"Ruby's being modest. She was holding her own before I made it over for the take down."

"Mixed martial arts champion, this one. My karate training fell short. I've since expanded my studies, and challenge you to a rematch."

"When?" Marian asked.

"I'd like to say soon."

"Take a break, would you?"

"I can't yet." Ruby's eyes darkened.

"I'm sorry. I didn't think. Longhorn gets transferred on Tuesday. The orders came down this morning."

Jasmine frowned at Ruby.

"I'll fill you in later, Jazz. Right now, we have a client to see."

"Who?" Marian asked, and grabbed the in-custody list off her metal stool.

"Veronica Epstein."

"Nice woman. I hope this morning goes well for her."

"It will. I brought my secret weapon." Ruby put her hand on Jasmine's shoulder. "Speaking of secrets, Cass would kill me if she knew I saw you and didn't even try. Lunch at Chestnut with us, chocolate indulgence included, in exchange for great-granny's beauty tips?"

"No deal. I can't get away for lunch. Ask me again sometime."

"I will. We stay on the champ's good side, Jazz." Ruby shot a sidelong glance at Marian as they walked back to Veronica's cell. "I'm instilling such valuable knowledge in this one."

"If I know Cass, she's already delved into horror flicks."

"You know her. And don't pretend you're any less obsessed."

"Have you seen 'Sinister Switch' yet?"

"No, no." Ruby waved her hands. "We're not going there again. Cass would talk to you until she lost her voice about horror vids with the proper incentive."

"Cass needs no inducement to talk horror."

"True. Worth a shot."

"I'll leave you with your client." Marian returned to her post at the door.

Ruby stepped first into the confined space. Dingy brick enclosed them.

Veronica raised her head from her arms, and

pushed back matted auburn tresses to reveal brown eyes rimmed in red. "Ruby, thank God you're here."

Ruby took her hand and locked eyes with her. "It's a pleasure to meet you, Vera. I spoke with Carter after I got off the phone with you, and my paralegal updated him this morning. He'll be here for the hearing."

"Thank you. I can't believe I was so stupid."

"Vera, let's figure out how to move forward. First, we're going to have a hearing." Ruby motioned for Jasmine to sit, and did the same. "This is Jasmine Sinclair. She'll speak at your hearing today." After they shook hands, Ruby continued, "Your blood sample came back at point-one-two-one. That nudges you over the gross-misdemeanor threshold, Vera. That's why they held you overnight, and why we're going to go in front of the judge today."

"I want to go home, Ruby. I want to go home to my kids."

"I know it. We want the same for you. We're going to make that happen. Have you ever heard of an ignition interlock device?"

"I heard something about it on the news."

"It's a small device that's installed on your car. Before it'll start, you have to set your finger on the testing console for a blood sample. Your car won't start unless you're under the legal limit."

"Is it painful?"

"No. The latest technology allows for a blood draw invisible to the naked eye. You may feel a tiny prick, no worse than a mosquito bite, and you won't see any puncture marks."

"Will I have to have it installed?"

"No, you have no priors so it won't be mandatory. But you could voluntarily agree to its installation as a condition of release. Judge Mason cares about public safety. Are you willing to volunteer to an IID?"

"Yes, absolutely. Whatever it takes."

"Good. I'll meet with you and your family at five this afternoon. My paralegal sent the specifics to Carter. Do you have any questions?"

"No. Thank you, Ruby. And you, Jasmine."

Jasmine reached out and placed her hand on Veronica's. "We're here for you."

"Marian or Rich will escort you into the courtroom when it's your turn. We'll be right by your side, Vera."

CHAPTER 5

He pulled into the parking lot of Alfred's Antiques & Collectibles, smiling as he imagined her face when he showed up with her present.

Entering the shop, he admired the carvings on a delicate writing desk. Maybe he'd come back sometime and buy her this, too. He glanced around and wished he could buy her all the treasures in the shop—anything to make her happy, to make up for what he had done.

At the sound of the entry chime, a gentleman in dress and demeanor appeared from the back. "Hello, Jerald," he called out once, and then again as the man kept his attention diverted on the desk. Alfred Whitehorn approached and tapped his shoulder.

His client looked up, face breaking into a grin, gray eyes lighting. "Hey Freddy. I'm here to pick up an order for Tony Priestley."

"You're in a good mood, Jerald. Are your experiments going well?"

Uh, yeah, they're going good."

"What a marvel. And to think, you're a patron of my humble shop. How does your lovely wife like her newest piece? It was quite unusual and distinctive."

"She thinks it's . . . extreme. I'm just here for the necklace." He tapped his phone, and held it out to Alfred. "Here's a note from Tony saying I could grab it for him."

"Anthony is a wonderful lad. Not every boy would go to such lengths for a special someone. How do you know Anthony?"

"Well, you know, it's like I've known him forever."

"He hardly seems old enough for that kind of friend, to have become so woven into a life that one forgets the particulars. I, on the other hand, have outlived many friends of that kind. Compared to me, you're not much past a lad yourself, Jerald. It is all as seen through the eyes of the beholder, isn't it? Do you know Elizabeth?"

"Nope."

"Are you a business acquaintance?"

"Yeah, that's it."

"I try to stay apprised of young Anthony's business happenings. I count on him for a good chat. Would you care for a cup of coffee? Only one other client can drink it so strong. Stronger, actually." He tapped his aristocratic nose. "Her brew smells delightful but undoubtedly wreaks havoc inside. I fear for her stomach lining."

"I need to buzz, Freddy. No tea today. I mean, coffee. I'm just here for the necklace."

"Very well. It is a stunning piece." Alfred reached underneath a display case and produced a pretty green box decorated with yellow ribbon. "This will elate Elizabeth. It is a shame that you have not met her. She has such charisma, and her laughter is quite contagious."

"She sounds legit. Tony asked me to do him a large."

"You must have spent some time with him. I dare say you sound like him, Jerald."

His client's brows furrowed. He clutched the box and turned to leave.

"Excuse me," Alfred called after him.

He stopped and turned, gray eyes darting.

"One of my best clients flouts procedure. You can make haste after you sign. I need my documentation in order."

"Oh, yeah, I'm scrambled." He returned to the counter and grabbed the stylus to scribble his signature.

"That will do. Thank you, Jerald. Please do come back soon. I unloaded a new shipment yesterday. The new items are brilliant, and rare."

"I'll tag you, Freddy. Thanks."

"Yes, off with you. Chemistry is a demanding field."

"Yeah, I have lots to do with my experiments and

all," he said, and backed toward the door.

"Until next time, Jerald."

He waved the green box into a hat rack, and caught it before it could smash into a crystal display. After righting it, he gave Alfred a last glance and bolted out the door.

Alfred averted his gaze.

Ruby and Jasmine pushed through the heavy oak door.

"Pause, Jazz. Take a moment to appreciate that you tackled a milestone." She waited a beat. Clasping Jasmine's shoulder, Ruby steered her toward the elevators.

"It's a blur. It's a complete blur." Jasmine shook her head in disbelief.

"It'll sink in."

"How did I do?"

"You did well, Jazz. Pointing out that Vera's husband and teenage children showed up for her was a nice touch. That she's a family woman means she has roots here, a support system."

Jasmine sighed in relief. "I like her. Do you always like your clients?"

"Yes. My greatest strength and weakness is my ability to see good, to see potential."

"How is that a weakness?"

"It can creep into the case analysis. We strive to know the situation in its entirety—its nuances and dynamics. We seek the truth first. We work with facts. At times, we wish they were different. You'll see soon enough. Would you like to observe the intervention?"

"Yes. I want to see how this case plays out. I want to be in on all of it."

They stepped into an elevator.

"How are you with waterworks, sloppy displays?" Ruby asked.

"I'm great."

"Good, that makes one of us."

"When you work with at-risk teens, you figure out how to ride the rollercoaster of their emotions."

"You're already handy to have around." Ruby nudged Jasmine with her elbow. "What did you find made the difference to nudge them from at-risk to on-track?"

"I showed up for them. Over and over."

"Yes, and that's what we do for our clients. Showing up with consistency and compassion matters."

They stepped onto the sidewalk.

"Take a break," Ruby urged. "Wander for an hour, clear your head. And please pop into Anton's on your way back. It's the bakery across the street. We're regulars. Tell them I sent you, order whatever you want, and have them throw in the usual for the rest of us. They'll add it to our tab."

"You're a vision," Cassandra said. "We were brainstorming, and my stomach started rumbling."

"I don't know how you two consider this food, but here it is." Jasmine set a bulging bakery bag and a beverage carrier on Ruby's desk. She grabbed two cups and held the first out to Ruby. "Caramel macchiato for you."

"Thanks, Jazz."

She passed the second cup to Cassandra. "And a double-chocolate latte, extra whip."

Cassandra grabbed it with an appreciative smile. "Did Colin get his mint mocha?"

"Yes, on my way down the hall. He attacked the baked goods. Judging by that bag's size, there's still enough for ten."

Cassandra shook her head and grinned at Ruby. "Isn't she adorable? She doesn't know our capacity for consumption. I suppose one needs to see it to believe it."

"True. Fuel us with caffeine and sugar, and keep it coming. Jazz, what the hell is that?" Ruby pointed to Jasmine's right hand as she prepared to take a bite.

"It's a muffin."

"There are no chocolate chips."

"It's a Morning Glory Muffin. No refined sugar, no grains."

"No flavor."

"It's real food. Sustainable fuel. You'll both crash, and I'll have to carry you to Chestnut."

"Would you? You're an even better intern than I

thought."

"No, and I'm surprised you fit into your suits if that's your regular fare."

"My mother has been known to call me 'a fatty trapped in a skinny person's body,' and she might be onto something," Ruby said.

"She did not," Jasmine said.

"A direct quote, Jazz."

"You don't know Ruby's mom. She's dead on," Cassandra confirmed.

"That's terrible. My mother is an osteopathic practitioner. 'Let food be thy medicine, thy medicine shall be thy food.' Know who said that?"

"Hippocrates."

"How about this one. 'Tell me what you eat, and I will tell you who you are.'"

"I'm sugary goodness," suggested Cassandra. "Let me do Ruby."

"That's a little forward, Cass, in front of our new intern." She gave Cassandra a cheeky grin, and turned to Jasmine. "Jean Anthelme Brillat-Savarin."

"How does anyone keep up with you two?"

"Caffeine. Lots of it. Did you have Anton throw any in that green goop? What, exactly, is that? According to Brillat-Savarin, you're slimy and potentially radioactive."

"No, it's caffeine-free. One doesn't need cheap jolts with real, balanced nutrition."

"What gives it that unnatural glow?"

"It's completely natural. Algae, top-grade. It's the

latest super food."

"Ruby's usual combo is strong coffee and jelly-loaded danish. Let's see, she's potent and abrasive with a gooey center. Nailed it," Cassandra proclaimed in a sing-song voice.

Ruby chuckled.

Jasmine smothered a laugh. "I don't think that's what Brillat-Savarin had in mind."

"Want to try my smoothie, Cassandra?"

"Beware, Cass. I don't buy that's a benign glow. Let her go first, and then wait to see if she mutates."

Cassandra's eyes lit up. "That'd be awesome."

"Straight out of one of your horror flicks."

"Never mind." Jasmine retracted her drink.

"Wait, is there chocolate in it?" Cassandra asked.

"No."

"I'll pass."

"Hopeless."

"Don't give up on us, Jazz," Ruby said. "We have such potential."

Ruby rapped the doorjamb as she breezed into the meeting room and plopped down next to Jasmine. "Reviewing our intervention file?"

"Yes," Jasmine said. "I can't believe how many programs are available."

"You don't have to memorize them, Jazz."

"I want to know as much as possible before walking in. It's my first intervention."

"Is it? Well, hopefully you'll get your drinking under control and there won't be a second. We're here for you, Jazz."

"You know what I meant."

"Yes, firsts are nerve-wracking. You think you're nervous; imagine how the Epstein family feels. You and I are there for moral support. Amy's the pro at this sort of thing."

"Is it depressing?"

"No, not really. You'd think so. Yes, Amy addresses the seriousness of the current situation. And then she offers the most important thing when a family member suffers from a life-altering disease like alcoholism."

"What's that?"

"Hope."

"Sounds heavy."

"It is. We won't go in with empty stomachs. That brings me to why I'm here. Are you ready for lunch?"

"But we just ate."

"That was hours ago."

She raised a skeptical brow and checked the time. "Ruby, that was two hours ago."

"Jazz, you'll learn we defense lawyers get our three square and snacks when there's a lull in the action."

"What lull? We have an intervention this afternoon."

"I know. This is as close to a lull as we get. Are you in?"

Jasmine looked at the screen, torn.

"It'll still be there when we get back."

"All right. I've never been to Chestnut."

"You're in for a treat."

As soon as Jasmine and Ruby emerged from the meeting room, Cassandra pounced. "It's about time. I'm starving." She put her arm around Jasmine and propelled her down the hallway. "Colin told me we're celebrating you, too." She glanced at Colin as they passed his desk. "Are you coming?"

"Of course." He motioned Cassandra and Jasmine ahead, and fell into step beside Ruby. "We'll let the two women of the hour lead the way."

"It was just a routine bail hearing," Jasmine tossed back.

"Nonsense," Cassandra said. "It was a milestone for you. We pause to enjoy our successes, right Ruby?"

"That's right. We always make time for chocolate cake."

They reached Chestnut, and Jasmine craned her neck to take in the décor.

"This was a bank before it was repurposed in the 40s as a restaurant. The carvings are exquisite," Colin said.

"Go ahead, you two," Ruby said. "Explore. Cass and I will get our table."

Cassandra and Ruby moved to the reservation stand. The hostess stood tall and poised in her tailored black dress. Pearls dangled from her ears and hung in three strands at her throat. "Ms. Miller, welcome. I recognized you from your billboard. Please, follow me."

"Now that's service. You're a VIP now, Ruby," Cass whispered. "I need a splashy billboard for Dayton Law Office."

"You certainly do."

Jasmine and Colin met them at the table.

"Have you seen the vault door?" Jasmine asked as she sat next to Ruby. "It should be in a museum."

The waitress hovered until they'd settled, and then descended for drink orders.

"Coffee, and keep it coming." Ruby said.

"I'll have the same," said Cassandra.

"As will I. I'll need cream and sugar, and keep that coming."

"Basically, he wants candy coffee," Ruby added.

"I could bring out whipped cream and caramel sauce. Our chef makes them from scratch."

"Perfect."

"And for you?"

"I'll have oolong tea," Jasmine said.

"Would you like a minute to look at the menu?"

"Ready?" Ruby asked her table. When they nodded, she said, "No, we're ready. Go ahead, Guests of Honor."

"I'll have the Waldorf salad."

"Cass, what's come over you?"

"Make that two, please." Jasmine smirked at Ruby, and gave Cassandra an encouraging nod.

"What?" Cassandra asked, avoiding Ruby's gaze. "I

want to save myself for dessert."

"I don't understand that logic at all," Ruby said. "You have no max when it comes to chocolate."

Colin cleared his throat. "I'll have the salmon. It sounds delicious."

"I can assure you it is. It was flown in from Alaska this morning. The cherry plank our chef grills it on puts it over the top."

"Wonderful."

"I'll have the filet medallions," Ruby said. "And I'll substitute the sweet potato casserole for the broccoli."

"Will you be ordering dessert?"

"Yes, we'll order that now. We'd leave with broken hearts if you ran out. Three volcanic-fudge tortes with ice cream, please." Ruby gestured to Jasmine. "And whatever she'd like."

"In the spirit of celebration, make that four."

"Hear, hear. And pair our dessert with Moscato, please."

"How many bottles?"

"One. We like to keep our celebrations separate from our interventions."

Jasmine turned to Colin. "What was it like when you worked at the county attorney's office?"

"Schuler served as county attorney then," he said. "There were problems. Certain paralegals had more interest in gossiping about their kids' antics, and their no-good ex-husbands than working. The rest of us had to pick up their slack." When the server returned with their drink orders, Colin paused to dollop whipped cream and drizzle thick sauce onto his coffee.

"It's almost too pretty to drink," Jasmine said. "Were you a barista?"

"I prefer the term 'coffee artist,'" Colin said. "We all had to pay for school somehow." He saw Ruby's pained expression, and said, "I'm sorry."

"Sorry for what?" Jasmine asked.

"It's all right, Colin. I sold a number of antiques during law school. I'm certainly not alone. Alfred's Antiques does great business." She added cheer to her voice, and said, "The county attorney's office had your usual office dynamics. Not everyone was an all-star like Colin."

"And our fearless leader," he said.

"Overall, people's positions made sense for their commitment level and ability. Chatty Cali was on her thirteenth year as an entry-level paralegal."

"Then Johnston took office and things changed. For instance, Cali is the Community Prosecution Division's Senior Paralegal."

"That makes no sense," Jasmine said.

"Few assignments do," Colin said.

"What do you make of it?"

"He's legally trained and politically adept but lacks business savvy," Ruby said. "He's ill-equipped to manage human resources. That's the aboveboard explanation."

"And the underhanded one?"

"At our office, we don't accuse without proof. Right, Colin?"

"Right, Ruby."

Cass stabbed at her salad without taking a bite.

"Hey, Cass. What'd your salad do to you? Get something else if it'll take that glum look off your face."

"No, they gave me exactly what I ordered." She stared at the creamy greens and waved her fork over them as if willing them to disappear.

"Guess they don't have magical forks at Chestnut. Order something else."

"I wouldn't want to waste—"

"Do you feel like you're celebrating?"

"No."

"You know you want cheese-smothered ravioli." Spotting the gleam in Cassandra's eye, Ruby called over the waitress. "I'm sorry. This Waldorf salad was made beautifully. Jasmine is really enjoying it. But Cassandra would like it removed and replaced with the four-cheese ravioli."

"Absolutely, I'll put the ravioli in right away. At Chestnut, we strive to give each guest a pleasurable dining experience."

"You're doing superbly. Thank you."

"You're my Houdini." Cassandra raised the back of her hand to her forehead. "I'm famished. Those sweet potatoes look good."

Ruby passed the silver-edged dish. "Fine, but only until yours comes."

Cassandra speared into the candied top, and scooped out three heaping spoonfuls. "Now I feel like I'm celebrating."

"Excellent. Have as much as you want, Cass. I'll take an equal amount of your ravioli and call it even."

Cassandra's next portion was half-sized.

"It's your turn to toast, Colin," said Ruby. "Start thinking, and make it good."

"Your last won't be hard to top."

"It was hard to get inspired by the transition to a virtual file system."

"It was an important milestone."

"Important, but dull—as my toast reflected."

"You quoted Martin Luther King."

"What did Ruby say?" Jasmine asked.

Ruby held up her hand. "First, let me provide the context," she said. "Cass was against the new system, and charged with disposing the physical files. Not a good combo, it turned out. She decided to do so by filling my office with shreds."

"'All progress is precarious, and the solution of one problem brings us face to face with another problem,'" Colin recited. "'May the consequences of progress be met with an appropriate and equivalent response.'"

"One of my better pranks. Ruby's first toast is my favorite. She made it right after we launched our firms." Cassandra raised her coffee mug, and waited for Colin to lift his.

In unison, they said, "'May we never regret this

bold endeavor,'" before clinking their mugs and beaming.

"Have you?" Jasmine asked Ruby.

"No. It's been, at times, terrifying, thrilling, and everything in between. And always worthwhile."

They raised their mugs and clinked again. "Hear, hear."

CHAPTER 6

The oven clock read 5:16 P.M.—fourteen minutes before she had to have dinner on the table. Nothing could be out of place.

The table was perfect. Fresh daisies had pride of place in her grandmother's porcelain vase—the only special little something she'd allowed herself. Looking at the yellow petals, she had hope. Tonight would go well.

She toyed with the skirt of her blue silk dress, wondering if he'd notice it and remember the good times. The night they'd met, and he'd twirled her around all night. He'd looked dashing in a suit as dark as his hair. The size difference had thrilled her as he'd moved her across the dance floor.

Yes, tonight would be different. She'd make sure

everything was perfect, and give him no reason to get upset.

On impulse, she straightened the place settings, and took a picture. She imagined it was a table at the restaurant she'd dreamt of opening. Smiling to herself, she propped her phone on the counter, held her grandmother's vase, and waited for the flash. Seeing herself in a striking dress with beautiful flowers, ready to welcome home her handsome husband, she could almost convince herself she was happy.

His car blasted into the driveway.

Heart pounding, she put her phone away and replaced the vase on the table. His beer was icy cold. The steak was medium. She'd cut a small piece from the bottom to ensure the pink. This one wouldn't end up thrown against the cream wall. She wouldn't have to scrub for an hour to remove the blood. She wouldn't be so stupid to not get his steak right again.

He slammed the garage door and strode into the kitchen.

She forced a bright smile and cheerful tone as she greeted him. "Welcome home, Jerry. Everything's ready. The steak is just how you like it."

Ignoring her, he swept up the tidy pile of mail on the counter. Rifling through the stack, he pulled out a card and clutched it in his fist. "Who's Dr. Prim?" He waved the card at her. "Why is he wishing you a happy birthday?"

Unable to stop them, her hands trembled. At a

loss, she clasped them together, knowing she held a bomb with no way to defuse it. Helpless, she held up her hands. "Because it's my birthday."

"Are you trying to get smart with me?"

"No, Jerry."

He closed the distance between them, grabbed her wrist with his left hand and the back of her neck with his right, forcing her gaze up into his. Hard steel. "Are you sleeping with him? Is that what's going on here? I go to work to pay for this house, your car—everything. And you're off fucking this Alan Prim? Get you hot that he's a doctor?"

"No, Jerry. He's my dentist. I'm sure he sends every patient a card."

"Are you calling me crazy? Are you saying I'm imagining things?"

"No, Jerry, no."

"So you are fucking him!"

"No, I'm not." Her voice quavered.

"Should I call your boss and tell him what a slut you are? You're already on thin ice, missing work like you do. It's another sign you're unstable. You can't get to work, can't keep track of your goddamn keys, can't even keep track of who you belong to." He tightened his grip. "You're mine, or have you forgotten?"

"No, Jerry. I know. Please let go. You're hurting me."

"Not as much as you're hurting me by spreading your legs to your goddamn dentist. What about my feelings?" He threw her against the wall.

She landed on her left hand with a crack. Cradling her wrist against her chest, she sat shaking, tears streaming down her face. "I'll do better, Jerry. Not be so forgetful. Whatever you want me to do, I'll do it."

"You're going to find a new dentist. A woman. I can't even trust you to get your teeth cleaned. You don't deserve a present for your birthday. It wasn't even important enough to remember. You're so damn old it's ridiculous to celebrate at your age."

Twenty-nine, she thought. Mind scattered by the pain shooting from her wrist, it drifted to the evening of her twenty-fifth birthday. Silk brushed her legs. She was desirable, his princess, and he was her prince. Her sister threw the surprise party for Susan; its high attendance shocked no one. She was different then. She had dreams. Dreams Jerry called adorable like the stuffed animals she'd kept into womanhood. She'd figured out they were silly. Jerry had told her so enough times that she'd packed them away and given them up.

Jerry yanked her up by her left wrist and back from the past. Agony shot up her arm as she cried out.

"Are you listening to me? Or are you too busy fantasizing about your damn dentist?"

"Yes, I mean no. No, Jerry, I don't want anything from you."

He squeezed her wrist. Voice as hard as his eyes, he said, "So you're saying I do nothing for you." He felt her tremble, and tightened his grip. "I do everything for you! There's food on this table because of me. There's a roof over your head because I put it there. I'm king of this fucking castle and you expect to be treated like a queen. You're just a slut—whoring yourself like you women do." He punctuated his words with violent jerks to her arm, wrenching her shoulder from its socket.

She choked back sobs, knowing they'd only fan the flames of his fury.

With a sweep of his hand, he upturned the kitchen table.

The last connection to her grandmother crashed to the floor.

As she looked at the shards, something inside her snapped. She wondered which was more broken, and if either could ever be fixed.

"Look at what you've done. Clean it up. I've had enough of you. Don't you dare ask me when I'll be home." He slammed the garage door behind him.

She glanced at the disarray. Her gaze fell on the oven clock—5:44 P.M.

After locating her phone in the mess, she photographed what happened when she dared to dream. Tears blurred her vision as she saw on the small screen the reality of her life.

"Another successful intervention at Miller Law Office," Ruby said, and locked her office suite.

"Ruby, there was weeping," Jasmine said.

"Weeping is appropriate and beneficial," Amy said.

"It showed Veronica how important her commitment to sobriety is. Wouldn't you agree, Ruby?"

"Yes, the healing power of tears. I caught some shine in your eyes, Jazz."

"Well—"

"Good. Keep caring, Jazz. You'll be a better lawyer for it."

Amy nodded in agreement, and said, "That went as well as we could have hoped. Vera committed to long-term treatment as a resident."

"Aurora was a wonderful choice," Ruby said. "She completed and submitted her application, and we have her set to enter treatment tomorrow."

"I hope she succeeds. Her whole family showed up for her today. That matters, right?" Jasmine asked.

"Right. And they showed up for her at her arraignment. Jazz pointed that out to the judge. She took first chair, and handled herself admirably.".

"That's high praise from a top-notch lawyer. You should be proud. Allow me to buy you dinner."

"After lunch at Chestnut, I'm not too hungry. Do you think she'll succeed, Amy?"

"Alcoholism thrives on shame, on secrecy and denial. Today we shone light on it. Yes, Jasmine, I think she'll do well. What does this do for her case, Ruby?"

"Clean record, BAC a hair over the gross-misdemeanor threshold, speedy and voluntary enrollment in the most rigorous rehab program in the country, and voluntary installation of an IID. The case is clean. I anticipate negotiating for a careless. That'd mean a blemish on her record. A significant one, but not the oozing sore of a DUI conviction. I'm starving."

"After that delightful metaphor, my appetite has waned," Amy said. "Count me in for something light."

"Chinese takeout anyone?" Ruby asked with a hopeful grin. "No takers?"

Amy and Jasmine shook their heads.

"How about Good Globe?" Amy asked.

"Conveniently located right next door to Chan's Chow."

"I love Good Globe," said Jasmine.

"It seems you're out-voted."

"All right, democracy carries the day," Ruby said. "But if everything is glowing, I'm bolting to Chan's."

"Nine-one-one. What's your emergency?"

"I'm calling to report a murder. This is Stuart—"

"Mr. County Attorney, I'd recognize your voice anywhere."

"Yes, it's me. Stuart Johnston."

"I beg your pardon, but I have to continue this conversation according to protocol."

"Yes, of course."

"Please state your emergency."

"There's been a murder. The victim is Jerald Combes. I'm at his lake cabin. His wife, Susan

Combes, fled the scene in her car. I saw her. It's imperative that you locate her immediately. They live on three-one-eight-one Baker. She's mentally unstable and has already killed once."

"I've located your position, and dispatched units to your location and to the Combes residence. Are you in a safe place?"

"Yes, I'm in front of the cabin."

"Please remain where you are until peace officers arrive."

"I will."

"Between you and me, Mr. Johnston, I voted for you. I appreciate your commitment to cracking down on crime. I'm so sorry you're part of this tragedy."

"Thank you. He's a dear friend. I want justice for Jerry."

"Would you like me to remain on the line until law enforcement arrives?"

"No, I need the time to pull myself together."

"All right then. Take care now."

"Thank you."

He signed off, leaned against his car, and folded his arms across his chest. When he saw flashing lights, he crouched down and lowered his head.

An officer approached and laid a hand on Stuart's shoulder. "Are you all right, Johnston?"

He raised his head. "Strauss, thank God you're on duty—a man I can trust. I'm sorry. Give me a minute. I'll pull myself together."

"Take whatever time you need."

Stuart shook his head and rose. "I was able to positively identify . . . him. The victim is a close friend of mine. More like a brother, really, since our crew days at Princeton. I was able to positively identify the . . . him. God, I can't believe Jerry's gone. Murdered by his own wife. He warned me she'd been unstable. I never thought she'd take it this far. But I saw her drive away with my own eyes."

"What's her name?"

"Susan Combes."

"Physical description?"

"Brown hair, medium length, petite frame."

"Walk me through what happened tonight. Whose cabin is this?"

"Jerry's."

"What brought you here?"

"Jerry called me around seven. He'd had another fight with his wife."

"That happen a lot?"

"Yes. She's the jealous type—tracks his whereabouts, has a suspicious mind. Quick to flip her lid, as Jerry would say."

"He say anything else to you?"

"Jerry was heading down this road when he called. He'd caught his wife's car in his rearview mirror a few miles back. He said he'd calm her down and send her home. He wanted me to come over after that to help him figure out what to do about her. She was getting worse. Violent."

"She make any threats?"

"Frequently. Jerry bought her a new kitchen knife. She said she'd slice him up like a stuffed turkey, good riddance, and find herself a real man."

"When did she say that?"

"Tonight. I told Jerry time and again you can't reason with crazy. Damn it, why wouldn't he listen?" Stuart clenched his fists and turned away for a minute. He scrubbed his hands over his face, turned back, and said, "Times like this, it's hard to be objective. But as county attorney, it's my job. I'll help facilitate the charging process with my office. It could be she's already grabbed what she needed and fled."

"Appreciate your cooperation, Johnston. I'll send a detective over to get some more specifics. You know the drill."

"Yes, of course. Anything. I want to help. It's difficult being here, knowing that he's inside."

"We'll get you out of here as soon as we can."

"Can you do me a favor, Strauss?"

"Within reason."

"Don't get fancy on this one. Follow procedure perfectly—nothing more, nothing less. I want this to stick. I want justice for Jerry."

"You have my word."

CHAPTER 7

"Law office, Ruby speaking."

The sleeves of an oversized orange sweatshirt swallowed the caller's hands and covered her mouth. Brown hair curtained her face. In a muffled voice, she said, "I need to speak to a lawyer."

"I'm Ruby Miller. Criminal defense is all I do, and I do it well. Let's start with your name."

She lowered her hands, pushed back her hair, and wiped her eyes with a sleeve. "Susan Combes."

"How can I help you, Susan?"

"I've been arrested for muh—" A sob broke free, and interrupted her answer. Her face disappeared behind orange.

"Money laundering?"

Susan shook her head.

"Manslaughter?"

Again, she shook her head.

"Murder?"

Susan looked up. "Yes," she whispered. "My husband. I didn't do it."

"Where was he found?"

"The lake cabin." She put her head down and burst into tears.

"What's the address?"

"Two-one-four-two Grays Bay Boulevard, Minnetonka. They're saying—"

"Susan, I'm not yet interested in what the cops are saying happened. I'm going to go there and see for myself. Meanwhile, have a good cry. Do whatever you need to do to pull yourself together. Say nothing to the police. If they ask you anything about this case, you're going to tell them you want your lawyer. Once you get off the phone with me, they'll process your prints, collect demographics from you, and put you in holding. I'll be in to visit you once my team conducts an investigation at the cabin."

"Do you believe me?"

"My mind is open. I'll figure out who did it, Susan. Fair enough?"

"Yes."

"Where were you arrested?"

"My home."

"One second." Ruby pulled up a directory on the stationary supercomputer on her desk. "I have your home address. It's nine now. I'll be there by one. Hang in there, Susan."

Ruby disconnected, packed her briefcase, and left her office. "PSC, call Justin Kottke."

"Kottke."

"We have a hot one. We need to move on it—now. Meet me at two-one-four-two Grays Bay in Minnetonka. Lake cabin. Usual rates, big case. Murder. Wife accused of killing her husband. How long until you arrive?"

"What if I had a hot date?"

"Since the woman you're swooning after is oblivious, I'd say you'd be willing to cancel on any poor excuse for a substitute."

"Harsh, and accurate. Damn it. Heading out now."

"See you soon. PSC, disengage and call Jasmine Sinclair."

"Hi, Ruby."

"I hope you powered down."

"I zoned out to that show Amy recommended. It just ended."

"Good. I'm heading to a murder scene. Want to join me?"

"Absolutely."

"Be there in ten. PSC, disengage and tag Anton's."

"Anton speaking."

"Ruby speaking."

"Ciao, Gioia!"

"It's good to hear your voice, Anton, and not just because it means there's a cannoli in my near future."

"You need a late night fix."

"Yes, do I ever."

"Anything with the cannoli?"

"I'm heading to a crime scene. Give me the usual."

"Cops sampler, and a black-and-strong coming right up."

"And throw in something healthy. Got any green goop ready to go?"

"So you are taking your new intern. Jasmine, Morning Glory and GreenPower. I like her very much."

"Your mind is a steel trap, my friend."

"How is she working out?"

"Great. She's willing to dive right in."

"When will you be by?"

"I'm getting to your door now." Ruby set her PSC to standby and parked. In one fluid movement, she was out of the car and hurrying into the familiar scents of fresh baked bread and strong coffee. Tearing her eyes away from the tempting baked goods displayed in tidy rows, she focused on the man behind the counter wearing a white baker's coat. "Hey, Italian Stallion. There's the man with the goods in the flesh."

"You're too much. I'm tossing in the last pastries. Nice and hot. I'll put it on your tab." Anton moved his hefty frame with surprising speed. Brushing flour from his hands, he enfolded Ruby in an enthusiastic embrace, and pulled back enough to give her cheeks loud kisses.

She balanced herself on the counter as he released her abruptly to hand her a giant bakery bag and a coffee kit.

"Thanks, Anton. This smells like my idea of heaven."

"At the rate you're going, you might get there sooner than you think."

"Not you, too. You own a bakery. You should be on my side. I'm one of your best customers."

"We started offering healthy options for a reason."

"Somehow, I didn't picture the angel at the gates to sugary delights chastising me."

"See you in the morning, I suspect."

"You know it. I'll rally the team at eight. The proper fuel will discourage a coup against the fiend dragging them out of bed on a Saturday morning."

"I'll have Angela deliver."

"You're a saint. You deserve those manly wings."

"Scoot." He tossed a cinnamon roll at her head.

She caught and sampled it. "Divine. *A presto!*" She waved the roll, and walked out to the sound of his great guffaws.

Back in her car, she accelerated into traffic bound for dancing, bar hopping, and blind dates. "PSC, message to Colin Lewis. Murder case. Client is Susan Combes. Victim is client's husband, Jerald Combes. Please pull data on both. Prep file for meeting at eight sharp, conference room. Expecting six, counting you. Angela will deliver. Settle up our firm's account when she does."

Ruby's unit sounded.

"PSC, recite message."

Will do.

"Respond, eternally grateful. End message. Call Amy Larson."

"Need a head shrinking, my dear?"

"Not yet. It's still shrunk from dinner. I picked up a murder case. The client is Susan Combes. She's charged with killing her husband. I'll need you to profile. Eight work for you?"

"It would be my pleasure. Should I pick up Anton's on my way in?"

"Thanks for the offer. Angela's swinging over."

"Anything edible?"

"I told Anton to throw some nondescript glowing items into the mix, along with the real food."

"That was very thoughtful."

"Fuel increases productivity."

"Right, it was a practical move."

"Precisely."

"See you at eight, Ruby. Good luck."

"Yes, luck—'I'm a great believer in luck. The harder I work the more I have of it.'"

"Thomas Jefferson, I believe."

"Yes."

"Go make some luck."

"That's the plan."

Ruby dropped her PSC in the cup holder, and pulled in front of a brick apartment building.

Jasmine ran out in business casual with brown flats, and flew into the passenger seat.

"Hey Jazz. Nice outfit. Ever been to a crime scene before?"

"No, can't say that I have."

"First rule—never arrive empty-handed, or on an empty stomach." Ruby handed her a cup and a small bag. "Here, your green goo and something healthy. Don't ask me what's in them. I stopped at Anton's for coffee and baked goods. There's the cop stereotype for a reason. Our shared vices are excellent fodder for bonding. Bonded equals more inclined to inform. And it's the humanitarian thing to do. Err on the side of compassion—rule two."

"What are you looking for?"

"I'll know it when I see it. Go in with a clear mind. Often, the cops arrive with a conclusion, and look for evidence to support it. We're looking for evidence, period. If we don't gather what they miss now, it may be lost. Ready?"

"As I'll ever be."

"First time's the hardest. It doesn't get easy, but it gets easier. If there ever comes a time when getting near death doesn't elicit a reaction, resign."

They pulled over in front of the cabin.

"It's like daytime out here," Jazz said.

Black and whites parked across the yard. Squad lights filled the blackness with red and blue. Spotlights illuminated the driveway and the path leading to the front porch.

Ruby noted that there was no white outline in the lit area. The CSIs would make quick work of the outside, she figured, and then she could make her own observations up close. Not one to waste time, she turned to her intern, and said, "Stay in the car, Jazz. Figure out who owns the adjacent property. Research the owner or owners. I'm going to get the lay of the land." Ruby grabbed the large bakery bag and coffee kit.

"Good luck. My grandmother always said it never hurts to have the golden lady on your side."

"No, it never does. Thanks, Jazz."

Ruby strolled over to a slim man in a black jumpsuit.

He had set up his work station away from the yellow tape and heavy foot traffic streaming in and out of the cabin, and in close proximity to the white van with black letters declaring its purpose: CRIME SCENE INVESTIGATIONS. His long brown ponytail streamed across the white letters labeling him a crime scene investigator.

"There's dedication," she said. "Hard at work at quarter to ten on a Friday."

He turned toward Ruby's voice.

"You have photographs, Jimmy?"

"You know I do. I'm not known as the best photographer in the unit for nothing."

"I know it, and you know it. They call you in on all the big cases for a reason. When will I get to admire your work?"

"Would you settle for when the county attorney hands it over?"

"Come on, Jimmy, I brought sustenance. You get skinnier every time I see you. My grandmother called these crullers. Came by my sweet tooth honestly. You interested?"

"You know I am."

"I have some hot coffee to wash it down."

"Even better."

"I need a quick peek, Jimmy. I'll be done by the time you fuel up. As the defense, I have a right to these pictures."

"Well . . ." He eyeballed the bakery bag.

"I sprang for the good stuff. Nothing but the best for the best."

"Deal. Hand it over."

"As soon as you pull up the photos."

He tapped at his laptop, and spun it so she could see the screen.

Ruby opened the bag.

After snagging a cherry cruller and a white frosted donut, he took a generous bite into one and then the other.

"You happen to know who's on charging duty tonight?"

"Hollins," he mumbled around pastry, flakes falling from his mouth.

"Hollins?"

He swallowed, swiped a hand over his cheek, and wiped cherry jelly on his pants. "Yeah, and he has plenty of direction."

"Johnston's been talking to him?"

"Screaming, more like. Can't help but hear him. Johnston was first on the scene. Made the ID. Called it in. The vic's a real good buddy of his."

"What's Johnston after?"

"Warrants for the wife's car, for her arrest. He's been hollering for updates for the PC statement. Wants it all done by the book."

"No special treatment for his buddy—no extra samples, more photos?"

"Hell no. He was very clear on that. Strictly follow procedure." He lowered his voice. "He'd send your client to Mardova tonight if he could."

Ruby pursed her lips. "How long before the scene's cleared?"

"Fifteen."

"I'll stay outside until then." Ruby set down the coffee kit. "Pour yourself some coffee, Jimmy, and enjoy it while I peruse your fine work." Ruby scrolled through photos and made notes on her PSC. She grabbed her stylus and sketched a rough diagram.

"You see, it's open and shut. Looks like Johnston will get your client that one-way ticket to Mardova."

"It's not so much about what I see, Jimmy, as what I don't see."

"You're always good for a riddle, Ruby. Going to elaborate?"

"Of course not. I'm still in observation mode, Jimmy. I hear Kottke coming."

"You have to admit his bike is prime."

"Ogle it later, Jimmy. The sooner you finish up, the

sooner you get to go home to Sarah."

"That's not an incentive, Ruby."

"I thought you two made up."

"So did I. Can't figure her out for the life of me. Any suggestions? You know, you being a woman and all."

"I say bring her a cruller."

"She hates sweets. Gets after me for rotting my insides."

"I was going to say chocolate next. That's out. Flowers? Is an apology in order?"

"Probably. How the hell am I supposed to know?"

"Did you miss a special occasion?"

"Well, how am I supposed to figure out something I forgot?"

"Do you have a shared calendar?"

"Yeah, Sarah set it up a while back. Never looked at it though."

Ruby waited.

"Hey, that's a fine idea. Damn it. I should have thought of that."

"When did you get married? When's her birthday?"

He grabbed his phone from the workbench and accessed the calendar. "Let's see. Her birthday is the fourth of August."

"That's not it. But make a note so you don't miss it."

"Come to think of it, Ruby, we did have a summer wedding. I have a bad feeling about this. Yup. There it is. The seventh of May. She even made a note about the year we were hitched. I spaced on our tenth."

"Way to go, Jimmy."

"Thanks a lot. I'm an idiot."

"It's only Friday. Plan a flashy evening for Saturday. It'd make sense to not do a big-deal date on a weeknight. You were saving it for the weekend."

"Yeah, I better hurry up and get home. Any ideas what I should do?"

"You're on your own there, Jimmy. I'm done here. Good luck." She headed back to her car.

Justin Kottke had dismounted, removed his helmet, and shaken out his thick mahogany hair, unaware he had a captive audience. He unzipped his leather jacket, and called over, "Hey Ruby."

Jasmine darted from the car, and intercepted Ruby. "You know him? He's quite the specimen."

"Yeah, you stop noticing. We went on a date a few years back, before he left the precinct and turned PI. Had a fun time, no spark. I still find his mind sexy as hell."

"So he's available?"

"You could try, Jazz. Fair warning, he's madly in love with a horse whisperer. She's clueless. Come on." Ruby strode over to Justin with Jasmine at her heels.

"Jazz, meet Justin Kottke—finest investigator around. This is the newest addition to our team.,Jasmine Sinclair."

"So you got around to hiring an intern. How's it going so far?" he asked Jasmine.

She stood silent, mesmerized by the flecks of gold

in his chocolate-brown eyes.

"Ruby put you in a sugar coma?"

"No, no, I'm fine," she said. "This is the best job I've ever had."

"Speaking of, let's get to work. Kottke, team meeting at eight tomorrow. That means you, Jazz, if you want in."

"Of course I do."

"Hopefully, we'll get some shut-eye before then," Ruby said.

"Where'd you put the Anton's?"

"With Jimmy."

"I'll take care of distribution."

"I was counting on it. When you're done here, head to the Combes' residence. After this, Jazz and I will head over to the jail to interview Susan."

"What'd you observe about her so far?"

"She's no hardened killer."

"Any kind of killer? Heat of passion? Self-defense?"

"We'll know soon enough, won't we?"

"True. Nice to meet you, Jasmine." He shot her a grin, and strolled over to Jimmy.

Jasmine turned her dreamy smile on Ruby, and snapped out of it when she saw Ruby's amused expression. Summoning a serious look, she asked, "Are you sure Justin doesn't need a hand?"

"What for? To grab his ass? Sorry, Jazz. You're stuck with me. Although it's nice to know you have a vice after all."

Jasmine blushed.

"Don't let Kottke distract you from why we're here. Kottke handles forensics. He'll do a thorough walk-through, and send any samples to a lab in Bloomington. I do my own, independent investigation, and compare notes with him later. What did you notice as we were driving up?"

"Lots of personnel. Is this the usual amount for a murder?"

"Yes. On top of this horde, there's another one at the residence. What about the location?"

"Remote."

"Yes, it's at the end of the road. One neighbor a significant distance away. It's a good place to commit murder. I suspect the road is visible from the neighbor's porch. Did you spot the light on the porch as we were driving up?"

"No, I missed it."

"Hopefully so did the killer or killers. Let's find out if anyone was on the porch, shall we?"

CHAPTER 8

"Why aren't we using the front door?" Jasmine asked.

"It's visible from the crime scene. We want to fly under the radar. Cops get cranky when they don't get their coffee and donuts, and when they think we're interfering with their investigation. We're within bounds here. Witness interviews are part of mounting a defense. Nothing is stopping them from walking over to speak to . . ."

Jasmine consulted her notes. "Carol Lawrence. Seventy-two. Recently widowed. Late husband, Jeffrey. Currently works as a librarian, part-time. She has an apartment in the city—her primary residence. Ran a 5K last month with her daughter. Made the local news. Also has a son."

"Well done." Ruby knocked on the porch door.

"She must have been up and moving," Ruby noted when the porch light flicked on and the inside door opened. "I'm Ruby Miller and this is Jasmine Sinclair," Ruby called to the woman crossing the porch. "We're looking into what went on at your neighbor's. You notice the activity going on over there?"

"Yes, yes. I've been up wondering if anybody was going to ask me about it."

"No officers have been over?"

"No. Aren't you peace officers?"

"We're not. I'm a lawyer. Jasmine here is an intern with my office. Our client is Susan Combes. We're here to figure out what happened tonight."

"I'm Carol Lawrence. Call me Carol. Pleased to meet you Ruby, and Jasmine."

"Likewise," Jasmine said.

"I don't know how much help I can be." She stood at the door and rubbed the age spots on her hand.

"You might know more than you realize. Mind if we ask you some questions?"

"Not at all. It gets so quiet here at night. In some ways it's nice. But it's also nice to have visitors." Her brow furrowed. "Although I should ask about the circumstances. I don't know what happened over there. There are so many uniforms."

"Jerald Combes was found dead. We want to figure out what happened."

"Oh my, right next door. Do you think it's safe for me to stay here? I forget to lock my door half the time. Being out in the middle of nowhere gives a person a sense of security—a false one, from the sounds of it."

"We have no reason to think you're in any danger. But if you'd feel better, by all means stay elsewhere until this is cleared up. Do you have somewhere else to stay?"

"Yes, an apartment in the city. It's near my daughter and grandbabies."

"Sounds like you'd be more comfortable there, Carol." Ruby held up her PSC. "Do you mind if we record this?"

"Go on ahead."

Ruby engaged the recorder with a few taps. "I notice you can't see the Combes' cabin from the porch steps. May we come in?"

"Of course." She fluttered her hands, moved back, and waved them in. "Where are my manners?"

"It's a lot to process." Ruby stepped inside, and motioned for Jasmine to join her. She set her PSC on a wrought-iron coffee table. "Carol, where were you this evening?"

"I was on this very porch."

"Were you sitting?"

Carol pointed to a paisley loveseat. "I was curled up there, reading my book."

"Do you mind?" Ruby gestured.

"No."

Carol took a seat across from Ruby, and motioned for Jasmine to take the other chair.

"Thanks, Carol." Jasmine said, and took a seat.

Ruby sat on the loveseat and drew up her legs. "Like this?"

"No, my feet were facing the other way."

Ruby made the adjustment.

"Yes, like that."

"When I turn my head, I can see out the screen," Ruby said. "We're facing the road. When it's light out, can you see the traffic coming down this road?"

"Yes, we usually don't get a lot. Not like tonight. I'm near the end of the road, you know."

"Are you referring to the emergency respondents?"

"No, this was before the flashing lights started coming."

"What did you see?"

"A car and a truck came barreling down the road at about six-thirty, I'd say." She held up a slightly crooked finger and pointed toward the road. "It was still light out."

"Are you familiar with Mr. and Mrs. Combes?"

"No, they keep to themselves. He uses the place much more than she does. He's said hello, and asked me to let him know if he's too loud. I had to go over there last weekend. There was quite the ruckus, but it quieted down quickly enough."

"Would you recognize their vehicles?"

"Yes, I've seen that truck before. It's his. I don't know whose car that was. It might belong to Susan. I've seen a black sedan parked over there before, but never this car. Bright blue."

"Did you see anything else?"

"About ten, fifteen minutes later this rattletrap comes puttering down the road. I remember thinking it was on its last legs. It made an awful racket."

"How long were you on the porch?"

"Until late. It's just me. Jeffrey passed on a couple months ago. They say it gets easier. I'm still waiting for that to happen."

"I'm so sorry for your loss, Carol." Jasmine reached over to lay her hand on Carol's.

"Thank you for that." She sighed and patted Jasmine's hand. "I've fallen into a routine. Every Friday, I come here after work. After dinner, I head out here to read until I can't see my book. I watch the fireflies dance and listen to the crickets until I'm falling asleep in my chair. You can't get that kind of peace in the city. It makes me feel closer to Jeffrey when I'm here. We loved sitting on this porch together."

"Sounds like you made wonderful memories with your husband," Jasmine said.

"You're nice to listen to an old lady ramble. I'm sorry. You have a mystery to solve, and here I am going on."

"You have nothing to apologize for, Carol," Ruby said. "We want to hear what's on your mind. Did anything else disturb your peace and quiet?"

"Yes. The truck came roaring past here."

"What time?"

"It was starting to get dark by then. About seven, I'd say."

"Anything else?"

"I was heading in to make tea when the truck drove by. I made myself a pretty little tray, and carried it out here. I was just finishing my cookies when the truck came back down the road."

"Did you see the truck leave again that night?"

"No, but a car flew past just as I was taking my tray into the house. And the rattletrap was right behind it."

"Was it dark out by then?"

"Yes. I don't move as fast as I used to. No reason to."

"How could you tell what kind of vehicles they were?"

"I figured it was two cars from the headlights, I guess. And that rattletrap—Christ Almighty, I'd place that noise anywhere. Wake the dead. I bet my dear Jeffrey heard it."

"Could other vehicles have come down this road while you were inside?"

"Not likely. We're up closer to the road than I wanted to be. I told Jeffrey we should've built further off. That man didn't listen. He drove me crazy half the time." She swallowed hard. "I'd give anything to have him back telling me I'm a stubborn old woman. I'd tell him he'd turned into a grump of a geezer. We brought out the worst in each other, and the best."

"Sounds like your match." Jasmine said simply.

"I miss that man something terrible."

"It means what you had is worth missing. It's

natural to feel sorrow along with joy. It's important to feel both."

"You're pretty wise for a young thing."

"You're pretty sharp for a stubborn old woman."

Carol laughed and squeezed Jasmine's hand. "Thank you, dear. I needed that."

"Carol, did you stay inside after you brought your tray in?" Ruby asked.

"No. I came back out here."

"I know it was dark, but did any sounds, any scents stand out to you?"

"Now that you mention it, I smelled smoke coming from the woods."

"Is it unusual to have fires in this area?"

"No. People have always enjoyed circling around a good bonfire. It brought me back to my girlhood. My parents loved to take us camping. We'd take out marshmallows, graham crackers, chocolate, and make s'mores."

"Ah, the real deal."

"Now they have that Soy More treat. I don't care for it."

"I don't either," Ruby said. "But the group that goes wild for the glowing green goop loves soy." Ruby glanced over at Jasmine.

Carol missed the exchange. "There's nothing like a golden marshmallow straight from the fire and chocolate sandwiched between crisp sweet crackers. It was one of the best parts of summer. We'd take turns gathering more wood for the fire. That's what I smelled. Burning wood."

"Do you remember sensing anything else?"

"I was drifting off when a car came down the road."

"Could you tell anything about it?"

"Yes, I recognized it by the sound. I've seen a car over at the Combes cabin with Jerald's truck. A black sedan. It sounded like a small jet rocketing down the road—almost as loud as that bike that came by here a short while before you came knocking."

"What happened after you saw that car?"

"The flashing lights started coming. Once they set up those spotlights I could see I was right. The black sedan was parked over there, and Jerald's truck."

"How did you see the Combes' driveway?"

"I peeked out the kitchen window."

"Do you know who the driver of the sedan was?"

"No. Jerald would answer the door whenever I went over there. You know, to complain about the noise. He'd walk outside and talk to me on the steps. Then he'd go back inside and things would quiet down. He had a charming way about him."

"Did you like him?"

"Oh no, I've never trusted a charmer. I learned that the hard way with the man I dated before my Jeffrey. I had a heck of a time shaking him loose."

"Thank you, Carol. I'll give you my card in case you think of anything else. You've been superbly helpful." She rose and gestured for Jasmine to do the same.

"Oh, I'm glad. These seem like such little things to remember. Would you like a Soy More for the road?"

"No, thanks," Ruby said before Jasmine could speak. "It doesn't contain any of my food groups."

"What are those, dear?"

"Caffeine and sugar."

"With a diet like that it's a marvel you're so skinny."

"I prefer svelte."

"I couldn't agree more," Jasmine crossed her arms and leaned back with a satisfied smirk.

"What should I tell the police if they make their way over?"

"The truth," Ruby said simply, and handed Carol her business card.

Carol picked her reading glasses up from the coffee table and adjusted them on her face. After peering at the card, she said, "The new face of criminal defense in person on my porch." She tapped Ruby's card on her thigh, beaming. "I thought you looked familiar. My granddaughter is a puny thing, kind of like you. Seven years old, and she wants to grow up and be the boss of her own law firm. She practices by bossing her little sister around. Her mother and I are happy she has women like you as her role models."

"I don't know about being a role model."

"She's being modest, Carol. I know I look up to her. Give us a call. I'm sure Ruby would love to show your granddaughter around. Have her sit at her desk.

Play lady lawyer for the day."

"What a marvelous idea! I'll call my daughter first thing in the morning."

Carol stayed on the steps and waved until they were out of sight.

"Thanks a lot, Jazz."

"All I wanted was a Soy More. Would it have been so hard to accept her offer? I would have eaten yours, or offered it to Justin. With a body like his, he must appreciate health food."

"You have a knack for payback with a smile. Let's go talk to the driver of the black sedan."

"Who?"

"Mr. Stuart Johnston, Kaye County Attorney. Have you met him?"

"No."

"You're in for a treat. If you were a reporter, he'd flash you his thousand-volt smile. He'll likely charm you anyway, since you're a woman. Me, he's not too fond of. I think he forgot my gender, and I prefer it this way."

Ruby and Jasmine approached Stuart.

"I heard it's your buddy in there," Ruby said. "I'm sorry for your loss, Stu."

"Thank you, Ruby." He turned toward Jasmine. "I don't believe I've had the pleasure."

"Jasmine Sinclair, I'm Ruby's intern."

"I see." He shifted his gaze back to Ruby. "Jerry's wife must have lawyered up."

"Yes, Susan Combes hired me."

"Trying to get her off, are you?"

"Trying to figure out what happened," Ruby countered. "Sounds like you're trying to do the same."

"I know what happened—saw it with my own eyes."

"You witnessed a murder?"

"No, but I was on the phone with Jerry. Your killer client was tailing him. She'd picked a fight at home and followed him all the way to the cabin. He thought he could reason with her. I told him he couldn't argue with crazy. It wouldn't end well." Stuart became more animated as he fell into the cadence of his story. "He tells me he's going to talk to her, calm her down. And the next thing I know I'm pulling in as his wife is pulling out."

"Of the driveway?"

"Yes, of the driveway."

"How did you know it was her?"

"I recognized her blue car, her face. She had this wild look in her eyes, and a kitchen knife in her right hand. She's good for this, Ruby," he finished by shaking his fist.

"You noticed a lot, Stu, for just thinking you were dropping in to hang out with your buddy."

"I'm a very observant man."

"And I'm a very observant woman. Nice to see we have some common ground, Stu. I know we had our differences when I worked at Kaye—"

"That's an understatement."

"Yes, it is. But we both want to figure out what

happened, don't we?"

"I already know what happened."

"Okay then, let me put it this way. My team is seeking the truth. I wouldn't want any personal feelings to hinder this search. The system is designed to dispense justice. It can only do that if we both play by the rules. Can I count on you to play by the rules, Stu?"

He puffed out his chest. "Ask any of the boys here. I've given them clear instructions to follow protocol perfectly."

"I'm aware of that order, and the one to have all evidence sent to your office as it's collected and tested. It'd sure show good faith if you forwarded what's collected to my office by Monday morning. Technology makes it so easy to expedite and disclose discovery, doesn't it? We're all working around the clock on this so I think that's reasonable, don't you? After all, your office managed to push through formal charges at an astounding rate."

"I'll have discovery forwarded as soon as it's received. You'll be able to see for yourself that your client stands no chance. Short of blood on her hands, we couldn't have a stronger case against her. Plead her out, and move on."

"If she's good for it, then she'll have to be held accountable for her actions. You'll understand I'm not going to take your word for it, of course."

"Of course. You can see for yourself."

"Can I expect to see any warrants in the discovery

packet?"

"Yes."

"For?"

"Here. Susan's car. Her arrest."

"I can assure you, Stu, that the protocol my team follows is quite different than law enforcement's. Some would say more thorough." She locked eyes with Stuart. "I know it's your buddy in there. You don't mind us going above and beyond, do you?"

"No, no, of course not. Anything to secure justice for Jerry."

"I appreciate your cooperation, Stu. It'd sure help to have the star material witness in my office on Monday morning. You and I both know you don't have to talk to me. But it might help move things along. I know you're a busy guy, but surely you can spare some time for your buddy. What do you say?"

He considered a moment, and said, "Yes, certainly. Anything I can do for Jerry."

"Excellent. Nine work for you? I'll have my paralegal confirm with your office."

He nodded, and said, "Excuse me, I can't be around this tragedy any longer." Stuart gave a perfunctory wave to Ruby, and said to her intern, "Nice to meet you, Julie."

"Jasmine."

"My apologies, Jasmine."

"Not necessary, Mr. Johnston. I know you have a lot on your mind. I'm sorry about your friend."

"Thank you for that." He hustled up the hill.

"What did you think of him?" Ruby asked.

"Is he prone to getting names wrong?"

"No, it's one of his special politician skills."

"What happened at the office?"

"He asked me to tweak case law and facts to support the arguments he wanted to make. In no uncertain terms, I declined."

"What happened?"

"He found a more malleable law clerk."

"What's he usually like?"

"Choreographed, charming, insincere."

"He was flustered, but who wouldn't be in his shoes? His buddy was murdered."

"Yes, I'm aware. What would you expect from someone whose buddy was murdered?"

"A demand for special treatment, I guess."

"And how might one feel toward the lawyer defending the person you're convinced slaughtered your buddy in cold blood?"

"Angry."

"What did you sense?"

"Hate. Animosity."

"What appearance does he want to convey?"

"He's playing nice. Cooperating."

"He's chosen an interesting time to dedicate himself to doing everything by the book. Well, Jazz, let's keep moving. We have a long night ahead of us."

CHAPTER 9

Ruby and Jasmine located Jimmy, who hefted a crate into the white van and stopped in the middle of grabbing another. "We're getting ready to take off," Jimmy said. "Good thing. I'm in enough hot water with the wife."

"How much longer do we have the lights?"

"I'd say ten, twenty tops."

"Mind if we do a walk-through?"

"No, we're done. Packing equipment at this point, and—you know, the vic." He cleared his throat and aimed his words toward Jasmine. "Brace yourself, kid. We're transporting the deceased to the morgue, but I gotta tell you, what we left behind isn't pretty."

Jasmine swallowed hard, and said, "I'll manage."

He gave her an approving nod.

"Mind if we look around?" Ruby asked. "We'll stay outside until you guys clear out."

"It's all yours," he said, and hefted another crate.

Ruby led Jasmine across the lawn and stopped near

the driveway. The yellow tape had been removed.

"Let's play out the neighbor's timeline," Ruby said. "Carol Lawrence has no emotional attachment to this case. Thus, she's our most credible witness. Notice the tire tracks?"

"Yes."

"We're going to find out if they're consistent with Lawrence's account. If so, they corroborate her story. Corroboration builds witness credibility in the mind of a jury."

"Do you think this will make it to a jury?"

"I don't know. But I work every case as if it will. We have to start to get ready for trial at the case's inception. We could lose valuable exculpatory evidence, or overlook something that could become important later as we fit all the pieces together. Make sense?"

"We only get one shot at the crime scene."

"Exactly." Ruby motioned for Jasmine to focus on the hardened ground before them. "According to Lawrence, Truck and Blue Car cruised in about six-thirty. We observed Stu get into his black sedan and drive off. The ground has hardened from when it rained this afternoon. It's easier to spot tracks now." Ruby crouched next to a deep track, and photographed it with her PSC. "Our clever paralegal has linked our PSCs to various databases. One runs tire tracks. Here we go." Ruby held out her PSC. "We saw Johnston's car in this spot with our own eyes, and here's the track mark, consistent with Stu's vehicle. We can't get to exact make and model, but it's a start. Make sense?"

"Yes."

"Let's keep moving. Did you notice the tracks around the truck?"

"Yes."

"Play it Stu's way—Jerry pulls his truck in, Susan pulls in her car. They fight, she kills him. She didn't dispose of the body—it's inside. Who drove off in the truck and came back?"

"That's why we're figuring out the traffic flow."

"Exactly. Hand me your PSC, please."

Jasmine passed it to Ruby.

"See here?" Ruby entered the law firm's system and opened the tire application. "Photograph and trace the tracks on the left side of the driveway, around and behind the truck. I'll continue on the right."

They worked in silence—crouching and photographing, standing to wait for results from the database.

"Well, Ruby. Nothing too exciting over here."

Ruby rose and tucked her PSC into her pocket. "What do you have for me, Jazz?"

"Well, the tracks are all the same, and consistent with Jerald's truck."

"What else did you notice about the tire marks?"

"They're consistent with pulling in, out, and in again."

"Good. Nice work."

"But we already knew this."

"Now we have corroboration. Lawrence is one observant lady. You might even call her Lady Luck after I tell you what I found."

"What?"

"I'll start parallel to the truck. These tracks extend to where the driveway ends and are consistent with a midsize car. I can tell this car drove in, and backed out. Further down the driveway, tracks start for a smaller car."

"The rattletrap?"

"Perhaps. What does the track placement tell you?"

"It was parked behind the midsize."

"The black sedan pulled all the way into the driveway. That means . . ." Ruby waited for Jasmine.

"Both the midsize and the smaller car were gone when the black sedan pulled in."

"Correct. I think you're warmed up. Let's play out the cops' version." Ruby walked over to the right side of the driveway.

"Blue Car pulls in next to Truck. Wife gets out. Husband waits for her on the driver's side." Ruby positioned Jasmine next to the truck. "Johnston referred to a kitchen knife. She's killer pissed, and delivers the first slice on the driveway, bad enough for this blood pool." She motioned to the discolored earth by the driver's side. "How's he going to get inside? Crawl? Stagger? Run?"

"There are drag marks leading away from the truck

toward the cabin."

"Right. But what about these footprints? The toes point toward the cabin."

"I'd say male by their shape and size."

"How many sets?"

"Two."

"What's their condition?"

"What do you mean?"

"Well-formed? Distorted? Walking with one's weight balanced yields a well-formed print in muddy conditions. You'll notice that where the drag marks don't overlap, the prints are well-formed. Where they coincide, they're smeared. What does that tell you?"

"The prints happened before the drag marks."

"Yes. Go up to the porch and follow the path in the opposite direction."

"Other prints, not as deep, heading back to the driveway."

"The ground had time to set. What's their placement in relation to the drag marks?"

"To the side."

"Take the prints leading to the cabin. I'll take the ones leading away."

"Let me guess—there's another app for this."

Ruby grinned. "You're a quick study, Jazz."

Jasmine bent down, and held her PSC over a print.

Kottke emerged from the cabin.

She popped upright. "Hi, Justin."

"Jasmine." He nodded.

"You clear?" Ruby asked.

"Yeah, I have samples right here." He patted his leather bag. "Candace is heading into the lab now. She'll run them as soon as I get there."

"Of course she will, sweet talker."

"That's funny considering you weaseled your way into a crime scene with Anton's."

"We can't all be ex-cops."

"Thank God for that."

"Want to stick around for the reenactment?"

"No, times a wasting." He frowned. "She's not good for this, Ruby."

"I know it."

They looked at each other in unspoken agreement.

"Have I told you lately I love how your mind works?"

"Goes both ways, Ruby."

"Entry codes for her house and car are in her file. You hear about the warrants?"

"Yeah, one for here, one for her arrest, and one for her car. Why not her house?"

"I was wondering the same thing."

"What does it mean?" Jasmine asked.

"Well, for one thing, it means they grabbed her and left her house intact, presumably," Ruby said.

"I'll do a full sweep."

"Great. We'll be a ways behind you. I'll tag you after we interview Susan."

"See you. Welcome to the team, Jasmine," he tossed over his shoulder as he walked away.

Jasmine sighed as she watched him take long

strides, and jolted as she looked over to see Ruby watching her with a smirk. "Welcome back, Jazz. Ready to continue our investigation?"

"Yes, yes. I have the prints. What's next?"

"You play Susan Combes. I'll play Jerald."

"Why can't I play Jerald?"

"Do you have a spare outfit in my car?"

"No."

"That's what I thought." Ruby positioned herself on the driver's side. "Susan comes at Jerald with a kitchen knife. She cuts deep enough to bring him down—significant, according to the size of the pool, but not enough to bleed out. Would you consider yourself average size for a female?"

"Yes."

"So would I. Jerry goes down." Ruby fell to her side. "If Jerry struggled, it would've been harder to get him up the steps. Let's make it easier for her. Jerry's passed out from shock and blood loss. Move him into the cabin. Avoid the blood trail, please."

Jasmine hooked an arm under Ruby's shoulders, and hoisted her weight.

"Interesting instinct. Remember the drag marks."

Jasmine grabbed Ruby's wrists and pulled. Ruby moved scant inches. "We're going to be here all night."

"Want to switch?" Ruby asked.

Jasmine huffed and gripped Ruby under her shoulders.

"How much pressure is on your feet right now?"

"I'm really digging in."

Ruby laughed. "Not so skinny now, am I? Where are the woman-size shoe prints? Or barefoot prints? Release me for a minute."

Jasmine dropped Ruby and shook out her arms. "I could get you there, eventually."

"What if I were a hundred pounds heavier?"

"No way."

"Look down."

Jasmine bent and examined the ground.

"It's hardened since this afternoon, and still you can see your prints. Notice how they aren't as well-formed? You dug in your heels to drag me. Where are the corresponding prints? We have shoe impressions alongside and underneath the drag marks, but nothing consistent with dragging someone from behind."

"Want me to keep going?"

"No, but I admire your commitment. Let's head up the steps."

Jimmy walked out the front door. He shook his head at Ruby's rumpled appearance. "You out here practicing for your rematch with Marian?"

"Something like that."

"You need me to hang around for a while, keep the spotlights on?"

"No, we'll be inside by the time you break them down. Get home to your wife and work on wowing her with those anniversary plans."

"Thanks for saving my ass, Ruby."

"Any time, Jimmy."

"You landed a good gig," he told Jasmine.

"Most of the time I know it." She rolled her shoulders. "Good night, Jimmy."

They stepped aside as personnel filed past carrying a large black bag.

Seeing Jasmine's stricken expression, Ruby asked her, "How many grown men does it take to carry a murder victim?"

"You're making riddles? That's morbid, Ruby."

"No, I'm solving a murder. Want to join me?"

"Yes."

"Answer the question."

"Two."

"So what?"

"It's an observation. Let's follow the trail." Ruby pointed down. "It leads inside—no hesitation, no pooling by the front door. If Susan and Jerald arrived at the same time, and she slashes him in the driveway, is she going to run up and open the front door before hauling in the body? Go ahead." When she looked up and saw Jasmine standing stark still and stiff as she stared at the front door, Ruby said, "I'll lead."

Jasmine sighed, and stepped to the side.

Ruby braced herself and opened it. She motioned Jasmine to follow as she stepped inside. "Nothing but a blood trail leading through the entryway and down the hall," she said, and bent down to examine the trail. "Notice anything off about it?"

"No, uh, it seems pretty clear cut."

"Doesn't it? It's thicker in areas and moves in short

bursts. That could be consistent with dragging. Pull, take a break. Pull, take a break. What's going on alongside the trail?"

"Drops."

"Yes, gravitational drops. What are they doing among drag marks? Are you sure you want to continue?"

"I'm sure."

"They've removed the body, but it will still be hard to both see now and to un-see later. Murder scenes stamp a distinct and deep mark in one's memory."

"I'm in this, every step." Jasmine jutted out her chin.

"Let me go first, and if you don't follow that's fine. Understood?"

Jasmine nodded.

Ruby walked down the hall and let Jasmine follow at her own pace. At the threshold, she stopped and took a minute to adjust to the red, to the smell. She let the layered wave of emotions rise, and rode it out until it subsided. Then she turned her attention to the thick crimson smearing white walls.

Jasmine peered in. Her complexion turned ashen. She rubbed her hands over her eyes yet the vision lingered. Opening them again, she covered her mouth.

Ruby steered her out of the room. "Focus on my voice. Look at me. Breathe. In and out. That's it."

Jasmine complied.

Ruby waited until Jasmine's eyes focused and her

breathing steadied. "Are you with me?"

"Yeah. Sorry."

"There's nothing to apologize for. You can stay out here. I don't think any less of you for being affected by human tragedy. I'd think less of you if you weren't."

Pink crept into Jasmine's cheeks. "I'm ready. It's just—"

"A shock, I know, to see it in real life. Crime dramas don't convey the visceral stomach punch. Even though the victim has been moved to the morgue, death lingers. You made it into the room, and you didn't projectile vomit on me. Thank you for that. It's enough for your first day."

Ruby reentered the room. She forced her thoughts away from imagining the deceased laying in the tub. Away from the glazed unseeing look that haunted her dreams. Restricting her thoughts to the curved pattern.

Finished, Ruby shut the bathroom door behind her.

Jasmine paced the hallway.

"How are you doing?"

"Better."

"You can wait outside."

"Are we done here?"

"No."

"Then I'll stay."

Ruby nodded, and said, "It appears all the action happened in this area. We'll still walk through the rest of the cabin. Appearances can be deceiving."

CHAPTER 10

Ruby and Jasmine closed up the cabin and went out into the stillness of night.

Gazing at the lunar-reflecting water, Jasmine said, "It really is beautiful here. I can see why Carol comes here to find peace."

"You did well with her. You have good instincts."

They returned to Ruby's car.

"Would you like me to drop you at your apartment?"

"No. Sorry about back there."

"Unnecessary, Jazz."

"I want you to know I can take it. Do the job."

"You've had a stellar first day, Jazz."

"Thanks." Jasmine settled into her seat.

"PSC, call Levi Hollins, voice only."

"Levi speaking." A brisk male voice stated.

"Levi, it's Ruby."

His voice brightened. "Ruby, I'd love to catch up, but I'm in the middle of something."

"I'm aware. Heard you caught a big one tonight."

"Yes, I'm almost done organizing the discovery that keeps flooding in for the file."

"Fantastic. You see, I caught the same one as you."

"Your practice is good, I take it."

"It is. I talked to Johnston at the scene. He's eager to keep the ball rolling. Did he ask you to forward discovery to me?"

"He did—to the defense. That it's you is a pleasant surprise. I was about to look up the defendant's counsel. You saved me a step."

"Good. I'm on my way to see my client. I'm happy to swing by, and speed up the transfer by using my PSC."

"Sure, come by. I'll be here another twenty to thirty."

"That's all I need."

"I'll let security know you're heading up."

"Thanks, Levi. See you soon."

"Do you always meet with the charging attorney?"

"Only when there are red flags."

"Which are?"

"You'll catch on during our conversation—not sure if Levi will, but I suspect that you will."

Ruby parked and led the way into the atrium. "The prosecutor's office occupies the top seven floors on the court side. We're heading to twenty-two."

"I've never seen it this quiet."

"It's a bit eerie when you first come through after hours. You get used to it." Ruby signaled to the officer at the desk. "Ernie, still working hard I see. You push off your retirement again?"

"I'm still a spring chicken. Who's your friend?"

"Jasmine Sinclair, nice to meet you."

"Pleasure."

"Mind if we head up?"

"Levi told me to expect you. Go on. Try not to cause too much trouble now, Ruby."

"Nothing a spring chicken like you couldn't handle."

As they entered the elevator, Jasmine said, "Twice in one day."

"You did well here."

"Feels like ages ago."

"This is a walk in the park compared with your hearing."

They arrived on twenty-two and walked down the lighted corridor to the front entry. Ruby rang the bell, and waited.

A man with salt-and-pepper hair standing on end appeared. "Good to see you, Ruby. And this is—"

"My intern, Jasmine Sinclair."

"Nice to meet you, Jasmine. Excuse my appearance. It's been quite the evening. For you two as well, I'm sure." He directed them into the first office on the right. "It's smaller than my last office, but it suffices."

"Levi had the corner office in the Community

Prosecution Division before he was transferred here, to Violent Crimes, a couple months back."

"Four months."

"Sorry, it's hard to track the transfers. Johnston did heavy restructuring, didn't he?"

"That's one way to put it."

"How would you put it?"

"You know it's a political office, Ruby."

"Yes, very well."

"I stay out of politics."

"Let's start the download, shall we?" Ruby handed over her PSC, and Levi linked it to his computer.

"Thirteen minutes to completion," he said.

"That gives us a little time to chat." Ruby eased into a chair. "I have to say the new assignments surprised me."

"I would never say they weren't appropriate. But I will say they were surprising."

"I considered Ms. Wright the most qualified to manage the Drug and Property Unit—not Stark."

"That seems to be the consensus."

"Stark is first chair on this case."

After a sharp inhale, Levi started coughing.

"I second your sentiments," Ruby said.

Once Levi regained his breath, he said, "Sure, he came from Violent Crimes, but he doesn't have the chops for a first-degree murder case. I'm sorry. I overstepped. It certainly has been a long night."

"For us, too. We can talk about something else. I'm working on a timeline. When did Johnston arrive on-scene?"

"At seven-fifty."

"Do you know when he placed the nine-one-one call?"

"At seven-fifty-five."

"When did the first responder arrive?"

"Eight-oh-one."

"You have a mind for details, Levi."

"Thanks, Ruby."

"When did you complete the probable-cause statement?"

"Well, I added to it to place formal charges."

"What about the PC to support the warrants?"

"I'd have to pull that up." He tapped at his keyboard. "Let me see here . . . it was at eight-nineteen."

"You work fast."

"To be honest, Johnston drafted most of it. He said he started it right after he talked to dispatch. He wanted to help speed things along for his friend."

"When did he send you a draft?"

"The transmission was received at eight-oh-nine. I reviewed it and entered it into the system."

"Your name is on the PC statement?"

"Yes."

"Did anything seem unusual about Johnston's draft?"

"I didn't give it much thought. I entered it into our system's template, submitted the corresponding paperwork, and arranged for its presentation to a judge."

"Think about it. Eight minutes after the first responder arrived, Johnston had a PC statement drafted. Does that seem fast?"

"Yes, that's fast."

"Didn't you work with him on charging when he was in drug and property?"

"Yes, I did."

"Did he wow you with his ability to zip through a PC statement?"

"No, his speed wasn't memorable."

"It was average. That's my recall, too. I'm impressed he managed such a steep increase in productivity. Maybe he'd have some tips. You know how I love efficiency."

"You certainly do."

Ruby's PSC signaled. "Well, the transfer is complete." She grabbed her PSC and held out her free hand. "Thanks, Levi. Great to catch up."

He gave it a hearty shake.

"Likewise, Ruby."

Jasmine rose. "We'll get out of your hair so you can take off."

"Congrats on your new job, Jasmine."

"Thanks."

"And Levi? I wouldn't mention this conversation to Johnston. He's not my biggest fan under the best circumstances. You understand that I'm just doing my job. But he's taking this personally, don't you think?"

"Yeah, he is. It's his—"

"Buddy. Yeah, I know. Thanks again. We'll show ourselves out."

They left the Violent Crimes Division behind and rode down in contemplative silence.

Ruby led Jasmine through the atrium, waving at Ernie as she passed, and into a connecting tunnel. "Have you been this way?"

"No. Are we entering the jail building?"

"Yes, the Kaye County Law Enforcement Center. Doesn't it feel different?" Ruby placed her palm on the wall. "Concrete. It's still used for jails and not much else—not because it's cheaper than newer, and better, materials. It sets the ambience they're after."

"You paint a pretty picture."

"I want you to know what to expect so this dank setting doesn't distract you. Lady Luck has struck again—Susan's arresting officer is here. What are you going to pay attention to?"

"Not my surroundings."

"Right, not here. Save that for the scene, for the residence. We're here to people watch. Officer Strauss first, then our client."

They locked up their belongings. Ruby held her PSC as they entered the screening area. A bulky officer entered from a side door and ushered them through an archway. When the metal detector stayed silent, he said, "Officer Straus will receive you in Conference B. Do you require instructions?"

"No, thanks, Brutis."

Ignoring Ruby, Brutis hulked to the doorway.

"Enter now." He passed through and stood as sentinel on the other side.

"A riot, isn't he?" Ruby tossed over her shoulder as she breezed past.

"Hilarious," Jasmine whispered.

Ruby guided Jasmine down a fluorescent corridor. She paused at a heavy door. Metal clanked as it yawned open. She ushered Jasmine into a large concrete box with a single black table. Metal chairs lined the wall. Grabbing one, Ruby pulled it to the table. "Have a seat," she said.

Jasmine sat at the edge.

"Don't expect comfort. It's minimalist in here."

"I figured that out, thanks."

Ruby placed a chair across from them, and sat next to Jasmine.

"How old is this place?" Jasmine asked.

"Its bones are older than your great-grandparents. It's had facelifts over the years, yet it remains a cadaverous place. It'd be colossal if the retributionists had gotten their way. Do you know what the compromise was between the rehabbers and the retters?"

"The rehabilitationists got funding for restorative-justice programs, and the retributionists got Mardova."

"Nice one, Jazz."

"We learned that during Intro to Criminal Law."

"You're about to meet a real-life, die-hard retter—Officer Gary Strauss. Ask yourself, how would a retributionist filter information?"

The door clanked open, and a broad, rigid man entered. The bright lights washed out his pale face and hair, giving the impression he had unremarkable features. His mitt of a hand swallowed Ruby's and then Jasmine's. His chair scraped the floor as it shifted under his weight.

"Officer Strauss, you've undoubtedly had a long night. We'll make this brief before we meet with Susan Combes."

"Good, and then you can tell your client the jury verdict will come back quick—guilty. This one is open-and-shut. Once you see the evidence, you'll advise her to plead."

Ruby pushed to her feet. "Absolutely not. My client has a right to a zealous defense!" She pounded the table.

His bulging nose and ruddy cheeks gained definition as his face reddened. Fuming, Strauss panted under his efforts to maintain control.

"I'll leave no stone unturned, no report unread, no evidence uncollected. I will triple and quadruple check your work, and the work of all men and women under your employ in this matter."

"That's a ludicrous waste of your time. We found the knife. It has your client's prints on it. The county attorney himself saw her flee from the scene. He identified the deceased, and we verified with prints and a blood sample. She's a nut job. Ask Stuart Johnston. Ask her neighbor."

"Neighbor?"

"Deanna Connelly."

Ruby sat and smiled. "Your reputation precedes you, Strauss. You play by the rules, and follow protocol precisely."

Strauss nodded. His breath eased and features faded.

"I do the same, Strauss. I play it straight. I'm not seeking to avoid justice for my client. I want to secure it for her. Understood?"

"Yes, yes. I've heard you're solid. We're all a bit on edge. It's been a long night. And Stuart is pushing us all hard. It's his—"

"Buddy. So I've heard. I'm ready to see Susan Combes now."

"I'll show you back to your client."

"Thanks. I appreciate that you took the time to meet with us."

Strauss showed them into a meeting room. With a parting wave, he left them alone.

"I didn't know the rooms could get smaller."

"Shallow breaths, Jazz, or we'll run out of air."

She looked mortified.

"Sorry, bad joke. Breathe easy."

"That was . . . bizarre. What happened with Officer Strauss?"

"By checking in with the arresting officer, you can sometimes discover evidence before the initial client meeting. I riled Strauss a bit, and he sang like a canary. It is rather macabre in here, isn't it? Makes you long for birdsong and sunshine."

"Yeah. That's a distant, fond memory at this point."

The back door to the room opened. A slim woman in standard-issue orange walked in, eyes fastened to the floor.

Ruby moved to her client, put her arm around her shoulders, and ushered her to a chair. Once Susan was seated, Ruby began in quiet tones. "Happy birthday, Susan. Has anyone else wished you that today?"

"No." She looked at her hands. "No one."

"Did you see your husband today?"

"Yes."

"Let's attend to the formalities so we can update you on our progress. I'm Ruby Miller, and this is Jasmine Sinclair. You've verbally hired my firm. Please review the representation agreement." Ruby held out her PSC.

Susan reached for it with her left hand, then retracted it and bobbled the PSC with her right. "I'm sorry." She hastened to prop up the PSC.

"I'll give you the highlights. You're free to fire me as your lawyer at any time. It lists the conditions under which I could fire you as my client—essentially if you ask me to lie, cheat, or commit a crime. You're confirming my authority to gain physical access to any property under your ownership, to your financial accounts, and to your medical records as I deem necessary to represent you. My fee is at the bottom, along with the requisite permissions to transfer that amount from your personal account. It's a flat-fee, and covers everything through the case resolution. Possible resolutions are dismissal, or sentencing. Let me know if you have any questions."

Ruby and Jasmine waited while Susan reviewed the agreement.

"I can't pay that amount. Jerald's in charge of our finances. Our paychecks go into an account under his name. He transfers six hundred into my personal account each month for household expenses."

"One-hundred-fifty-thousand dollars was transferred into your personal account from your husband's—today. Happy birthday."

"That makes no sense."

"A lot doesn't make sense, Susan. We're going to find out what happened. We'll take everything one step at a time. First, do you have any questions about the representation agreement?"

"No. I just can't believe . . . Why would he give me that money?"

"It will all make sense in the end, Susan. I promise." She gave her a reassuring smile. "If you agree to the terms, please sign." Ruby set a stylus on the table.

Susan curled it in her right hand and signed.

"Every question I ask has a reason. Don't try to figure it out. Answer as best you can."

"I've been going over and over it. I don't know anything. I saw Jerry alive, and then all of a sudden the police . . . I don't know what happened. I don't know anything."

"Susan, it's okay if you don't know the answer to a question. This is going to be hard, but it's necessary. We're right here with you. We'll get through it together."

Jasmine gave Susan a gentle smile.

"Okay?" Ruby asked.

"Okay."

"Stuart Johnston claims he saw you driving away from the cabin holding a kitchen knife."

"No, no. That's impossible. I was in my house all night." Tears streamed down her face.

Jasmine squeezed her right hand.

"They think you left a trail a kid could follow into the woods to the gingerbread house."

"I don't understand."

"Any idiot would conclude that you killed your husband. Susan, look at me." Ruby waited for Susan to wipe her eyes and lift her gaze. "We're not idiots. And I don't mean everyone who investigated your case is, but mindlessly following protocol left much undiscovered."

"So you believe me?"

"Yes, of course you didn't kill your husband. We've set about proving it."

"How?"

"I wondered at your physical ability. You're accused of hauling a man from driveway to bathroom, and lifting him into a tub—not a feat for weaklings. Your dominant hand is your left. I know because you reached out from habit before withdrawing and extending your right. You signed awkwardly, and you've cradled your left wrist as if injured. Is it?"

"I think so."

"Did you tell the officers as they handcuffed you?"

"Yes. They didn't care they were hurting me—just like Jerry." She looked pained. "I shouldn't say that about my own husband."

"Is it true?"

"Yes."

"Please don't apologize for speaking the truth, Susan. It's exactly what we're after, and it's going to set you free. It's very rare for a woman to kill her batterer."

"No, Jerry's not . . . he just gets upset. I make him so mad."

"He gets out of control?"

"Yes."

"What has he broken of his?"

"Well, I'll have to think about it . . . Nothing, I guess."

"He's only broken what's yours, hasn't he? He's had enough control to target your belongings. I see marks around your neck. What happened, Susan?"

"I, I made dinner. And he found a card from my dentist. He's very protective of me. He wants me for himself."

"I know it."

"And I made him so mad."

"You're not responsible for his emotions."

"Before I knew it, he had me up against the wall. His hands were around my neck. And then he threw me down." She fixated on where the concrete met the floor. "I landed on my wrist. He pulled me up by it. I told him it hurt, but he didn't stop. I tried to get help. I made it to the neighbor's."

"Deanna Connelly's house?"

"Yes."

"Did she help you?"

"No, she wouldn't let me in."

"Where was Jerry?"

"He acted like nothing happened. He told her it was me. That I'm crazy, out of control." She looked up at Ruby. "Maybe I am."

"What makes you say that?"

"I keep losing things. They show up in plain sight. I couldn't even find my car keys to go to work this morning. Deanna wouldn't give me a ride."

"What did you wear for your birthday dinner?"

"A blue dress. I wore it when we first met. I wanted to make it special. I'm so stupid. I even took a picture in it."

Ruby glanced over at Jasmine. "When did you take it?"

"Maybe fifteen minutes before he came home."

"What did you use? A camera?"

"No, my phone."

"Where's your phone, Susan?"

"It was on my bedside table.

"Where's your blue dress?"

"In the hamper."

"Were your shoes in the photo?"

"Yes, I propped my phone on the counter and took it full-length. It's so silly."

"You should feel free to take whatever pictures you want in your own home. What shoes were you wearing?"

"They're white and blue with sparkles."

"High heels?"

"Yes."

"Do you keep shoes at the cabin? Clothes?"

"No, I've only been there a few times, back when we first bought it."

"What did your husband get you for your birthday?"

"Nothing."

"Did you ask for anything?"

"No, I don't ask him for anything."

"What's the last present your husband gave you?"

"A kitchen knife."

"When?"

"Around midnight."

"Why?"

"I don't know. He didn't say anything about it being a birthday present. And this morning he said I —I didn't deserve a present."

"Does he cook?"

"No."

"Did you ask for a new kitchen knife? Complain

about your old ones?"

"No."

"Susan, what happened after you went to Deanna for help?"

"Jerry was there, and Deanna didn't believe me. He told me to go inside and clean up my mess. And then he took off. He told me to not ask him where he was going. That's the last time I saw him."

"What did you do next?"

"I cleaned up the kitchen."

"Did you throw away what was broken?"

"Everything except my grandmother's vase. I put it in a box under my bed."

"And then?"

"I went to bed. I just wanted today to end."

"Anything happen before the cops showed up?"

"You'll think I'm crazy."

"Try me."

"It started like a dream. I had this strange feeling that someone was watching me."

"Hair standing up, heart pounding in your chest?"

"Yes, like that."

"What did you do?"

"I got out of bed, and checked. There was nobody there, of course. And Jerry's side of the bed was cold. So I went back to bed, and just as I was falling asleep, I heard Jerry's voice—crystal clear."

"What did he say?"

"'You're mine, Susan. Mine and nobody else's.' I'm losing stuff, hearing voices. Nobody sees Jerry like I do. Makes him mad like I do. Am I losing my mind?"

"No, but Jerry sure wanted you to think so. Have you ever wielded a weapon against him?"

"No, no. Never."

"You've never held up a knife and warned him to back off?"

"No. I just kept hoping . . ."

"Hoping what, Susan?" Ruby prompted.

"That I'd stop making him so mad. That we'd go back to being happy like we used to be. That he'd go back to being the man I fell in love with, and that he'd remember why he fell in love with me. But I just kept screwing it up, and now he's gone."

"Susan, you're not at all to blame for what he's done to you. Even if he was around, he wouldn't do anything to make things right. We're here to help you clean up the mess he's left behind."

"I can't tell you how much it means to me that you believe me. What'll happen to me?"

"We'll investigate through the weekend, and meet with you on Monday morning before your bail hearing. That's when the judge will determine your release conditions. We'll have a medic tend to your wrist right away."

"Thank you, Ruby. Thanks, Jasmine."

"You're very welcome, Susan. Remember, you have a lawyer. Remind the cops of that if they try to question you. I'm a phone call away."

On their way out, Ruby stopped by central command. She knocked on the wide slot in the bulletproof glass. When an officer slid it open, she said, "Hey McElroy. Is Strauss still around?"

"He's on his way out the door. Is this urgent?"

"Yes. Call him back in, please. We'll wait in Conference B if that's available."

"It is. You know the way. I'll send him in."

They settled into the same chairs.

"I suggest staring at the wall if you need to clear your mind. It's a lot at once."

"How do you keep all the details straight?"

"Do you think in pictures?"

"Sometimes."

"Visualize the cops' version, and the evidence-based version. It's important to keep both in mind."

Strauss barreled in. "What's the emergency, Ruby? My wife is expecting me."

"We'll be brief. My client needs a medic. She has an injured wrist—her left. Your officers didn't cause it, did they?"

"No, of course not. I hand-picked them for that unit."

"Doesn't it make you wonder who did injure it?"

"I have no time for games, Miller."

"I'm not playing them, Strauss. Why would she choose slicing, hauling, and hefting with an injured wrist?"

"People have two hands, Miller."

"And certain tasks require both, Strauss. She had an easier way to dispatch her husband. Why wouldn't she choose that?"

"What are you talking about?"

"She could've poisoned him—effective, and eliminates the size difference as a concern. He's six-foot-two, two-twenty-six. That's quite the Goliath to take down when you're five-four and weigh in at one-eighteen. You follow?"

"We can't discount the evidence."

"I'm not asking you to discount the evidence. On the contrary, I want you to follow it to its source."

Officer Strauss rose and propped himself on his fists as he towered over Ruby and Jasmine. "It's a clear trail leading right to her. I don't have time for this. I have an investigation to run."

"No, I'm investigating. You're missing the truth by looking through the lens of your conclusion."

"She's guilty." He hammered his verdict into the table with his fist.

"Very well, then." Ruby rose and motioned for Jasmine to do the same. "See that Susan's wrist is tended to, Strauss. Enjoy your down time with your wife. Excuse us. We have a murder to solve."

Ruby strode out with Jasmine at her side, and didn't look back.

CHAPTER 11

Ruby stayed silent as she snaked through traffic and exited onto the highway. Jasmine stared out her window, mentally sifting through what had happened. Slicing through the silence and Jasmine's thoughts, Ruby looked at the unit mounted to her dashboard, and said, "PSC, call Justin Kottke, visual on."

When he appeared on-screen, he studied her for a beat, and said, "You look pissed."

"I am. Strauss is point person, and leading the investigation into the ground. But he's following protocol perfectly. Damn him. Give me some good news."

"The house is clean. Spotless in the hygienic sense. Susan must have spent quite some time on it."

"Factor that into the timeline. There's no way she could drive back and forth, commit murder, and arrive home in time to sweep up after her bastard husband. He's a batterer, Kottke."

"I know."

"How?"

"Simple. What kind of husband has surveillance equipment inside his house?"

"Nice find, Kottke. You do earn the big bucks."

"Then why don't you pay me them?"

"Smart-ass. What was his set up?"

"Video in the kitchen. Audio and video in the bedroom, and a bug in the lampshade—husband's side."

"Tell me it's a two-way."

"It's a two-way. How did you know?"

"Something Susan said. Could you trace the transmission?"

"We'd need an e-guru of Flick's caliber for that."

"Keep an eye out for one of those. I'll work on it on my end. You'll find a box of shards under Susan's bed. Leave it for me. You'll find a blue dress in the hamper, and blue-and-white heels in the bedroom closet. Photograph, collect, and drop them at the lab. Her phone is on her nightstand."

"Already have it."

"Perfect. Review Susan's pictures from this evening."

"Yesterday evening. Anything else?"

"Yes, slow down time. After you do that, upload the photos of her wearing said dress and shoes to her case file."

"Yes."

"This is bullshit, Ruby."

"It's so good to hear you say that. Let's keep at it. I want to solve this before Monday."

"Before Monday." He ran a hand over his rugged shadow beard. "If anyone can do it, we can."

"We will, Kottke."

"And you're going to take your own advice? Get some sleep?"

"I'm not tired."

"You look exhausted."

"You don't look so hot yourself."

"I disagree," Jasmine said as she popped her head into view.

Kottke laughed.

Ruby disconnected and whacked her hand on the wheel. "Can you believe that guy?"

"I think he's wonderful."

Ruby gaped. "Sleep deprivation has addled your mind."

Jasmine crossed her arms. "He's top-notch. You said it yourself. He points out that you look worn out, which, might I add, you do, and you—"

Ruby cut her off by clutching her gut and laughing hard enough to bring tears to her eyes. "No, Jazz, I meant Strauss."

Jasmine cleared her throat. "Well, then."

"Thanks, Jazz. I needed that."

"What's next?"

"I'm going to drop you off. You've put in an admirable first day. The second will be as, or more, intense."

Jasmine gave Ruby a suspicious look. "And what are you going to do?"

"Swing by Susan's house for a quick walk-through. Kottke had a head start. He photographed and collected. Before long, he'll finish his reports and call it a night."

"And you'll do the same?" She crossed her arms.

"As soon as I'm done with my reports, I'll do the same."

Ruby pulled away from Jasmine's apartment building, and hesitated before turning to the PSC mounted on her dash. She said, "Engage, call Arianna Ramirez." When her friend's heart-shaped face came into view, Ruby began, "I just visited a new client. Her name is Susan Combes. She looked like you. When I walked out of the airport in Seattle and there you were, car packed with everything you had to your name. We'd spoken on the phone, and you'd sounded off. But I hadn't seen you in six months. I barely recognized you."

"You'd forgotten the extent of my exotic beauty?"

Ruby cracked a smile. "It was your eyes, Ari. They were so dull. I was ready to kill him that day if we stayed. I couldn't drive fast enough."

"I didn't recognize me either."

"I look at you now, and have hope for Susan."

"What's she on the hook for?"

"Murdering her batterer."

"Any chance she's good for it?"

"She has a physical defect that makes the act impossible."

"In English?"

"Her husband fractured her left wrist. She'd need it to do what they're trying to pin on her."

"When do you want to bring her by?"

"She doesn't know you exist yet."

"And you're seven steps ahead of yourself."

"Or three steps, depending on how this plays out."

"All right, let me know when I enter the picture. And try to give me some notice."

"A woman needs you. You're the best at what you do. Team meeting at eight. Take notice."

"Fine, flattery has secured my presence."

"I thought knowing you in pigtails with a snaggletooth would be enough."

"Nope, it was the flattery, which you negated. You know very well it wasn't a snaggletooth."

"Hey, did I mention your exotic beauty?"

"That's my girl. Call any time."

"Thank you, gleaming gem of the Latina community. Your beauty is only exceeded by your benevolence. To bestow such kindness on a woman of ordinary face is—"

"Ruby, you're too much at two in the morning. I need my Hollenbeck to keep up with you."

"Your taste in espresso is as impeccable as your visage."

"*Dios mío*, Rubina. Enough."

"My new intern is trying to get me into drinks that glow."

"Yuck. You considered that grounds for termination, right?"

"Considering her commendable performance on day one, she stays. I've done my best to prevent her poor taste buds from shriveling in protest. I fear I'm too late. Her tongue may be entirely devoid of buds."

"Sounds like the opposite of our diet."

"Yes, and it's worked for us since we were teenagers. Though I've wondered why it didn't have the same transformative effect for me as for you. Who doesn't want to be an exotic beauty?"

"Yes, you poor ugly duckling. Let's see, blonde hair, emerald eyes, killer smile that you use when it suits you. All grown up, and the new face of criminal defense. Great tagline, by the way. I loved the billboard. That teal suit really popped."

"That's weird, our connection's fuzzy."

"Nice try. The new tech is crystal."

"What was that?"

"Stop shaking the screen. You're making me dizzy."

Ruby set her PSC back in its holder. "Seriously, Ari. I have to go. I'm hoping to catch Kottke."

"The teal suit leaps into action."

"Thanks, I needed a boost."

"What are snaggle-toothed friends for?" Her grin revealed straight, gleaming white teeth. She laughed as she signed off.

As she drove through Susan's neighborhood, Ruby noted the sprawling homes. She saw no lights in any windows, no action on the street. Not a night-owl community, she assessed. After parking behind Susan's car, she noted at the red sports car. Between the standard and the flashy sat Kottke's motorcycle. She hadn't missed him.

Ruby left her headlights on and approached Susan's car. Knowing Kottke would have collected prints and scanned for fibers and fluids, she skipped sealing up, and opened the driver's side door. Ruby swiped a finger over the dashboard—dust-free, polished. Susan took care of what was hers.

Picking up a car remote from the cupholder, Ruby pushed autostart. The car came to life. She turned on the interior light, and noticed the driver's floor mat was soiled compared to the spotless passenger's. Unable to make out a shoeprint, she moved on. She engaged her flashlight application and examined the seats. A dark, oblong stain marked the passenger's. Consistent with a bloody knife, she noted. She signaled the garage door with the remote clipped to the visor on the driver's side, and moved on.

After turning off both cars, she grabbed her briefcase and used the garage entrance. Kottke wasn't kidding, she mused. She'd never seen a kitchen with such sparkle. Feeling transported to Alfred's shop, she walked to the stove and touched the dials in wonder.

Justin walked in. "I wouldn't mess with that. You've been known to get a coffeemaker sparking. I'd hate to think what you're capable of with that thing."

"Have we entered a time warp?"

"Bizarre, isn't it? She did a great job cleaning this place, considering what she had to work with." Justin opened a closet and motioned Ruby over.

"Whoa. Alfred would love to get his hands on these for his shop." Ruby clicked photos. "I wonder how much time she spent in here, making the king of the castle his meals."

Justin cocked his head. "Should we feel sorry he's on a slab?"

"Sorry he's not around to finish the job he started?" Ruby walked into the dining area. "See the dents in this wall? This is where he threw her. He had his hand against her windpipe, strangling her. You've read the femicide report. All the risk factors for fatality were there. Her life was in danger."

"Yet he's the one who ends up murdered."

"And she ends up in jail on her birthday facing a life sentence on Mardova."

"She won't be there for long. We hit the jackpot." Justin pulled out a phone from his leather bag. "Susan's. I ran it for spyware, and found WifeSpy. These programs have obvious names. The difficulty lies in finding them. I managed to find it. My e-skills end there."

"I've heard of it. People travel everywhere with their phone. It taps into the GPS. It also forwards communications to the linked unit, and allows for call-tapping. He could see every message, every email, and listen to every call. She couldn't make a move without him knowing about it."

"And that still wasn't enough." He reached back in, and removed electronic devices. "Surveillance equipment. Flick would be nice to have right about now."

"I know, I know. I'll find a replacement. In case you hadn't noticed, I've had a busy night."

"Well, we don't need e-skills for this." Justin pulled out a stack of papers and waved them. "I found it in the office. One guess what it is."

"His will."

"How do you do that?"

"Simple deduction. And few documents would put that satisfied smirk on your face."

He swiped a hand over his face and set down the will.

"Everything in order?" Ruby asked as she flipped through the pages.

"Somewhat."

"I see what you mean. Susan stands to inherit Jerald's estate. If she's legally unable to do so, it all goes to none other than Mr. Justice-for-Jerry. Where's Susan's will?"

"I assume that's rhetorical."

"Obviously." She started to pace, agitated. "Jerry wouldn't have spent good lawyer money on a legal document pertaining to his wife's property. As far as he's concerned, she has no property. She herself is property—his." She whirled to face Justin. "Find the dress and shoes?"

He patted his bag. "Yeah, and you'd be hard-pressed to find a speck of dirt."

"She took care of what was hers."

"Not the type to leave a mess behind."

"What about her bedroom? Anything strewn about in haste to flee?"

"She wasn't running."

"Her account is she was sleeping. I believe her." Ruby patted the surveillance equipment. "We'll know soon enough."

"We know Susan didn't do it. Any ideas on the real killer or killers?"

"Yes, but I want to run probabilities and review discovery first."

Kottke raised a brow. "You've been holding out on me, Ruby."

"Don't look at me like that. We've been too busy investigating to review discovery."

"Fair enough. How is Hollins?"

"He doesn't understand the new assignments any more than we do."

"Not surprising."

"No, but I was surprised at how fast Johnston drafted the PC statement. And his behavior is off. He asked for no frills for his best friend. He made it clear to the cops, but wouldn't admit it to me."

"I have an idea how you phrased it. Boxed him in, did you?"

"I did. He'd been at the scene for a long time by

that point. And suddenly he had to run."

"I know where you're going with this, Ruby. Why would he kill his buddy?"

"What are the classic motives? Greed—the inheritance." She ticked off a finger. "There's jealousy. But if he's after his buddy's wife, why would he send her to Mardova? Maybe Jerry had a mistress. Abusers have double standards. She looks at another guy; he breaks her belongings, her bones. Meanwhile, he's cheating. I'll head down that path in the morning. He may not have strayed far from home. The neighbor, Deanna Connelly, refused to render assistance to Susan."

"I'll track down his work history and contacts, and follow that trail in the morning."

"Good. Do you still have that contact at the bureau?"

"Sure do. Agent Mitzu."

"Reach out to him. KSCO isn't helping us on this. Throw a potential killer county attorney into the mix and we could need federal backup."

"Why can't you make an easy request?"

"Because you always make it happen. I wouldn't want to underutilize your talents."

He rolled his eyes. "You drop Jasmine off to get some shut-eye?"

"Yes, and not without protest. She insisted I get some rest, too."

He laughed. "Good for her. She needs a strong spine for this work. You feed her your usual line? 'I'll head home right after I'm done with my reports.'"

"Maybe. Why is everyone so concerned about whether I sleep?"

"We care about you, ace." He tugged her hair. "And we'd hate for our bold leader to drop from exhaustion."

"Yeah, yeah. I'll catch a couple hours."

"Slumped over your case files doesn't count."

"Agree to disagree. You finished here?"

"Yeah, I have some forensics to drop at the lab—prints and fibers from Susan's vehicle. When are you going to invest in a portable lab? Jimmy got his last week. You gotta see it in action. It uses lab-on-a-chip technology. DNA results in under a minute."

"I've noted your request. It took Jimmy a year to get his. Maybe you'll have better luck. I'll put it right up there with an espresso maker for the office, requested by—"

"Colin." Kottke zipped his leather jacket. "I'm off. I'll leave the electronics with you for when you find our new e-whiz."

Ruby sighed. "Wish me luck."

"You'll need it. Flick was the best."

"Let's hope you're wrong."

Kottke laughed as he strolled out the garage door, leaving Ruby in silence.

She stood in the corner of the dining room, surveying the scene, imagining what it had looked like hours before. Table set, the smell of food cooking. Grabbing Susan's phone, Ruby propped it on the counter and saw Susan, smiling in a blue dress and sparkling shoes, holding a blue-and-white vase spilling over with flowers. She visualized what happened next. Susan rushing to set everything right for her husband. Jerry ramping into rage.

Ruby left the phone on the counter and moved to the wall damage. An elbow, a wrist—she wondered which part of Susan's petite frame had left the noticeable dent. An elbow, she decided, as she reenacted Susan's fall.

What did Susan feel?

Fear, she decided. It would have risen in Susan's throat and pumped her heart almost to bursting. Pushing herself up with her right hand, Ruby clutched her left as she ran, following Susan's path through the living room and out the front door, where she stopped and stood. Ruby noted the short sprint to Deanna Connelly's. It was after midnight then, as now. The moon softly lit the path. Clumsy with terror, Susan had made it to her neighbor's steps. She'd placed her faith in Deanna. If only she made it to the neighbor's, Jerald wouldn't hurt her.

But Deanna's front step was not home base; Susan wasn't safe.

He'd followed her—calm while she was terrified. Enjoying himself, Ruby figured. Enjoying his effect on her. She reentered the house—not a home. Susan's cage, in ways she hadn't even known. He'd watched her moves even when he was away. Tracked her like prey.

Ruby walked upstairs to the second floor. She scanned a guest bedroom, decorated in sage and neutrals. Immaculate. Rarely used, she figured, and not by any visitors of Susan.

The next room held office furniture. After finding no memo cubes, no electronics, she wondered if it was ever used, or if, like the rest of the house, it was kept for appearances.

After moving on to the master bedroom, Ruby stepped into the walk-in closet and noted the tidiness. Susan's doing, Ruby figured. She photographed the empty slot among Susan's heels. Jerald's shoes sat in tidy rows in multiples—not a single pair in a particular brand and style, but an array of colors in each. Someone liked his appearance very much, Ruby assessed. She photographed the set of loafers missing a triplet, and flipped through brands—Boss, Armani, Ferrero. He spared no expense for himself.

His wife's wardrobe was a different story. Ruby recognized Koreanna and Peony from low-end fashion outlets. Toward the back she found nicer clothes, worn with age. *Your life wasn't always like this*, Ruby thought. *You once wore beautiful dresses and danced. You thought you'd married a prince. How long did the honeymoon last? Was it over before it even began?*

She left the closet and took in the sleek décor—silver and black with splashes of red. He'd marked his turf. Ruby suspected that Susan had to please him wherever she was in his domain, including the master's bedroom. His needs and desires were paramount; hers meant nothing, and were too insignificant for him to notice.

Ruby knelt beside the bed and located a violet box. Inside, delicate remains rested on tissue paper. Though broken, Susan had tucked it away.

She took care of what was hers.

You're one of us now, Ruby thought. *We're going to take care of you.*

Ruby repacked the remnants, closed the house, and stood on the driveway for one last look at the residence. She hoped, when this was over, Susan would have a home.

CHAPTER 12

Ruby set a violet box on the counter. "Is this one-of-a-kind, Alfred, or could you work your magic and obtain another?"

He put on his spectacles and inspection gloves before examining a shard. "A wonderful creation made by human hands, meticulously painted and well-preserved until it met its unfortunate fate. What kind of mind allows violence against such beauty?"

"Isn't that the million-dollar question?"

"What do you mean, my dear?"

"The man who shattered this piece did the same to a beautiful woman. He twisted loyalty and love to ensnare her. On the outside, she's still beautiful. I suspect, though, that inside she looks quite similar to this."

He set down his spectacles and pinched the bridge of his nose. "Yes, for all of society's advancements, we have not eradicated violence within homes, nor stamped out crime from the streets."

"I know what to do for this woman's case. But I don't know how to put her back together."

"That you want to do so will make a difference. Perhaps you aren't the only one that can help your client. Many believe in your work, Ruby. You need only ask."

"I'm glad you think so, because I need your keen ability to track down anything. Her husband targeted this piece for what it represented—that connection to her past, her loved ones. He worked on severing those connections, on isolating her. And now she's sitting in a jail cell facing a life sentence on Mardova—the ultimate isolation. Interesting, isn't it?"

"Where is her husband?"

"They tell me that he's on a slab in the morgue, and she put him there."

"Ah, yes, Jerald Combes. Quite unfortunate. It made the morning news. He was one of my best clients. I saw him yesterday morning, unexpectedly."

Ruby jerked up her head. "Mind if I record this?"

"Of course not, my dear."

"PSC, record on. Interview of Alfred Whitehorn. Alfred, you stated that Jerald Combes was in your shop yesterday—Friday, the ninth of May. Correct?"

"Yes."

"What time?"

"I'd finished my morning routine. A tad past nine, I'd say."

"What brought him in?"

"He was here to pick up a piece of jewelry for a friend. Business acquaintance, more like."

"Who's his buddy-slash-business contact?"

"Anthony Priestley."

"Did he say why Priestley wasn't picking up his own jewelry?"

"No, he said he was 'doing him a large.' I remember the language because it was most unlike Jerald."

"Anything beside his jargon strike you as odd?"

"He seemed flustered. Jerald has made many purchases, and yet he started off before signing for the item."

"What has he purchased?"

"Kitchen-related antiques and collectibles."

Ruby tapped her PSC and held it up. "Here's a photo of the cleaning supplies found at his residence."

Alfred adjusted his spectacles. "Yes, I procured these pieces for Jerald. He was a very loyal client."

"You're his sole supplier?"

"His antiques-and-collectibles acquirer. You make me sound like a common peddler." He sniffed and whisked a white handkerchief from his pocket to clean his spectacles.

"I'm sorry, Alfred. I have the utmost respect for you and your business. There's no acquirer-client privilege. Mind if I see his file?"

"Certainly."

"Did he say why he bought these items?"

"They were for his wife's collection. I suppose she kept them as conversation pieces, and to remind herself of the wonders of the modern kitchen."

"No, Alfred. She used them. Jerry bought them for her to make sure she didn't take any shortcuts in serving him."

"That's preposterous. I had no idea he did anything of the sort."

Ruby laid a reassuring hand on his shoulder. "I'm sure you didn't, Alfred. Jerry had many people fooled."

"I do not consider myself a fool. One moment, please." Alfred disappeared in back, and returned a few minutes later with a bound black book. He set it in front of Ruby. "It contains anything one would ever want to know about homemaking antiques and collectibles. And I will transfer a copy of Jerald's file to you."

"May I have Anthony Priestley's as well?"

"Yes, indeed."

"Thanks, Alfred. Did Jerry sell anything to you?"

"Only once, perhaps six months ago. He had antique farm equipment."

"Did you think it was unusual for a chemist to have farm equipment?"

"Yes. I inquired, and he said it was on land he had inherited."

"Did you notice anything unusual about his appearance yesterday?"

"He had on a yellow-gold garnet ring—right hand, ring finger."

"Did Jerald not wear jewelry?"

"He did—always in good taste, and new. But I recognized this particular piece from elsewhere. It had a distinguished design—a golden lion overlaid the stone. Anthony wears one that I dare say is identical. I would have to study them to confirm."

"Anything else?"

"He was in a frightful hurry—no time for coffee, no interest in perusing the latest shipment. Jerald had requested first pick. I imagined his wife had quite the collection. I never dreamt—"

Ruby anticipated his train of thought. "Don't beat yourself up, Alfred. All we can do is help Susan."

"That poor woman. It's intolerable what he's done to her. If he were still with us, I'd have a mind to tell that wanker to sod off."

"I couldn't agree more. Did he buy anything else recently?"

"Yes, he purchased a large table, also wooden, custom-built by a very well-known craftsman for a mortician in Connecticut at the turn of the last century. A bit ghastly, but an undeniably rich history to the piece. I like to think those prepared on it for their final resting place received the proper respects."

"That's gruesome, and not a cleaning supply. Strike you as odd?"

"Yes, but sometimes clients deviate from their usual collections."

"Did he say he'd moved into morgue paraphernalia?"

"No, but he was rather vague on his reason for the purchase. I figured he'd find a place for it in his lab."

"His state-of-the-art lab at Tycon Industries? No way would Tycon allow something bathed in blood over a century old into their facilities. Sanitary wood is an oxymoron."

"No, not Tycon. His personal lab."

"Tell me more about Jerald's personal lab."

"It was the reason for unloading the farm equipment—to make room for his private lab, where he could do the experiments that would take his industry by storm. Come to think of it, he's usually verbose about his experiments. Yesterday he was very close-lipped about them."

"Let's walk this through. He comes in to pick up jewelry. The jewelry is for whom?"

"For Elizabeth Priestley—Anthony's mother."

"Any other details? Anything unusual about how he moved, what he said, how he said it?"

"He nearly had a casualty on his way out—a hat rack from the gilded age. I pretended not to notice, but you know me, my dear."

"Little escapes your attention."

"He called me Freddy."

"Freddy? You don't strike me as a Freddy."

"I'm typically not, but Anthony calls me Freddy. I

presumed it was a slip. Maybe Anthony told him to see Freddy, and it stuck. Interesting, isn't it?"

"Yes, I'm finding it all fascinating." Ruby leaned across the counter and gave Alfred a sound kiss on his whiskered cheek. "Thank you, thank you, and thank you." Ruby scooped up the book and her PSC.

"Anything else?"

"Not unless you have e-skills you've been modestly hiding."

"Why?"

"I never thought I'd say this, but I miss Flick. I need to run a trace on electronics."

"You needn't look any further. My best client, and a dear friend, has substantial e-skills. You could say he's the best in the business."

Ruby checked the time. "Any chance he's up at six-twenty on a Saturday?"

"Certainly. That boy is up and active at five like clockwork. He's coming in this morning for a spot of tea. We settled on seven. I have nothing pressing. Should I see if he's interested in joining your investigation? What you're unraveling captures the imagination. He's the inventive sort."

"Yes, please. If he's onboard, send him right over." Ruby sighed. "Flick's sweet tooth put mine to shame. It's funny what you miss."

"I think you'll be pleasantly surprised with my recommendation."

"I bet I will. You have impeccable taste, Alfred. Do you mind doing a follow-up interview with

Kottke later today?"

"Not at all. Do let him know that if I give him helpful information, he needn't kiss me."

Ruby laughed. "I can't promise he'll be able to resist that handsome face. Add the British accent and you're irresistible."

"Go on now. The game is afoot."

"*The Adventure of the Abby Grange*."

"Very good. Do tell me when you figure out what it all means."

"I have a theory. Unlikely as it seems, it has pushed all others aside and is now the sole contender. For now, I'll leave you in suspense."

"Coffee to go?"

"Yes, please. You're so good to me, Alfred. Or should I say Freddy?"

"Not if you'd like me to deliver a technology specialist." He poured her coffee from a shining silver pot.

She sipped the strong brew and sighed. "Thanks, Alfred."

"There's a tray of crumpets on your way out along with the raspberry jam you've taken a liking to. I suggest you take pity on your mistreated stomach."

Ruby went to the tray. She set down her coffee while she slathered a biscuit and took a greedy bite. Humming in satisfaction, she raised her cup toward Alfred before juggling her book, coffee and biscuit, and bustling out the door.

Alfred shook his head in amusement.

"Well, well, if it isn't my eager intern tagging me bright and early on a Saturday," Ruby said.

"I'm up and ready to go," Jasmine said. "Any work for me?"

"Yes, as a matter of fact. I had an interview this morning."

"And you didn't tag me to join you?"

"Sorry, Jazz. It was unplanned. If you want in, I can swing by. I'm heading back to the office now."

"Of course I want in. I called you at six on a Saturday, didn't I?"

"Half past, but still impressive. This work sucks you in, doesn't it?"

"Yes, when will you be here?"

"In five."

"Christ, I have to finish my face."

"You realize I'm picking you up to investigate a murder, right?"

"I need lip color if I'm going to have a chance with Justin."

"I already told you, you don't have a chance. Go nude, and he wouldn't notice."

"We'll see about that."

"Channel your persistence elsewhere, Jazz. Two minutes." Ruby signed off, and pulled in front of Jasmine's building to wait.

When Jasmine slipped into the passenger seat, she wasted no time. "Tell me about the guy who's getting transferred. You know, the guy Marian mentioned yesterday. Is he a client?"

"Hell no, he's not a client. I see you've found another outlet for your persistence. Remember our chat about what we look for in our clients?"

"Yes."

"He's a prime example of the opposite."

"Tell me about him."

"First, let me tell you about a young girl—Tara Baxter, seventeen years old."

"Was she a client?"

"No, I met her at Kaye High. You'll learn soon enough I do a yearly talk there, and have every year since I was a student. It's evolved over the years. I assemble the girls, and talk about dating red flags—how to spot a keeper, a stalker, a loser, an abuser."

"'Real Romance,' you mean."

"Yeah, Amy coined it."

"I've heard about it from my work with at-risk teens. It stuck with them enough to tell me about it. I didn't know you're part of it."

"For thirteen years. Four years ago, Tara approached me after my talk. I was in my third year of law school, like you."

"And you were working at Kaye County."

"Yes. I'd had a lot of girls come up and tell me their stories. That I'd shared mine made them feel comfortable sharing theirs. I'll save my story for another day."

Jasmine nodded.

"The previous day, Tara was late to school. She got in her car and drove a mile or so before her tire blew. A few minutes later, her ex-boyfriend showed up and offered to give her a ride. She said no and called her dad. When her dad pulled up, her ex had backed her against her car. He shook her by the shoulders and screamed at her. Her dad grabbed him and threw him off. The auto shop confirmed the tire had been slashed. Classic abuser tactic—create an emergency situation, and then offer to fix it to be the hero."

"What happened after that?"

"She told her friends that he had slashed her tire. Impossible, they said. He loved her so much."

"What happened to her?"

"He escalated—showed up wherever she went, hacked her social media and sent nasty messages about her to her friends and family."

"What did she do?"

"Everything right. She secured a harassment restraining order against him. The prosecutor's office charged him with stalking. She was ready and willing to testify."

"Let me guess, he violated the HRO."

Ruby nodded. "One night, she came home after studying with her chemistry partner—a boy. When she pulled into her driveway, he was waiting in the shadows. He had her pinned on the ground before she knew he was there. She was his, he told her. If he couldn't have her, nobody would. He'd fucking kill her."

"Terroristic threat."

"Yes. He started to cry, and told her nobody could love her as much as he did. He begged her not to make him do it, as he squeezed her throat."

"Domestic strangulation is a felony in Minnesota."

"Yes, and with good reason. A battered women's organization studied femicides by intimate partners, and each included strangulation in the escalation to murder."

"Did she survive?"

"Yes. Once again, she did everything right. She hit her panic button. By the time the cops arrived, she'd lost consciousness. They charged felony domestic assault—strangulation. He bailed out, promised to change, to stay away from her. Even judges want to believe in redemption, especially in the young. Eric Longhorn was eighteen years old, and on a mission."

"He didn't stay away, did he?"

"No, he didn't. The night he got out, Tara was afraid to go anywhere, to do anything. She didn't know where he was, what he'd do. He'd called thirteen times from different numbers."

"I've heard of spoofing. You can punch in any number into the app, and that's what will show up."

"Exactly. Tara went to bed unaware he'd broken in and was waiting for her to lie down. When she did, he attacked. He stabbed her fourteen times and left his mark—a red Valentine's heart. 'Be mine,' it read. He was out the window and driving off before her father could break down her door. His little girl was already dead."

"That's heartbreaking."

"Yes, it is. I wanted so badly for her to be a survivor of domestic violence—not its casualty."

"How do you deal with such tragedy?"

"We learn from it to help the living. You see, she'd done everything right, and so had her parents. They'd reported, and had installed a reputable home-alarm system. And they did things that weren't legal but were understandable. They bought her a handgun. It was still in her nightstand."

Jasmine dabbed her eyes. "What happened to him?"

"He tried to pin it on Tara's chemistry partner. Longhorn planted a trail that threw off the police. Her parents hired an e-whiz who found spyware on Tara's phone. He'd been stalking her for months. Why do you think I'm telling you this story?"

"It's about a violent abuser. And we know Susan was battered by the man she's accused of murdering."

"Yes, go deeper. We have to understand this heinous mentality to solve this crime. What's the thought process of an abusive and controlling man? How does he see his victim? What tactics does he use to keep her under his control? What's his goal? After Tara refused Longhorn, he murdered her on Valentine's Day. On Friday, Susan Combes turned twenty-nine. Happy birthday to her." Ruby spat out the words. "It's an angle to consider. There are many ways to ruin a life."

CHAPTER 13

Ruby and Jasmine stopped by Colin's desk.

"You have a visitor, Ruby," he said, and handed her a cup of coffee. "He's in the meeting room. He claims Alfred sent him. You won't believe who he is."

"Let me guess, he's our new e-guru."

Colin opened and closed his mouth. "I, I don't even know what to say."

"That's a first. Jazz, you can work in the conference room. My reports are in the file. You'll also find this morning's interview. The rest of the team will start filing in soon."

A wicked gleam came into her eye.

Seeing it, Ruby said, "Don't expect Kottke anytime soon. He likes to stroll in right on time. Arianna Ramirez will be here before he is."

"Who's she?"

"The love of his life."

Jasmine sighed.

"Now it registers. There are plenty more hunks in the sea, Jazz."

"Maybe the e-man has potential."

"Fish elsewhere. We have a murder to solve. Besides, I doubt it. He's an e-nerd. You should've seen Flick."

Ruby strode to the meeting room, and stopped at the threshold, taken aback by broad shoulders and a lean-muscled frame covered in black slacks and a blazer. She cleared her throat. He turned from the window. "Alfred sent you?"

When he nodded, a tendril of thick black hair fell over his chocolate brown eyes. They warmed as he shot her a grin that would cause heart palpitations in other women.

Damn it, she thought as she felt the thump. She wasn't immune after all. It'll fade, she reassured herself. As with Kottke, she'd stop noticing his appeal.

"I'm Emilio Martín." He extended his hand.

She took it, and held fast against the jolt. "Ruby Miller. Thanks for coming in on no notice."

"It's my pleasure to meet you. Any friend of Alfred is a friend of mine."

"Yes, likewise." She sat and motioned for him to do the same.

He did, stretching his legs as he cradled his head in his hands.

"You don't look like your average comp nerd."

"You don't look like your average defender of criminals."

"What do you mean by that?" Her eyes sparked.

He enjoyed their change from mossy green to gleaming emerald. "You first."

"Our former e-man, Flick, fit the image. Long hair, pulled back and bound by the oddest fasteners he could find. His ears disappeared under piercings. We asked for fair warning before he entered a room so we could grab eye protection. He dressed in neon."

"You've aptly described half my research-and-development team."

"Your turn."

"You don't look like you sell prior-owned automobiles."

"Ah, yes. You've nailed it. As in your profession, it's a stereotype for a reason." Flustered by his appreciative grin, she forged on. "Alfred said you don't drink coffee. I hope you don't mind that I do, by the pot. Would you like tea? What do you drink? If it's not bright green I may have it in stock. I run on caffeine and sugar. But I try to stock options." She caught herself rambling and clammed up.

"Are you always this expansive?" he asked, humor alive in his eyes.

"No. Maybe. It depends."

"I had tea with Alfred. I'm fine, Ruby. What's Ruby short for?"

"I've gone with Ruby since my hating-pink tomboy

phase." Over-sharing again, she mused, and sipped her coffee to prevent any further revelations.

"So it's feminine. Rubella?"

"Sounds contagious. My mother isn't that cruel."

"Rubanna?"

"Ruby. You can play your guessing game later. We have a lot of work to do. Alfred said your e-skills are second to none. Is he right?"

"That's accurate."

"I trust Alfred's judgment, but a jury would require more convincing. Tell me about your qualifications."

"I graduated from MIT."

"With honors?"

"The highest."

"And your experience?"

"When I was twelve, I started building robots. By the time I turned sixteen, they utilized technologies others had not yet imagined, much less invented."

"Okay, whiz kid. Let's get to the reason I require your services." Ruby rose, and a piece of paper slipped from the pocket of her slim trousers.

"Allow me," he retrieved the slip and returned it to her.

"You undoubtedly saw what it said."

"Why do you need permission?"

"Well, if you must know."

"Yes," he said, and reclined. "My very life depends upon it." He covered his amused smile when she sent him a warning look.

"It began when I first launched this firm. I was

twenty-six, and fresh out of law school. Although many tried, nobody could convince me I was too young, too inexperienced, too female, too blonde. I was determined. And also terrified," she heard herself admit.

"Bold endeavors trigger excitement and terror. It takes tenacity to proceed."

She nodded at his statement's truth. "I knew the law, and relied on logic to work my cases. I knew if I waited for permission from others I'd be paralyzed. So I granted it to myself. Permission to show such passion in court the judge instructs me to tone it down. Permission to annoy the hell out of officers who resist considering evidence I unearth during my own investigations. Permission to blast out of my comfort zone. It became a habit, these permission slips. And there you are, holding one in your hand. You can throw it away. It served its purpose."

"I'll take care of it."

"Thank you. As I was saying, our client is Susan Combes. Jerald, her husband, was abusive and controlling. Police arrested Susan yesterday evening on murder charges Are you familiar with the dynamics of domestic violence? If not, our consulting psychologist can give you a primer. To serve Susan well, you need to understand what Jerald did to her."

"I'm familiar." His jaw clenched.

"I pay standard consulting rates."

"Not necessary. I'm doing this pro bono. My

company encourages volunteerism."

"What company?"

"Tycon Industries."

"Small world."

"What do you mean?"

"Susan's husband worked for Tycon. Have you come across a Jerald Combes?"

"No, it's a large enterprise. Would you like me to obtain Jerald's personnel file?"

"Yes, thanks—if we don't already have it. You must have some good contacts at Tycon."

"Yes."

"Justin Kottke is our lead investigator. He's pursuing that trail. I'll connect you with him at the meeting." She stopped pacing and leaned both hands on the table, mesmerizing him with her intensity. "There's a theory I'm pursuing. It seems outrageous, yet the evidence supports it."

"You have my undivided attention."

She walked him through her theory before excusing herself to review her notes in her office.

Emilio walked back to the window to take in the city. He slid the paper from his pocket.

Permission to let someone else be the tech expert and stick to logic and law.

He wondered which captured his imagination more—the woman or her theory.

Arianna's chestnut hair streamed behind her as she hurried into Ruby's office and shut the door.

Ruby looked up. "Is the team ready to begin?"

"Yeah, but you left out something major. You're working with Martín?"

"You've heard of him?"

"Ruby, everyone has heard of him. Leave your legal cave once in a while."

"And?"

"He's a tech genius—started his own robotics company at sixteen, sold it at seventeen, invested in another company, and so on. He has the global tech market covered."

"So he's rich. Big deal."

"He's brilliant."

"Now that part I'm interested in, but it isn't breaking news. Alfred beat you to it. Wait, why would you know about a tech gazillionaire? Horses are your thing, tech is definitely not. You refused to install AutoTroughs for your horses."

"Of course I did. I wouldn't risk a glitch in the system. I get the formulas right every time, and trust my team to do the same. And nothing automatic can look at my horses and tell when they need a booster or a supplement."

"Yes, I know. You didn't answer my question, Ari. Why are you so jazzed about this guy? Maybe he's your thing."

"Martín is Spanish. His mother's family had a reputation for breeding the best horses on the continent. His mother left the family business. Nobody knows why. But Martín revived it. His ranch in Segovia is the horse lover's promised land."

"Ah, you want to use him to get to his horses." She grabbed her PSC and motioned for Arianna to follow.

"Ruby, it's not like that."

"It's okay. I want him for his e-skills."

"Right. And I suppose you didn't notice he's gorgeous?"

"I didn't say I'm blind."

As they entered the organized chaos, Arianna tossed back her lustrous hair and laughed.

Justin stopped mid-sentence as she drew his gaze.

Emilio's eyes were on Ruby as she crossed to the front.

"All right, team, listen up," Ruby said. "First, if you ate all the Anton's, heads will roll."

"No rolling required, boss." Colin held up a heaping plate. "This vulture didn't make it easy." He tipped his head toward Justin.

"You're my hero, Colin." She snatched the plate and turned back to the group. "We've added another member to our team—Emilio Martín, e-man. Word is his skills rival Flick's."

"Damn straight, Ruby," said Justin. "He's legendary."

"Alfred speaks highly of you all," Emilio said. "I'm honored to join the team."

"And he's a gentleman, like Alfred." Arianna added.

Justin looked from her to Emilio in dismay, and stayed silent.

"Grab whatever you consider food and drink and take a seat, please." She chomped on a frosted donut and chased it with black coffee.

"Does she always eat like that?" Emilio asked Colin.

"You mean food choice, pace, or position?"

"All three, I suppose."

"Yes, she fuels on caffeine and sugar, often inhaling and chugging on the go."

"That can't be good for her."

"Order her not to and see where that gets you."

"No, I'm not the type to take that route. The path of persuasion is more my style."

"You sound like Ruby."

"Do I? From what I've seen, that's a compliment."

Once everyone settled, Ruby brushed sugar off her slacks and launched right in. "Our client, Susan Combes, was arrested for murder in the first degree of her husband, Jerald Combes. Crime scene is the Combes' cabin. First on-scene was Jerald's buddy—Stuart Johnston, Kaye County Attorney. When police arrived, Jerald's truck was on-scene. A blood trail led from the driver's side into and through the house, and ended in the guest bathroom. Therein, a man identified by eyewitness Johnston as Jerald Combes lay in the tub with wounds consistent with a kitchen knife. A blood sample and fingerprints confirmed the ID. Johnston claims that he saw Susan pulling out of the cabin driveway holding a kitchen knife. Officers executed a search warrant for Susan's vehicle and found a knife on the passenger seat. The state sees this as an open-and-shut case."

"Let me guess," Colin said. "They're wrong."

"Got it in one."

"The first red flag was method. Why not poison her husband? Susan cooked for Jerald every night, including the night of the murder. And the motive was shaky. Where was Susan's escalation? Jerald escalated to breaking Susan's bones, to strangulation. Where were the signs she was ready to snap? Her life was in danger, not his—according to a risk assessment. What about the means? Why would she follow him to the cabin to kill him with a kitchen knife? Why not do it in the kitchen? She's pegged with attacking him in the cabin's driveway, and hauling him inside. Tell them about the reenactment, Jazz."

"We observed drag marks and a corresponding blood trail leading from the driveway into the cabin. I attempted to maneuver Ruby inside. Given adequate time, and after expending considerable effort, I could have succeeded. I made little progress in the ten minutes we allocated to the task," she finished with a wry smile.

"Must be all the Anton's," Justin said.

Jasmine allowed the laughter to fade before continuing in a serious tone. "Jerald Combes outweighed Ruby by about a hundred pounds. There's no way I could have hauled his ass up the steps."

"Thanks, Jazz," Ruby said.

Jasmine took her seat.

"We have supporting evidence Susan was incapable of such a feat. Susan told us that Jerald threw her to the ground on Friday evening. A jail medic confirmed that her left wrist is fractured."

"I had trouble dragging Ruby with two good wrists."

"Har har, Jazz. We get the point."

Justin rose and went to the front of the room.

Ruby gestured for him to have the floor and sat.

"I located Susan's phone. She photographed herself on Friday evening before Jerry came home." He brought a photo on-screen. "Blue dress, blue-and-white heels. I located Susan's dress in the hamper—no mud, no blood. Her shoes were in the closet and immaculate. By Johnston's account, she'd have had no time to change."

"Yes, and that's helpful exculpatory evidence, but it's circumstantial. The best evidence of Susan's innocence was provided by her abuser."

"What do you mean, Ruby?" Colin asked.

"We've seen other cases in which abusers have used electronics to monitor their victim's movements. We wanted to know what means Jerald used to monitor Susan. So Kottke swept the residence."

"Jerry installed video surveillance in the kitchen and master bedroom. He also had a two-way bug in the bedroom. That means—"

"We have conclusive evidence of Susan's

whereabouts during the murder," Ruby said.

"Way to steal my thunder." Justin said.

"Roar about something else. I anticipated hefty tech talk. Get into the specifics with Colin and Emilio. We've hit on this enough. Susan is innocent."

"Isn't that it, then? Don't you have enough to get her out?" Arianna asked.

"Yes," Ruby said. "But's complicated. We'd have to hand our findings over to the county attorney's office. Our prime suspect is currently Stuart Johnston."

"Kaye County Attorney? If I didn't know you better, I'd say you've lost it," Arianna said.

Ruby sighed. "I said it's complicated. Johnston generously agreed to meet with me on Monday morning. His cooperation made little sense at the time."

"He wants to keep tabs on our progress," Colin offered.

"Right," Ruby said. "This is a messy case. Let's keep untangling it. Amy?"

"The pathology is consistent with a male who lacked the empathy to plot this murder from a woman's perspective. He miscalculated by placing her actions within his paradigm of anger, control, and violence. He saw Susan as a pawn, devoid of her own feelings and thoughts. She's powerless, silent, and disposable, in his mind. And he failed to factor in her fractured wrist. It was beyond his notice. Insignificant. The setting of the scene is inconsistent with Susan's tendencies. It was messy, splashy. Susan took care of what was hers."

Ruby nodded in agreement. "She meticulously cleaned up her kitchen before going to bed, yet she didn't scrub at the blood trail or rinse out the tub?"

"Precisely, and this fits with the narcissism I described. In making his plan, he failed to factor in how long it takes to clean a kitchen," Amy said.

"And we're not talking about light cleaning," Ruby said, raking a hand through her hair. "I studied her cleaning supplies—collectibles, rather. She could have used a decrepit old mop, and yet the kitchen footage shows her on her hands and knees. The mop is missing, and so is a wooden bucket. Where did they go? These pieces seem inconsequential on their own."

"The owner of the neighboring cabin, Carol Lawrence, smelled wood burning."

"Yes, Jazz. Good." Ruby scanned her team, eyes glinting. "They could be coincidences."

"But you don't believe in coincidences," Justin, Jasmine, and Colin said in unison.

"No, I don't. It all means something. What else?"

"Friday was Susan's birthday," Jasmine said.

"Yes, that matters."

"Abusers love to ruin special occasions. Longhorn picked Valentine's Day," Arianna said, and searched Ruby's eyes.

"I'm okay," Ruby said for Arianna's benefit. "Ari's right."

"And it's another piece to consider," Amy said. "Who wouldn't figure in that a woman would wear an impractical outfit for murder on her birthday? The killer is male, and it's personal."

"Does it fit the profile for him to have an accomplice?" Ruby asked.

"Yes."

"Thank you, Amy. Jazz, walk us through the traffic flow, please."

"Yes, sir." She gave Ruby a jaunty salute.

"She's a natural fit to the team," Amy murmured to Colin.

"Yes, I adore her."

"Proceed." Ruby gave Jasmine an exaggerated bow and sat to gulp coffee.

"With Colin's help, I animated the traffic to and from the cabin. Colin?"

Colin tapped his PSC and an aerial view appeared on the center wall screen.

"At approximately six-thirty, a green truck drove to the cabin followed by a blue car," Jasmine narrated. "About fifteen minutes later, a rattletrap came down the road. It parked here, behind the blue car. At around seven, the truck left, and returned fifteen minutes later. Five minutes after the truck's return, the rattletrap and blue car left. Around eight, a black sedan pulled into the driveway where the blue car had been. It stayed until around ten-thirty, when Ruby and I saw its driver get in and take off."

"Whose car was it?" Emilio asked.

"Stuart Johnston's."

"What about the others?" Emilio followed up.

"I'll take that one," Justin said. "Thanks, Jazz."

She beamed at him and sat in her seat with a sigh.

Justin sauntered to the front of the room, smiling at Arianna as he passed. "I ran the truck's plates. It's registered to Jerald Combes. As for the other vehicles, Susan has a blue car. I collected mud samples from the driveway, and from the tire of Susan's car. They match. Her car was at the scene. The rattletrap was unidentified."

"Until this morning," Ruby added. "Alfred introduced another player into the mix. Jerald Combes was at Alfred's on Friday morning to pick up a piece of jewelry for a business acquaintance—Anthony Priestley." Ruby nodded at Kottke.

"Anthony Priestley is twenty-seven years old. The feds looked at him during their investigation into a coke ring run by a Mexican cartel, and nothing stuck."

"The same ring that was dismantled during the big federal bust six months back?" Colin asked.

"Same ring," Kottke confirmed.

"What kind of vehicle does Anthony Priestley drive?" Emilio asked.

"Nicely done, New Guy. Colin, put it on-screen, please."

Colin complied.

"It looks like a rattletrap," Amy said.

"There's more," Kottke continued. "There was a missing-person report filed yesterday night for Anthony Priestley."

"Who filed it?" Emilio asked.

"His mother and a woman who claimed to be his best friend—Elizabeth Priestley and Rebecca Phillips. Ms. Priestley's record is squeaky. Phillips is charged with felony possession of cocaine, and is currently represented by counsel."

Colin stood. "I have an update on that front. Ruby, I put it on your calendar but didn't want to disturb you. Ms. Phillips called to make an appointment. I booked her for seven tomorrow morning."

"She fire her previous lawyer?"

"Yes."

"Lady Luck strikes again."

"Do you want me to move the appointment?"

"No, that's perfect. Good work, team." Ruby retook control of the room. "We need to figure out what happened to Anthony Priestley. Is he a murderer? Did he chicken out and flee? Is he in a hidey hole somewhere? Is he an eyewitness who hasn't come forward? Is he even alive?" she peppered.

"Did Stuart Johnston and Anthony Priestley kill Jerald Combes?" Amy asked.

"Yes, we have to pursue all viable possibilities," Ruby said.

"Why would Johnston kill his best friend?" Jasmine asked.

"The motive could be a classic," Justin said. "Greed. I found Jerald's will at his residence. Johnston was set to inherit everything from Jerry if he knocked Susan out of the picture."

"He struck me as a killer."

"It's not just based on Jasmine's killer instincts," Ruby said. "Jazz and I paid a visit to Levi Hollins, the charging attorney—on paper, at least. Johnston spoon-fed him the PC statement. If you're writing a PC statement and submitting it to the on-duty judge at midnight on a murder case, wouldn't you also ask to search the house? He restricted it to the cabin and Susan's car. Why the car and not the house? Makes sense if you know where the knife is. What did we find in the house? Who would have had an interest in keeping it hidden?"

"Surveillance equipment. It confirmed Susan was in the residence all night."

"Right, Kottke. What were the forensic results?"

"It was Jerald's blood. The tox-panel revealed cocaine. Candace also found anti-coagulant."

"So we have in the blood trail an additive to stop blood from clotting. Here's another piece. Jazz, what did we notice alongside the blood trail?"

"Gravitational drops."

"Combine that with the pieces missing from Susan's kitchen collectibles—"

"And you have a person or persons laying a tidy trail to Susan Combes," Emilio concluded.

"Yes, and I bet one such person is Stuart Johnston. Kottke?"

"Johnston's prints were found on Susan's car—the door handle, the steering wheel."

"He was so cocky about his misdirection he didn't bother to wear gloves. Johnston didn't factor us into his plan."

"Why aren't we going to Rebecca Phillips and finding out what she knows about her friend?" Jasmine asked.

Amy Larson stood. "I'll take this one, Ruby. If they are involved in illegal activity together, Rebecca may have filed the report to cover his tracks. If Anthony is in hiding, then alerting her could cause him to go deeper."

"It is also possible she genuinely doesn't know his whereabouts," Ruby added.

"What do you have in mind?" Colin asked.

"We'll gather intel today and have a better idea of the players. We'll dig deeper into Jerald's activities. Alfred mentioned a farm property that Jerald Combes had converted into a private lab."

"I have more on that front," Justin said. "I spoke with Jerry's boss at Tycon. Jerry was gung ho about DNA experimentation and wanted to move forward with it—fast track it to human trials. His boss not only didn't give him the green light, he pulled the plug."

"How did Jerald react?" Amy asked.

"He was pissed for a while. Then he was fine. Before the project pull, he'd come in earlier than anyone and leave later. After, he'd come into work on time, do his job, and leave."

"When was his project yanked?"

"About seven months ago."

"We need to find out what Jerry was doing on that

property," Justin said.

"I traced it." Colin pulled up a photo. "Here's the public-access aerial. It hasn't been updated in ten months."

"Who owns it?" Emilio asked.

"Susan Combes."

Ruby pumped her fist and gave Colin a smacking kiss on his cheek. "Well done, you brilliant, beautiful man."

"What are we celebrating? I want in," Jasmine said. "Who wants a kiss?"

Focused on Arianna, Justin missed her hopeful glance.

"It figures Jerald would say he inherited the property," Ruby said. "Contrary to Jerry's belief, Susan exists apart from him. And her independent existence is recognized by the state. Her property was not his, and neither was she. She's authorized us to access her property as needed to conduct her case. It's time we do our own recon on the stalker's activities. Any ideas for surveillance?"

Emilio stood. "If I may, I can assist in this area." He tapped his own handheld device, which looked quite similar to the units Flick had supercharged for the team, and an image appeared on-screen.

"What's that? A robo-bug? Don't we have enough real-life bugs around?"

Emilio laughed and grinned at Jasmine.

"It is a bug, in a manner of speaking. It has an astral satellite's sight, a bumblebee's size, and an express chopper's speed."

"Thank God it doesn't look like a mash-up of the three," Ruby said.

"Its audio detection is four-hundred times that of a human. You're looking at the latest in drone technology."

"No way. That's a drone?"

"Yes, equipped for surveillance only. It isn't armed. If captured, it self-destructs."

"Into a poof of smoke?" Colin asked.

"I'll show you." He entered a series into his device, and the drone flattened and emitted a sticky substance.

"It looks like a squashed bug," Ruby said.

"Precisely."

"What's that goo?" Justin asked. "Acid?"

"No, that would certainly alert its captor something's off. It's histamine and irritant. It causes skin to break out in hives, ensuring the drone's prompt release, and likely further destruction."

"Under the captor's boot," Ruby said. "Clever."

"One finds much inspiration in the natural world to advance technology."

"When can we deploy the drone?" Colin asked.

"It's been my latest pet project so I've taken to carrying it with me."

"You keep a prototype in your pocket?" Ruby eyed his blazer.

"Don't be silly. It's in my office."

"Your office?" She raised a brow.

"Say the word and I'll release Jaspyr."

"He has a name," Jasmine said. "Like a pet robot. Would it break your heart if Jaspyr gets squashed?" Jasmine looked up, eyes wide.

Ruby rolled her eyes. "I'm sure he'd build another."

"Thank you for your concern, Jasmine. It would console me to know he met his end for a good cause."

Ruby scanned the assembled talent in satisfaction. "Team, let's spring Susan. Once we show up on Monday, we have to start playing our cards. Otherwise, we let the state's version stand, and Susan's held without bail for the duration of this case. We'll meet tomorrow, same time, to review what we collect today."

"Well, on that note." Kottke broke into raspy song. "I'm going down to Lucky Town. Going down to Lucky Town." He offered his hand to Amy.

She accepted and fell into step with him. Soon, her rich alto harmonized.

"I wanna lose these blues I've found. Down in Lucky Town. Down in Lucky Town."

Ruby grabbed her PSC and called over as she walked to the door. "When you're done goofing around, we have killers to catch."

"Ruby, you'll learn as you get older to never turn down the opportunity to dance." Amy responded without missing a beat.

Emilio held out his hand to Ruby. "May I?"

She held out her hand and jerked her head to the drone on-screen. "May I?"

"In my office."

"Yeah, your office," she echoed, amused. "Glad to see you've settled in. Grab it and meet me in my office, please."

Ruby pulled Arianna aside. "You have access to the file. Let Colin know if you need anything. You know best how to help Susan. I . . ." Ruby held up her hands.

"What you're doing for her matters." Arianna laid a hand on Ruby's shoulder. "I've prepared a room for her at my ranch."

"Thanks." Ruby clasped Arianna's hand. "I have to go give a certain someone a piece of my mind." She darted her eyes to where Emilio sat conversing with Jasmine.

"Go easy on him, Ruby. I like him."

"Jazz, you're with Kottke today," Ruby tossed over her shoulder as she strode to her office.

Emilio excused himself and went to Arianna. "We haven't yet met. I'm Emilio."

Arianna shook his hand. "I'm—"

"Arianna Ramirez. I'm fascinated by your work."

"Well, you're welcome at my ranch any time. It's a small operation, nothing like yours."

"Do not diminish your work so. It matters. It would be my honor to see it. And allow me to reciprocate and show you my ranch whenever it suits you."

"In Segovia?"

"Yes, if you don't mind a bit of travel."

"I'll take you up on that. Thank you," she said, dazed.

"It's my pleasure."

Justin fell into step beside Emilio as he entered the hall, and said, "There's something you should know about Arianna and me."

"Are you involved?"

Justin shifted. "Not exactly."

"Would you like to be?"

Teeth on edge, he said, "Yes."

"Then why, I wonder, did you dance with Amy?"

"Are you going to give me any trouble?"

"I think you're giving yourself enough, my friend. My interest lies elsewhere. If I may, I've kept her waiting." He clapped Justin on the back, and continued on to Ruby's office.

"Well, I'll be damned."

CHAPTER 14

Emilio found Ruby pacing.

"Where do you get off?"

"What do you mean?" He sat on her desk and admired a luminescent orb, appearing casual. His grip gave away his effort at composure.

"Why didn't you tell me you're a gazillionaire?"

"It's refreshing to be simply another team member working toward a noble end. I'd prefer it stay that way. This is your investigation and your team to lead, not mine. My e-skills are at your disposal, and any connections that may be useful. I have no desire for special treatment."

"Good, because you won't receive it. And my law firm is not some rich man's charity. I insist on paying you a consulting fee."

"As you wish."

"And you're right. I'm responsible for securing the best outcome for Susan. I require full disclosure from my team, and that means no material omissions. I don't care if you own half the free world. I care if you have the skills to pull off your part in securing justice for Susan."

"In the spirit of full disclosure," he said, setting the paperweight aside and rising. "I must tell you I'm captivated by you."

"You must be accustomed to having whatever you like. I have no interest in being bought, and the same goes for Arianna. Stay away from her."

His eyes darkened. "I don't buy women, Ruby. I always respect a woman's wishes." He leaned forward, and she felt the warmth as he breathed out his words. "Tell me you're disinterested."

"Right now, I'm interested in tracing the surveillance equipment, and in conducting our own surveillance."

He leaned back and studied her. "As am I. Give me half an hour to run a trace."

"You have it."

He shot her a grin and left her office.

Ruby shut the door behind her, and walked down the hall.

"Ruby?" Amy called from the conference room.

She poked her head in.

"I could see you twitching from here. Are you all right? I heard that Emilio has quite the effect on women."

Ruby turned a finger in a circular motion. "I can see those matchmaking wheels turning, Amy. Toss a wrench in, because I'm not hot for him or anything—just bothered. That man is impossible. He's presumptuous and . . ." She grasped for the right word. "Arrogant."

"My, he has worked you up. I think that Justin checked his emotions pretty well today, don't you?"

"What? Oh, yeah," Ruby said, distracted.

"They remain quite obvious to all except Arianna. It's not unusual for emotions buzzing between two people to be apparent to all but them. Watching the beginning of a love story is like those first weeks of spring. Everything is bright, full of hope."

Ruby relaxed at the mention of Arianna. "Yeah, it's a real kick to watch. Hopefully, when they finally get mushy, they don't do it in front of me."

"You're a hopeless romantic, Ruby."

"You know I want her happy. He's a good guy. He knows her history, and won't repeat it."

"I believe that's why Justin is taking his time. He doesn't want to spook her."

"Her hair will turn gray at this rate."

"She does have gorgeous hair."

"Hair and love. I'd rather talk case strategy."

"Relationships are messy, unpredictable," Amy pressed on.

"They sure are."

"And also thrilling, full of meaning."

"For some. I'm maxed out on girl talk. Mind if we

move on to talking about the case? I could use your help."

"Not at all. What do you need?"

"Another set of eyes."

"You have them. Whom or what are we going to see?"

"Susan's neighbor, Deanna Connelly. Susan fled to her house during an incident. Deanna sided with Jerald."

"Abusers can be very charming."

"Yes, and have double standards of conduct."

"You're thinking a romantic relationship?"

"Jerald got jealous over the damn dentist. That's a pretty tight leash. Maybe he gives himself a lot more latitude."

"Yes, double standards are common with abusers."

"Shall we see what place Deanna thought she held in Jerald's heart?"

"Absolutely. I think good-cop, bad-cop is in order. Am I to play bad cop this time?"

"That's a real stretch, Amy."

"I suppose I'll leave that part to you. It is such a snug fit."

"Thanks." Ruby beamed.

"The cops may have already interviewed her," Ruby said. "I didn't see it in discovery, but they could have done so this morning. What's your take?"

"She'll be reluctant to talk to us, initially," Amy

said. "We're on Susan's side. She'll show loyalty to Jerald again. I might be able to reach her, make her feel she has an ally."

"That's what I'm thinking. And she'll be upset at losing Jerry, ready to slap at someone. I'll offer my cheek." Ruby pulled into the Connelly's driveway.

"A short sprint from Susan's house." Amy noted.

"Yes. She made it, and found no help here. I'll have to hide my disgust for this woman. At least at the get-go."

"If we're right—"

"We do have an excellent track record."

"True. And if we're right, again, then we must remember she is another pawn. He twisted her love and logic as he did Susan's."

"She's not blameless like Susan. It's hard to think of the other woman as a victim."

"She's a woman who loved a man. We must understand her to connect with her."

"I knew I picked the right person for this."

They walked up to the front door and knocked. A curvy woman in a black dress answered. Her copious make-up failed to conceal the redness around her eyes and nose. "I already talked to the police," Deanna said. "I told them everything I know."

"Mrs. Connelly, we're not with the police. I'm Ruby Miller, and I represent your neighbor, Susan Combes."

Amy rushed forward quickly before Deanna could slam the door. "Hello, Deanna, I'm Amy Larson. I'm a psychologist. I'm so sorry for your loss." She offered her hand and an understanding smile.

Deanna took Amy's hand. "Thank you. I can't believe he's gone." She turned to Ruby. "And it's all your client's fault. That crazy bitch killed him. What else do you need to know?"

"If that's true," Ruby said, "then Susan will be held accountable for her actions. I'm here to gather as much information as I can."

"We think you're the person who knew him best, Mrs. Connelly," said Amy.

"You can call me Dede. You're right, I knew Jer better than anyone."

"Are you willing to talk to us?" Amy asked.

Deanna looked from one to the other. "I'll tell you the truth about your client." She spat the words at Ruby. "Jerry gave me an earful about her on the regular. Come in."

They walked into an explosion of pink and frills.

"You have a very pretty home," Amy said. "Do you live here with your husband, Dede?"

"Yes, though he's a deadbeat. It's no secret. Not like Jer."

"How so?"

"Jer was an angel. He went out of his way to do nice things for Psycho Susan. That's what I called her. Jer loved that nickname," she said with a faraway look. "He bought her an expensive kitchen knife she didn't even appreciate. That's the kind of guy he was—dependable, thoughtful. He took care of things around my house for me. He'd fix this. Tinker with that."

"He was handy with electronics?"

"He was the best. Nobody appreciated how talented he was, especially his boss and that bitch he was stuck with."

"Tell me about Susan," Amy said in a gentle tone.

"She wanted to chain him down. You know how a man needs space to roam." She fiddled with a lacy throw pillow. "Jer-Bear was strong, powerful, but he had a softer side. Yeah, he liked things his way. He knew his mind. And he was loyal." She tossed the pillow aside. "He stayed with her even though she was out of control. She'd lose things, forget appointments. She asked me to drive her places, but Jer said it was important she take responsibility so I always said no. I wouldn't have taken her anyways except as a favor to Jer."

Amy raised a brow at Ruby. "You've been very helpful. I want to get a sense of how well you knew him. How close were you two?"

"As close as two people can get."

Amy put her hand on Deanna's. "Did you love him, Dede?"

"Yes, so much." Tears dropped onto their joined hands.

"I'm so sorry for your loss. Did you have plans to be together?"

"He said someday. His wife was so messed up. Fragile, he said. He was worried if he left that'd push her over the edge. That was the last thing we talked about. If he ever tried to leave her, she'd snap. I think that's what happened that night. He tried to leave, and she made sure that he'd never be with another woman." Deanna's eyes flashed.

"Did Susan know you were fucking her husband?" Ruby asked.

Deanna whipped her head to glare at Ruby. "That's despicable."

"I agree," Ruby said.

Amy patted her hand. "I know, Dede. They were in a relationship, Ruby."

"Yeah, it wasn't like that. Jerry could open up to me about stuff he couldn't tell Susan."

"Likely story. You want the truth? He was stringing you along, Deanna. He was never going to leave his wife for you. He already had a Mrs. Combes, and he was never going to leave her. He was never going to let her leave him. She tried. She ran to you for help, Deanna, after he strangled her and fractured her wrist. You refused to help her get away from him."

"No, it wasn't like that. He was going to leave her. She killed him before he had a chance."

"You wanted to be Mrs. Combes? Look what he did to his wife, Deanna." Ruby held out her PSC and pulled up a bone scan. "See here? This is called a distal radius fracture." She scrolled. "See these bruises around her neck? They're consistent with strangulation. Do you see the damage he caused?"

"No, she did that. All of it. She's clumsy."

"It was her ninth fracture, Deanna. She'd only broken her pinky toe until she married Jerald. How would she strangle herself? It's physically impossible. She ran from this, Deanna. She fled from his abuse, and you wouldn't help her."

"No, no, get out of my house." She grabbed the pillow, and sobbed into it.

Amy laid a hand on her back. "We're leaving, Dede. I'm sorry that Ruby upset you. Here's my card. You don't have to talk to her. You can call me any time."

Deanna held out her hand for the card without raising her head. "Thank you."

"We'll show ourselves out."

"I hope your client rots in Mardova!" Deanna yelled as they crossed to the front door.

"You're not the only one," Ruby said, and closed the door behind her.

"Well?" Amy asked.

"I don't think she's an accomplice."

"Neither do I. She's genuinely in mourning."

"Yeah, she fell for everything Jer-Bear told her."

"And it goes against the profile to rely on a woman as part of the plan."

"Women are their pawns."

"Yes. They certainly didn't factor us in," Amy said.

"Damn right, and it's only a matter of time before they do. We'll be ready. You agree that there are two killers?"

"Yes. It fits."

"Thanks for coming. You were a superb good cop."

"I enjoy getting out and stretching my legs. Perhaps next time I can be bad cop."

"No one would buy it. Your halo is blinding."

Ruby cruised into her office suite. "Where's Martín?"

"Flick's old office." Colin replied.

Ruby did a double take. "Seriously? He could have had the meeting room, the conference room. Hell, he could have worked in my office."

"Why haven't you offered me that arrangement?" He motioned to his area.

"We need you front and center."

"Yes, I suppose you do. Emilio said something about liking the ambience in Flick's."

"Ah, the e-man—an elusive breed. Try and figure them out."

"How did the interview go?"

"As expected. Neighbor loved Batterer. Even when confronted with Wife's broken bones, Neighbor's blinded by denial."

"Why didn't he beat his neighbor?"

"In his mind, she was his plaything, not his property. And now she's a wreck."

"Did Amy calm her down?"

"Amy is a saint. She gave the woman her card."

"It doesn't sound like you're inclined to cut this

woman any slack."

"No. Cheating is bad enough—not neighborly, to say the least. But to refuse help to a woman afraid for her life is a new level of sordid."

"Jerry left a lot of damage in his wake."

"Yes, and we've yet to discover it all. I hope Emilio has something for me."

"I heard victory whoops so that's promising."

"He doesn't seem the type to whoop."

"Not every professional is as stalwart as you, Ruby."

"I'm not stalwart, just—"

"Reserved? Dignified? However you spin it, you could lighten up. Take a vacation."

"Nicely done. I didn't catch you on the lead up that time. I thought you were merely insulting me. Tell Charles not to pack his golf clubs quite yet."

Arriving at Flick's closed door, she knocked and waited.

"Yes, yes, come in already."

"Why would you shut the door if you didn't want entrants to knock?" Ruby asked, and stopped in her tracks. "Where am I?"

"You took longer than half an hour. I moved on to the next task. I figured I could use a tech center in close proximity to the team."

"You're enjoying yourself, aren't you?"

"Immensely. This reminds me of my first office. Bits and pieces of electronics that I repurposed."

Ruby eyed the contraption holding hot tea.

"You made your own tea maker."

"A FastFare, actually. Small yet mighty, much like our fearless leader." He shot her a cheeky grin.

Her scowl melted into a smile under his radiant enthusiasm.

"Colin was kind enough to stock it."

"You've been here for two hours, and already you're—"

"All settled in. I told you I work fast. Impressed?"

"Maybe if you let me take your drone for a spin . . ."

"Done." He sprang from his chair and grabbed his briefcase.

"How are you so bouncy without caffeine?"

"Adequate nutrition, Rubina."

"Rubina? Who spilled?"

"My source prefers anonymity. He or she also told me adequate nutrition is something you could use more of."

"That doesn't narrow down my suspect list."

"Good. Here, I've programmed this for you." He dashed to the FastFare. "Jacques, prepare one Rubina Special, please." When a plate and cup emerged, he said, "Go ahead, take it."

"What is it?"

"What does it look like?"

"Coffee and a cinnamon roll."

"Precisely. Try it."

Ruby eyed him warily over the rim as she sipped. "This is great coffee," she admitted.

"Yes, yes. Try the roll."

She took a tiny bite, and followed it with a large one as her taste buds danced in glee. "That is . . . Wow."

"Best roll you've ever had, no?"

"Don't tell Anton. Can I have another?"

"Absolutely."

"Wait a minute. Weren't you harping on me for my eating habits? Now you're offering me junk food. What's the catch?"

"They're fortified. Coffee is the real deal, loaded with antioxidants. And I combined it with the latest in supplementation to rival the nutrition of a GreenPower smoothie."

Ruby started backing away, shaking her head.

Emilio was too excited to notice. "Its patent is pending. And that isn't an ordinary cinnamon roll. It's made with a sweetener I had to hike through the rainforests in Jamaica to acquire. Has a zero glycemic impact on your body. The flour is from coconuts, but not just any coconuts."

"From the rare Kirkawack tree found on the island of Tikiluau."

He cocked his head. "No, don't be silly. From the palms of Bora Bora."

"Stop the madness. Stop the madness right now." Ruby forced herself to set the roll and coffee down. "I can't believe it. I'm surrounded. I've gone and hired another one."

"Another what?"

"Health freak. I'm outnumbered. It's only a matter of time before I'm drinking glowing goo and talking about the benefits of some obscure berry."

"It wouldn't be the worst thing, Rubina."

"Don't mess with my caffeine and sugar."

"Would it help if I told you this was a cinnamon roll like any other?" He held it out as a peace offering.

"Yes." She accepted it, and repeated, "It's just another cinnamon roll." She finished it off. "A damn good one, I have to admit."

"How about a compromise? I won't tell you when it's fortified food."

"I'd rather not know. Deal. And if I can tell that you've tinkered with it, it's not getting past these taste buds. They're finely honed and difficult to trick."

"I've already made it past them once."

"Beginner's luck. Get anything done besides make your freaky FastFare?"

Emilio moved behind her at his desk and caressed her arm.

She bolted up and skirted around the desk.

"You could have asked me to give you your chair."

"I could have, yes." His eyes glinted.

"Stop looking at me that way."

"What way?"

"Like you want to jump me on this desk."

"As you wish." He turned his attention to his PSC. "Juan, display on-screen."

"You unearthed a working screen."

"Who said it worked?"

"It appears one man's e-graveyard is another man's —"

"Tech center. Yes, I told you." He gestured to the screen. "I tracked down the transmission destination for the surveillance equipment found in Susan's kitchen and bedroom."

"You do work fast."

"There's more. I swept Susan's phone, and found spyware encrypted and buried."

"So did Kottke."

"Yes, and he did well. Stalker applications are common, but hard to detect, particularly ones with this level of encryption. I tracked down the source."

"Now I'm impressed."

"My heart flutters at winning the favor of a worthy woman," he said, exaggerating his accent.

"Knock it off." She bit her lip to hold back a laugh.

"You're not after me for my accent? Spanish is a romance language, Rubina."

"I'm not after you, period."

"I cannot say the same, Rubina." He said, and turned his attention back to the screen. "The source device is a cell registered to one Jerald Combes."

"As we expected."

"Yes, I was as unsurprised by that as much as I was surprised by this. Ask me the last time the surveillance equipment was activated."

"When?"

"Friday evening, at six-fifty-eight."

"That's around the murder."

"What does it mean?"

"It doesn't in and of itself disprove the state's theory. Wife takes Husband's cell after the kill and finds out he's been watching her. Where's the cell?"

"It's still active. Signal triangulates to—"

"Fifty-nine-oh-two Whittaker Road—the farm property. Yes!" Ruby exclaimed. "Now that not only disproves the state's theory, but it supports mine. No way is Susan transmitting from jail. Excellent work, really."

Unable to resist the joy radiating from her green eyes, he captured her mouth in a searing kiss before releasing her.

Confusion swirled in her eyes. Shaking her head to clear it, she stepped away. Her throat went dry. She broke his gaze. "Knock that off. We're working."

"Colin received a celebratory kiss for his discovery. As any other team member, I'd like the same treatment."

"That's not. That wasn't . . ." She ran her hand through her hair and turned away.

"You're adorable when you're flustered."

She whirled. "Call me adorable again and you'll see my karate training in action."

"Ah, a wonderful contact sport. I enjoy sparring myself. You'd be a formidable partner, I imagine. Yes, I'd enjoy that immensely. I'm picturing it right now." He reposed with his fist on his chin as if deep in thought.

"You're impossible to work with."

"We both know that had nothing to do with work. And before that, I'd say we made good progress. You and I have an efficient rhythm."

"Stop with your innuendos."

He raised an eyebrow. "That was purely for pleasure, Rubina. Do you have something against it?" He sent her a heated gaze.

"There you go again."

"What, Rubina?"

"Looking at me like you want to ravage me on your desk."

"There's more to the emotional spectrum than lust. You've grabbed hold of me, Rubina. You haven't meant to, you've made that clear. I'm no more comfortable with it than you are, but there's the truth. You need only tell me you're disinterested."

She remained silent.

"I'm going to deploy Jaspyr. Would you like to give me a goodbye kiss?" He asked, wanting to goad the fear from her gaze as much as he wanted to discover its cause.

"No, I'd like to give you a swift kick to your—"

"Rubina, you really are—"

"Don't you dare say it."

"Delightful." He smiled as her eyes flared and banished the shadows.

"I can assure you I'm not that either. Stop smirking."

"I'm not. I'm smiling. I find you enchanting,

Rubina."

"Stop that."

"Stop what? Complimenting you? Should I not tell you your beauty is only exceeded by your sharp mind, and I can't seem to resist either?"

"You definitely shouldn't."

"Why, are you a nun as well as a lawyer? I'd respect any vows you've taken. If not disinterest, then what is it? I suppose my tech center is not the most romantic of settings."

Ruby sighed. "No, I'm not a nun." When he said nothing, she continued. "I've dated, nothing has stuck. And I haven't wanted it to. I've wanted simple. I have my work."

"Very important work."

"You'd be complicated."

"That's the nicest thing you've said to me."

"You need your head examined. Stop by and see Amy on your way out. She'll set you straight in no time."

"Your concern warms my heart." He grabbed her hand, and held it to his chest. When she didn't pull away, he linked his fingers with hers.

"Emilio?"

"Yes, Rubina?"

"Go deploy your drone." She unlinked their hands and used hers to push him out the door.

He could still hear her laughing when he reached Colin's desk.

"I like having you around," Colin said. "She hasn't

laughed like that since—" he stopped short.

"Since?"

Colin hesitated, and then continued. "You're on the team. I suppose I should tell you about Tara Baxter."

"I hear you have a flair for technology. Why don't you tell me while we send Jaspyr on his mission?"

"Yes, absolutely. Let me switch over to auto-respond." He changed modes and bolted upright. "Where are we heading?"

"To the roof."

"But we aren't cleared for roof access."

"I have various real-estate holdings."

"This is your building."

"Yes, allow me to give you a behind-the-scenes tour, starting with its roof."

"Don't tell Ruby that you own the building."

"I wouldn't dream of it. She insisted that I accept a fee."

"That's Ruby for you, as quick to help others as she is to decline aid. She prefers to make it on her own. Don't stand in her way."

"My aim is to help her, not hinder her."

"What did she think of the Ruby Special?"

"She insisted on pretending it was junk food."

"She ate it? Huh, she ate fortified food. Isn't that something?"

"Is it?"

Colin studied him. "I say this as a happily attached man. I don't know if it's the genius factor, the gorgeous face, the accent, or a combo, but Ruby doesn't know what's coming. It's about time someone gave her a reason to surface from her legal cave."

"You've spoken to Justin, have you?"

"Yes, and I have excellent vision." He tapped his glasses. "I like you, but that'd change fast if you hurt her. She's family to us."

"I won't put her heart in any risk beyond which I'd place my own."

After a moment, Colin nodded and said, "Fair enough."

"What would Rubina think of your efforts to protect her?"

"It would irritate her." Colin grinned at the thought.

Emilio returned his smile. "What are brothers for?"

CHAPTER 15

Emilio entered Ruby's office and said, "You must have received my drone reports."

"Yes."

"And . . ."

"And there's a lot to do before Monday."

"Which means?"

"I have to work it all through. While you're here, I need info about your latest gadgets—the ones not on the market yet."

"I'd be delighted to discuss it over dinner."

"Now's not really the time for a date."

"Your objection is to the timing? You've been holed up in here for hours, Rubina."

"Yes, I don't micromanage. We all come and go as we please. We'll reconvene at eight."

"You also don't feed your team."

"Colin can dial for delivery as well as I can. Have him order lunch."

"It'd be quite late for that. I took the liberty of ordering a spread at the appropriate hour."

"What time is it?"

"Four. The others warned me not to interrupt you."

"And yet here you are."

"Yes, here I am."

"Did it glow green?"

"What?"

"Did your lunch options glow?"

"No. I took your aversion to real food and penchant for junk into account. Jasmine helped me with the selection. We decided on a mix."

"She has her own vices. Did she order you for dessert?"

"I have a hunger for you, Rubina. I'm not the type of man who indulges in a sampler. Understood?"

"Yes," she said. "Thanks for taking care of lunch. I sometimes forget not everyone fuels up on sugar and caffeine." She looked up hopefully. "Any of the junk left?"

"You cannot survive on caffeine, sugar, and tenacity, Rubina."

"I know. They're not good for me, and neither is sarcasm. But after two hours of sleep in forty-eight, they sustain me."

He brushed the pad of his thumb against the dark marks under her eyes.

Caught off guard by his tenderness, she held still and watched him.

He saw spine and fatigue in her sea-green eyes. "You're a fascination."

"Perhaps." She moved his hand aside. "Be fascinated later. Let's talk possibilities."

"Between you and me?"

"No, gadgets. We need solid evidence, safety, and a plan involving subterfuge. Think your techie mind is up to the challenge?"

"I know it is."

"There's that robust ego."

"There's nothing wrong with a healthy awareness of one's abilities." His heated look told her he meant more than technical prowess.

"No, there isn't. I figure it's only a matter of time before I find out if it's real or imagined."

"We've made ample progress, Rubina," Emilio said. "It's nearing the dinner hour. Your consultant must have three squares or his productivity will plummet."

"Nobody's stopping you."

"Our work will await our return."

She gave him her full attention and a wicked grin. "Where did you have in mind? Jet over to Denmark and dine at the world's best restaurant? We'd nibble toast points loaded with caviar harvested from the Caspian sea, sip the most sought-after wine?"

"Are you enjoying yourself?"

"Yes."

"Are you done?"

"For now."

"What's your answer?"

"No, thanks. I'd rather grab a burger and eat it in my office."

"May I make a suggestion?"

"Actually, I'm not done. I know about high-end. I've seen dear friends and clients seduced by it with lasting consequences. I have no interest in it."

He started to speak.

She raised her hand, palm facing him.

"I'm not an heiress or an aspiring actress. I have no interest in glitz, your fancy food, or your mountains of gold. All I'm after, Emilio," Ruby paused to tap his temple, and continued, "Is your mind. Got it?"

"Ah, so you've pegged me as a playboy and decided you're immune to my charm?"

"Yes. That sums it up."

Her verbal blow connected with his gut. Keeping his tone casual, he said, "As you wish. How about a classic that's survived the ages—pasta with meatballs the size of your fist?"

"You're persistent, I'll give you that."

"You took issue with fancy. We won't go for fancy. Unless there's another reason you're reluctant to be alone with me?" He looked at her in challenge. "You wouldn't fall for a frivolous Casanova's advances, would you?"

"No, no reason." Ruby jutted out her chin. "What

kind of meat are we talking? Soy blend?"

"No, the real deal. Grass-fed beef."

"Real cow." Her mouth watered as her eyes narrowed. "Who ratted out my weakness?"

"That I won't say. But I will tell you it cost me a bulk bag of espresso beans, and an espresso maker that'd do them justice."

"I hesitate to ask the brand, but you already know my affinity for the brew. Which one?"

"Hollenbeck."

"It's Arianna, then. Best friends since Kaye High and you turn her traitor with Hollenbeck."

"If you're nice, Anna might share."

"Anna? On a nickname basis now?"

"Yes. Believe it or not, some women enjoy my company. Seek it out, even."

"Some women stay with companions that throw them around their living quarters."

His expression darkened. "Which begs the million-dollar question."

"What do you think that is? Why do these women stay?"

"No, Rubina. Why do these men degrade, demean, and violate women? The responsibility is theirs."

Ruby considered him. Decision made, she slapped her thighs as she rose. "So . . . where's this meatball joint? I'm starving."

The Gabriella Blanca Center had pride of place in the city's center. Towering and majestic, it brushed against the gauzy clouds floating leisurely across the azure sky.

Ruby trailed her hand along the sandstone as they made their way to the impressive entrance. "You don't see architecture like this anymore."

"Its residents affectionately call it the Castle, particularly the pint-sized ones," Emilio said.

"Residents? I've often wondered what happens here."

"It's a comprehensive program that requires many volunteers—for life-skills classes, for its childcare program. It aims to break the cycle of abuse. Women and their children are welcome here."

"How long do they stay? How does the program work?"

"The program is designed to rebuild their confidence and give them dignity. Each woman works, and pays rent based on her income. She becomes better educated and a better mother during the program, which can take up to two years. Many women transform in astonishing ways in eighteen months, and are ready to go it on their own. Of course, they're not really on their own. They'll always have this community supporting them."

"So you're—what? A volunteer?"

"Yes, and there's my beautiful date for the evening."

A woman with glowing skin and youthful eyes held

her arms wide as she spotted Emilio. "Mijo," she exclaimed, and planted lavish kisses on his cheeks.

"Rubina, meet Gabriella—my mother."

"Your mother? So nice to meet you, Gabriella."

"*Bienvenido*, Rubina. Welcome, welcome. Please come in. And do call me Gabi."

"Call me Ruby. Gabi, is it a coincidence you share your name with the program?"

"My son went and named it after me. He didn't tell you?"

"Somehow he missed that part."

"He's humble to a fault."

"And Blanca? Middle name?"

"My mother's first."

Ruby shot Emilio a meaningful look. "Break the cycle," she muttered. "You excel in omissions."

"Like you, Rubina, my mother has no interest in the glitzy and the fancy. This center is the only thing I could get her to accept. Though I haven't given up trying."

"Oh hush, *Mijo*." She beamed at him. "I'm very happy with what I have. With a son like this, how could I not have everything?"

"You might give her the impression I'm an affable guy. She's determined to think otherwise."

"Yet she's here tonight."

"Yes, I am here. May I join the conversation, or would you rather continue without me?"

"My goodness you have spine. You'll need it with this one. He'd talk you into chocolate ice cream when you're wearing white gloves."

"It wouldn't take much to talk me into old-fashioned chocolate ice cream. Real cream and sugar, no substitutes."

"My mother is fascinated by the old," Emilio said.

"I am, yes. I make my food the old way—none of this zapping with rays. When you make it with your hands, you're adding love. I've always said so. *Verdad, Mijo*?"

"*Sí, Madre*." He kissed her crown and gave her a one-arm squeeze before releasing her. "I'm going to touch base with Angela and make sure she has everything she needs for the week."

Gabriella guided Ruby into an expansive, gleaming kitchen.

"This is unlike any kitchen I've ever seen. I've seen some of these contraptions in a client's kitchen."

"She enjoyed the old way?"

"She may have, had it been a choice."

Gabriella nodded in understanding. "It's modeled after a late nineteenth-century kitchen. Emilio and I toured a house from the Gilded Age preserved by the historical society—one of the Vanderbilt's summer cottages. Are you familiar?"

"Fairly. Cornelius Vanderbilt was an early American business magnate. He made his fortune in rail and water transport. I've always wanted to see the Vanderbilt summer houses, particularly The Breakers—the grandest mansion in Newport. It sounds magnificent."

"You're standing in a replica of its kitchen. My sneak of a son went and added it when he built this home for me."

"It must take a lot of work to prepare meals in here by hand."

"Oh, no, I enjoy this too far much for it to be work. And I have plenty of help. The volunteers also do brilliant work with my girls. We're a family here, you see—the volunteers, the women who stay here, and their little ones. They find a sense of belonging here, as well as love and acceptance for who they are. It inspires them to figure out who that is, to become their best selves. They feel safe to do so here."

"That's beautiful. I feel honored to be part of it tonight."

"I imagine Emilio brought you here because he knows you believe in this work. He's very involved with this program, and particular about whom he invites in."

She felt her heart space expand, inflated by Gabriella's warm words. Unsure what to say, she asked, "Who designed this place? Is the rest of it inspired by The Breakers? The outside looks more like something you'd find from the Renaissance period."

"As a girl in Granada, I saved my pocket money to tour La Alhambra. It's a beautiful palace on the city's outskirts. *Es increíble.*" Her eyes glossed over as she transported to her girlhood in her home country. "I'd spend hours sitting in the courtyard looking up at the sky. It was a second home to me, and much safer than my first. As a teenager, I was hired to give tours. By then, I knew it all by heart. It was my favorite place. Emilio first heard about it through bedtime stories. There wasn't enough good in his life, or magic. I tried to bring him both. And he has returned it to me a thousandfold."

Comprehension dawned. Ruby touched her hand to her heart before placing it on Gabriella's arm. "He built this for you. I mean, I already knew that. But it's not for show—for splendor and extravagance. He brought your favorite part of your home country here." She said with sheer awe in her voice.

"For me, yes, and for other women who are seeking a safe home. La Alhambra was not just a palace. It was also a fortress."

"He brought Granada to the center of Minneapolis. Is there nothing he can't do?"

"Not if he puts his mind to it," she said with a mother's pride, and patted Ruby's hand. "Now, how are you with a knife?"

"Rusty. Nothing like my friend Alfred. He's a history professor turned antiques dealer. He has many talents."

"Yes, we adore Alfred. I've known him for years."

"Yes, of course. It makes sense you'd know him. Alfred introduced me to your son."

"Alfred the Matchmaker. That man does wear many hats, no?"

"Those weren't his intentions. I needed an e-man."

"We both know my son is overqualified for a consulting position. He has a sweet heart. He'd never turn down Alfred. He's been like a father to him."

"I'll have to have a word with dear Freddy."

"I'm sure he had the best intentions."

Ruby softened. "Yes, he always does, and is impossible to stay mad at. Well, I have to tell you I'm an amateur at this." She dangled a knife, point down, from her fingertips and examined it.

"I have a feeling you're a quick learner."

Emilio stood in the doorway and watched his mother guide Ruby through chopping vegetables. The tension she carried eased as she laughed with his mother at her own clumsiness. He felt the tug—the same that had compelled him to bring her with him tonight, and walked to her.

"I hope one of the secret ingredients tonight isn't my finger," Ruby said.

"Nobody has lost any digits under her watch." He picked up a knife and slid it through carrots before moving on to celery.

Ruby gaped in disbelief. "And he's good with a knife. Unbelievable."

"I was trained by the best. She'll have you chopping like me in no time."

"I'd like to walk you back to your office, Rubina, but I have a young audience to prepare for," Emilio said as they left the ruckus of the dining room behind.

"For what?"

"Their bedtime story. They're eager to find out if Aragon and Tabitha outwit the evil sorcerer and live happily ever after," he said as they left the ruckus of the dining room behind.

"Do they?"

"I'm concocting this tale as I go. There will be slaying and valiant escapes to sate the bloodthirsty and adventurous, to be sure. Somehow, it will work out in the end. Every good bedtime story requires a suitably happy ending. Would you like to stay, Rubina?"

"Who wouldn't? I have to get back though. I want to run through everything again, make sure there's nothing I missed. Thanks for dinner."

"Thank you for your volunteerism. The Center greatly appreciates your service. Rather well done, I must say, for a beginner." He lifted her hand. "And with fingers intact." He kissed the inside of her palm before turning her hand to link her fingers with his. "Tomorrow, we're making Thai food, if you're interested. The rest of the week my mother plans Spanish fare. The weekends are for adventures in taste."

"I love Thai food—straight from the take-out container."

"I can guarantee it's better from Gabi's Kitchen. Think about it."

"I will."

"I'll walk you out. Before you get used to the layout, it's a bit of a labyrinth. But first—" Emilio guided her into the kitchen, and gestured to steaming mugs on a tray. "Another Saturday night ritual—a hot drink to go with the story." He poured a mug into a travel container and handed it to her.

"It smells like heaven." Ruby sampled. "And tastes like it smells."

"Hot Spanish chocolate—one of the finer things in life."

"This is my kind of fancy."

"It's an old family recipe. My grandmother safeguarded it. Back when we lived in Spain, this was one of my mother's small comforts. She didn't have enough of them in those days." He unclenched his fist and gripped a mug.

Ruby's brow furrowed. "What do you mean?"

He forced a smile. "It's time for fairy tales and happy endings. Everything else must wait. Thank you again for coming, Rubina."

"Tell Gabi I had a wonderful time."

"So did she. She's already taken you in as one of her own."

They stepped onto the sidewalk.

He waved a cab, and opened the door for her. "I'll see you tomorrow, Rubina, under much less pleasant circumstances."

"Yeah." Ruby sighed. "Let me know how your fairy tale ends."

"I imagine Aragon and Tabitha will do something

like this." He leaned down for a gentle kiss and the heat soon melded them together. Breaking contact first, he stayed close, waiting for her response.

"Well, try to keep it G-rated for the kids." She nudged him back and yanked the door closed.

With a wide smile, he watched until her cab disappeared around the corner.

Ruby returned to her office, sat at her desk, and wondered at the strange feeling. She'd wanted to stay. Shoving it aside, she dove into her work, surfacing at eleven to drag herself home. She thought of a man who'd build a castle for his mother and weave fairy tales for children. Happy endings mattered most to those who'd witnessed the dark. She figured, if nothing else, they had that in common. It was a start. One she was uncomfortable with, but she wasn't one for denial. Mind occupied with Emilio, she drifted into a dreamless reprieve from the monsters that haunted her while asleep and awake.

CHAPTER 16

Ruby walked into the meeting room, and stopped at the sight of her potential client.

A young woman clicked the long, swirled orange nails of one hand on the table and twirled her elaborate curls with the other. Her bronzed face hinted of beauty beneath a look-at-me mask. She shot icy daggers at Ruby from beneath a curtain of lashes. "Did you have to meet up so early? I sleep in."

Ruby sat and returned the frost. "Under the supervision of the Minnesota Department of Corrections, you'd be up at seven, every day."

"You're going to keep me out of prison."

"No guarantee of that."

"My last lawyer promised he would."

"Empty promises must not be what you're after, or you wouldn't be here. Would you like to start over, Rebecca? Maybe we could set a friendlier tone for this meeting."

"Sorry, I'm not usually such a bitch. I'm on edge." She offered her hand with a small smile. "I'm Rebecca. Thanks for seeing me."

"Apology accepted." Ruby shook her hand. "Pleased to meet you, Rebeccca. I'm Ruby. Welcome to my law firm. Thank you for sending your case materials over in advance. It gave me a chance to review your file. You're organized."

"So are you."

"I'm a lawyer. What did you expect?"

She pressed her lips together and puffed air. "I had low expectations after Peroni. And he was the best of the creeps I met with before the hire. If he'd have put as much effort into my case as trying to get laid I wouldn't be here."

"You didn't want to be told you're too beautiful to be a criminal?"

"No, or suck his small dick for payment."

"Ah, I see. You didn't want to pay him in sexual favors. Many of my colleagues haven't earned my respect. And many don't play by the rules."

"Do you always follow the rules?"

"Yes, always. If you can't work with that, I'll be happy to show you out. I'll even send you on your way with a travel cup of coffee and a scone—no hard feelings."

"I'll have my coffee here, if you don't mind." She reached forward and lifted her mug.

"Good. What's Anthony Priestley like?"

Pain clouded her sapphire eyes. She swallowed

hard before answering. "He never missed a Friday night dinner. My parents . . . Well, they're out of the picture. When he found that out, he started bringing me around. Not as his girl."

"Would he rabbit?"

"No, not without telling me and Lizzie."

"His mother?"

"Yeah. He'd at least let us know when we'd see him again. His dad bolted on his mom. Tony would never do that to her. We had plans."

"Which were?"

"He wanted to get out of the life."

"Drug dealing?"

"Yeah."

"Coke?"

"Yeah."

"Go ahead."

"Friday was going to be the big night. He wanted to meet before dinner, just the two of us. He had mag news."

"When was the last time you saw him?"

"Tuesday morning. He wanted to make Friday night special."

"Was it someone's birthday?"

"No, it was because of his big news. We went to the antique store."

"Alfred's."

"Yeah. How'd you know?"

"Lucky guess."

"He sprang for a present for his mom—a

necklace."

"What's she like?"

"She's fiery with curls like mine. Well, hers are natural, and red. And she has green eyes like yours, but brighter. Like a cat, Tony says. She's Irish, and quick to get worked up."

"And quick to forgive?"

"Yeah."

"What'd the necklace look like?"

"Rubies and emeralds. I could sketch it."

"You notice if he wore any jewelry?"

"Yeah, a ring. It was mag. It's all he had left of his dad. I can draw that, too."

Ruby handed her a stylus, and opened a sketch app on the guest tablet.

"No, I free style." She held up her nails. "My work. I need real tools."

"You mean—"

"Real paper, heavy stock. Charcoal pencils. Don't I look like an artist?" She smirked at Ruby.

"You don't, Rebecca." Ruby tapped a message into her PSC, and sent it before looking up. "Have you worn something like this . . . attire to court?"

"Yes. Skirt, heels, shirt. What's wrong with it? I look like a vid goddess."

"Of the porn genre. Court is conservative. It's serious business. Your future is in the hands of the judge making decisions about your life. I think there's more to you than this made-up front. You have an eye for detail. You're organized. You must have paid attention in school. Where did you go?"

"Jefferson. I graduated with honors."

"Did you always dress like this?"

"No, I was a real Miss Goody. That was before I grew boobs and boys noticed me."

"Let me put it this way. We don't want the judge to notice your cleavage and nothing else about you."

"Prude." She looked Ruby up and down.

Ruby mirrored her. "Prostitute."

Rebecca glared at her.

"Rebecca, I know looks can be deceiving, but some people don't take the time to see past their preconceived notions. Do you want them to imprison you for looking like a hooker? Some people think that's an offense worthy of a long lockup. They wouldn't be too concerned about getting the specifics about this case. Tramps like coke. Case closed."

"You know, I have a whole lot to say about your frumpy-ass suit."

"You'd have to get in line. And I'm more interested in figuring out what happened to your friend. It sounds like Anthony saw more in you than cleavage and legs."

"Yeah. Are you going to take my case?"

"Depends."

"On what?"

"On whether you're going to do your part as a member of your own legal team. I'll explain what's going on, and what I find. I'll answer questions. But you have to trust I'm the expert on case strategy. You may think you're more clever than the cops, but you're charged with felony drug possession. Let's start with something simple. Are you willing to dress conservatively for court?"

"You know, this isn't what that prick Peroni told me to do."

"What did he tell you?"

"The more skin, the better."

"Can you think of a reason he'd tell you that? A self-serving one?"

"Sure, I'm not an idiot. I figured he was getting off on it. But I had no reason to think the old guy behind the bench didn't think just like him."

"No, I suppose you wouldn't."

"So I was right—Peroni's no good?"

"No one's been able to catch him falling below the bare minimum, nor rising above it."

"He didn't even know the name of the cop that took me in. I tricked him, and asked if he'd talked to Mahowald. He said he'd played tag with him."

"I see your point. Officer White arrested you."

"Yeah. Mahowald transferred out."

"Sounds like someone did her research."

"I knew my file better than he did. It's not adding up. Why did they come after me? I'm a nobody. Low-level."

"When's the last time you heard from Anthony?"

"He called after he picked up the necklace. He was blazed about it. Couldn't wait to show it to me. We were still on for coffee." She dabbed at her eye, careful to not stab it with a sharp nail. "He said he was a new man. I pressed him, but he wouldn't crack. He told me I'd have to see it to believe it."

"What did you think about him getting out?"

"I doubted it was legit at first. You want out, you flee and hope both the cops and higher-ups don't find you. Blood in, blood out. But he swore it wasn't like that. He was in on the ground level so he'd get rewarded." She slammed her fist on the table. "I keep flopping between worried and pissed, ya know? The cops aren't doing anything about some single guy that's been gone for a few days. A spontaneous vaca, they said. He wouldn't do that to Lizzie. He pays all her bills. If he doesn't come back, she'd really be in a jam. And now I'm crunched and can't help her out. He better show up soon." She clenched her jaw.

"Anything else make you think he wouldn't just disappear?"

"Our buddy Cheeze went rabbit. His real name's Francis. He vanished. No word to any of us. I didn't put it past Cheeze, but no way would Tony not tell us. Not if he could help it." She raised her eyes to meet Ruby's. "That's the part that worries me."

Colin knocked and entered. "Paper and pencils."

"Where did you dig those up?"

"You have no idea what's behind the front desk."

"Anton's?"

"No, we devoured it."

"Damn it."

"Anything else?"

"No, thanks for the speedy delivery."

"Any time."

Rebecca watched him leave. "He's cute."

"He wouldn't be interested in you."

"Why?" Rebecca stood, eyes blazing. "Because I'm nothing but a two-bit, drug dealing whore?"

"No, because he's madly in love with his co-hab Charles who is the perfect specimen of a man—ask Colin." Ruby said, amused.

"Oh." She sat, and compressed her lips.

"Want to know what I think of you?"

"I don't care." Her captive gaze belied her words.

"I think you feel let down by your parents. You got the grades, went to an elite school on scholarship. The other kids got free rides, fancy stuff. You had to work hard for everything you got, and still you didn't have much. You wanted nice things—designer dresses, handbags."

Her eyes popped a bit before she looked away. "Maybe I dealt to pay for my sister's operation. Did you consider that?"

"The sister you don't have? You're an only. And yes, I noticed your poor excuse for clothing isn't off-the-rack. It makes you look cheap, though. You chose this world of quick cash and brand names. Has it made you happy? Has it given you the status you wanted?"

"I'm not here for a lecture."

"Neither am I. I'm wondering if you understand what's important to you, or if you've fallen for your own front. What's been the best night of your week?"

"Fridays."

"How many purses, designer clothes, and piles of cash would you give up to find your friend?"

"All of it."

"You haven't been building a life, Rebecca. You've been building a lie." Ruby held up her hand when Rebecca tried to respond. "Think about it later. Does Anthony have unusual smarts in the chemistry field—like one of those untrained tech whizzes?"

"Yeah, right. He barely passed our chem class, and that was only because I was his lab partner."

"How organized have you been with your illegal business?"

"Very."

"How so?"

"I kept notebooks—all my drops, all my connections. I kept records for Tony, too."

"Excellent. You have the notebooks with you?"

"No, I gave them to a friend for safekeeping."

"I'll need that info. Your case hinges on the drugs. They were found in your truck. If the search was legal, they stay in and it's an easy case for the state to win. If it was illegal, the drugs are suppressed and poof, the case goes away. The legality of the search was decided. You lost. The drugs stay in."

"So I'm screwed."

"You're not walking away from this. Now we do damage control." Ruby caught a flash in her eye. "You pay attention to details. Did the big fed bust six months ago disrupt supply?"

"Yeah, it did. The higher-ups changed. That's when Tony got in on the ground."

"Notice any change in quality when the supply stream commenced?"

"Yeah, it was prime. Not like the shit we were selling. It'd do the job, but not like the new stuff."

"You use your own product?"

"No, I'm no addict."

"Good, saves me from talking you into treatment. What kind of training do you think you'd need for that caliber of product?"

"Any idiot could find the recipe and basic cooking instructions. But this stuff was pure, refined. That'd require creating a new formula, top-grade equipment, and deep know-how of the process."

"Could you do it?"

"No way in hell."

"Or you'd already have done it, and cut out the middle. More profit for you. You'd be queenpin of your own organization."

"Yeah, I would have. It's the kind of thing I thought I wanted once." She studied her nails.

"A chemist could do it?"

"Yeah, definitely. A good one."

"We have our work cut out for us. We have to convince the prosecution you're worthy of a chance at redemption. We may have some bargaining chips to work with. Anthony was going straight. He wanted to give himself a better life. Do you want the same for yourself?"

"Yeah."

"I like that you didn't hesitate. Are you willing to work for it?"

"Yeah."

"Welcome to your own legal team, Rebecca." Ruby tapped the sketchbook with a pencil and held it out. "Here's your first assignment."

They locked gazes.

Satisfied by what she saw, Rebecca nodded and grabbed the pencil.

"I'll give you some space, Rebecca."

"Becky." She started to draw with a flourish, and paused to give Ruby a sassy grin. "Go team."

"That's the spirit."

"Let's get this meeting started," Ruby said. "Emilio?"

"Colin and I deployed Jaspyr to the farm property of Susan Combes. The farmhouse itself has fallen into disrepair and appeared to be in disuse. The main barn was a different story. We obtained access through the hay loft and captured footage of the activity on the main level."

Ruby posted stills on-screen. "These images show this unidentified man working in the lab. Its setup is peculiar. Patient beds line one area. Elsewhere, there's piping and glassware, and bulk chemicals on shelving units. What was Jerald Combes doing in this lab? And what is this man doing in the lab of Jerald Combes?"

"We had to look closer," Emilio said. "At the tools, the setup."

"Come on, you two," Colin said. "Enough with the suspense."

She held up her hand, and continued. "Another man comes onto the scene. One we all recognize."

"Stuart Johnston," said Jasmine.

"Yes, Mr. County Attorney—best buds with Jerald Combes. And there he is with another man."

"Who?" Colin prompted.

"Anthony Priestley. I recognize him from the missing-person report." Kottke grinned. "Taking a little thunder back from yesterday."

"Well done," Ruby said. "I sent this still to Alfred, and he confirmed it's Priestley. So it seems we have Jerald Combes in the pawn shop yesterday morning, and dead in his cabin less than twelve hours later. We have Anthony Priestley disappearing on Friday, and reappearing on Saturday."

"Busted! We have the killers!"

"I appreciate your enthusiasm, Jazz. We're not quite there yet. All right, team. How do we wrap up these bastards with a bow for the feds, and spring our client at the same time?"

"Let me guess," Colin said. "You have a plan."

"Yes, and it's a win for all except the killers. We'll get a vindicated client, and the deadly duo will get a one-way shuttle trip to Mardova, and the feds will get to dismantle another drug operation."

"I'm hesitant to ask how." Justin swept his hand over his face.

"First thing tomorrow morning, Mr. County Attorney and I are having a little chat—here, alone. Or so he'll think. I'll get him comfortable, get him pissed, and get his confession."

"Right before he attempts to eliminate you. Let's see, I vote no." Colin looked up and contributed before once again tapping on his PSC.

"Using yourself as bait. Brilliant. Let's add another kill to their list. Use me, Ruby. I'm an ex-cop."

"Sorry, Kottke. He won't be as furious about a male foiling his plan as a lowly female. Not that you can't get the pain-in-the-ass o'meter right up there."

"Seriously, Ruby. Your life for Susan's freedom isn't an exchange we're willing to make."

"I don't plan on it. We don't know how far Johnston has infiltrated his office. We'll have backup, and it'll be federal. We'll apprise your bureau buddy of the evidence we've collected."

"What will the feds think of your plan?"

"They'll love it as much as my team. But they'll realize they have no one imbedded, and no way to work someone in without sending up flares. I'll assure Agent Mitzu I'm confronting the county attorney with or without the agency's participation." She grinned. "But I can't do it without yours."

"You're insane, ace." Justin slugged her on the shoulder.

"I suspect they'll offer to outfit me with a wire,

and monitor the meeting—ready to intervene. A generous offer, but I trust this team more. Kottke, you're in charge of security for this op. Would you like to bring Agent Mitzu into the loop, or should I?"

"I'll do it. You'll walk out unharmed, Ruby. You can count on us."

"I don't mind a few knocks. Just keep me alive."

"I have a few prototypes in development that could be of assistance," Emilio said.

"Great, team with Kottke." She saw Colin's eyes light up.

So did Emilio. "I'll require Colin's assistance."

"He's all yours," she said.

As the trio walked toward the tech center, Emilio turned to Kottke, heated. "I hope you don't plan on her walking in there unarmed."

"Listen, pal. She's the driving force behind this whole operation. Everything you see here, all the progress we've made on this case—she's spearheaded it."

"Yes, yes. I know she's capable."

"She's capable, and not stupid. And she's a hell of a lot stronger than she looks. She could toss you on your techie ass. She trusts us to keep her safe, and I'm going to do just that."

"So that's the plan? Have firepower ready to extract her if necessary? There may not be time for that."

"What do you have in mind?"

"She insists on using herself as bait," Emilio said. "I have a workaround. We'll have to head to my uptown lab for supplies."

"Sublime. I'd love to see your lab." Colin said.

"Real nice," Justin said. "Get cryptic as we're planning how to save Ruby's life."

"Trust me," Emilio said. "Besides, you'll have to see it to believe it."

They headed to the elevators.

"She's getting under your skin, isn't she?" asked Justin.

"I'm not sure what she's doing, but it's very important to me that she's unharmed."

Justin studied him as he would a suspect in interrogation. With a brisk nod, he said, "You and Colin go ahead. I'll start rigging this place with eyes and ears."

"Yes, throughout the building."

"It's his," Colin added.

"I'll arrange complete access for our team. Its tenants will be perturbed when the building is closed Monday morning for security upgrades, but safety comes first."

"I like your style, buddy."

Ruby looked up and gave Amy an absent smile when she entered her office.

"Where did Jasmine go?" Amy asked.

"Jazz is in the meeting room."

"She's a wonderful addition to the team."

"Yes, we've caught many lucky breaks in this case. She's one of them."

"'Diligence is the mother of good luck,' Ruby."

"Yes, good old Ben's words still ring true."

"And it seems we have an inventor of Franklin's caliber in our ranks. Another fortunate development."

"Yes, Emilio is . . ."

"Yes?"

"He's . . . not what I expected."

"The neurosurgeon certainly didn't have this affect on you." She said.

"It's bad enough Alfred is meddling. You can both do me a favor and take off your matchmaker hats. I need you to don your psychologist one at the moment."

"You can't ignore a man like that forever."

"No, I already tried."

"And where did it get you?"

"It landed me in a castle chopping veggies and chatting with his mother." She held up her hands in dismay. "She's wonderful. You'd like her. It's all spun out of control. And the worst part is he's not pretentious and materialist. He makes up bedtime stories." She ended with her hands in her hair and a look of distress on her face. "What am I supposed to do with a man like that?"

"I have a few ideas, my dear."

"Never mind. You're not helping at all." She

finger-combed her choppy hair, and drew in a steadying breath. "I'd like you to write up a report. Profile the escalation of an abuser with his history. Document the relevant evidence of past conduct. I'll need it ready for court on Monday."

"Certainly. I'll see to it right away."

"First, do you mind walking through the best approach for tomorrow? I have one shot at eliciting a confession. I need to hit the bull's-eye."

"He enjoys recognition. Give him a chance to brag. Goad him into it. He'll need to feel he's in control of the situation. You're a snag in his plans that he can remedy—silence you and he'll bury the truth." Resolute, Amy stepped forward. "I'd like to be in the room with you."

"The best shot we have is if I go in alone. You know that."

"Yes, but I had to try."

"The three muske-techies will keep me safe."

"I admire your bravery, Ruby, to be willing to face a killer alone."

"I'll be fine. I know karate."

"A small comfort."

"I have to do this—for Susan."

"And Tara, I suspect. It won't bring her back, you know."

"I know."

"You were just a law student back then. You did all you could have done."

"No, I could have pushed the prosecutor harder."

Ruby rose and went to the window. She braced her hands on the sill. "I need to know I did everything in my power to stop this bastard from ruining Susan's life."

"Will it be enough?

"No." Ruby spun, eyes tormented. "But maybe then I'll get some damn sleep."

"It might help if you didn't sleep alone. I'd sleep awfully well if I had a gorgeous Spaniard telling me a bedtime story in that irresistible accent."

"Find someone else to set up. Jazz is right down the hall."

"I'll stop in and see her on my way out." Amy stopped in the doorway, and gave Ruby a serious look. "Consider me on-call."

"Thanks. When you're done finding Jazz the love of her life, please send her in."

CHAPTER 17

"So this is how you operate," Emilio said. "You tell your team that they can leave—the plan is in place, the parts are set. And then you proceed to stay."

"Something like that," Ruby said. "And yet you're still here."

"I'm accustomed to being the last one at my office."

"This isn't your office."

"No, this one isn't. Mine is down the hall." Emilio flashed her a grin.

Ruby chucked a memo cube at him.

He caught it.

"I'm working. Don't you have your tech empire to deal with?"

"I can do my work from anywhere with the right equipment."

"And even without it."

He tossed the memo cube in his hand.

She held up her hands as if in surrender. "I admit it. Your hodgepodge set-up is effective."

"It appears you're defenseless, Rubina."

"I most certainly am not." She dropped her hands and her eyes flared.

"I wonder—do you see me as a threat?"

"I don't."

"Good."

"You're a harmless e-nerd," she taunted, crossing her arms in challenge.

"Am I?" He had her up and out of her chair before she could counter. He shut and locked her office door as he pressed her against it, ravaging her mouth with his.

"I don't take what isn't freely given." He released her and stayed a breath away.

Acting on a force as great as thought, she moved into him, wrapping her arms around his neck and her legs around his waist.

He held back, offering softness.

She wanted heat.

She grabbed his generous bottom lip in her teeth. He responded by flicking his tongue over her lips and then plunging between them, clouding her senses with his flavor.

Pulling her mouth from his, her chest heaved with the effort. "This isn't going to happen," she managed. "Not here."

He spun with her, and set her on her desk. Hands on either side of her, he clutched the overhang until she thought it'd break. Pushing away, he moved to the window and rested his forehead on the cool glass.

Hesitant, she approached and placed her hand on his shoulder. "Are you upset?"

"Of course not. You may want to stand back a bit. I can still see quite vividly what I'd like to do to you on that desk."

"I've, I've never done anything like this."

He turned in surprise. "Oh?"

"I don't mean sex. There's been sex. But never in my office. I keep my lives separate—the professional and the personal."

He smiled. "I'd like to see where you live, Rubina." He linked their fingers. "Now seems like wonderful timing."

She held back. "It's not. It's terrible. I have work."

"Our plans are solid. All that's left is their implementation. That's not set to happen until nine." He caressed her cheek, and she stayed still, gazing up at him—a frightened doe with a steel spine. Was it any wonder he found himself falling for this fascinating, shifting blend of contradicting layers? Knowing his thoughts would send her darting, he said, instead, "We can figure out what's between us, or ignore it. Either way, it's there. What are you going to do about it, Rubina?"

"It's not much." She shrugged as she led him into her apartment. After toeing off her shoes, she sank her bare feet into carpet, an indulgence for home or the beach. "Colin says the color scheme is—"

He cut her off by spinning her around, yanking her in, and taking her mouth—hot, lusty, and lightly edged with humor. He broke the contact. "We can discuss your décor later, if you'd like."

He gripped her hips and boosted her up, tipped so he fell with her pinned underneath him onto her bed. His mouth claimed hers.

She grabbed his exceptional ass and gave it a hard squeeze.

She slid her hand around, between them, and found him. The next hard squeeze brought a moan, had him shifting his mouth to her throat.

She met every demand, and made her own. He discovered the rhythms of her body, the secret places to exploit and seduce, inflame.

He found her a fascination and a glorious surprise.

Her hands gripped his hair. She arched her back, trembling, urging him to join them.

He traced the firm curve of her breast, and tasted her silky skin, surrounding himself with her scent. The catch of her breath and her hand around him drove him to a keen and lusty ledge.

Lithe, ready, she slid her body to meet him. She felt his heartbeat pounding, matching the drumbeat of her own.

Her mouth clung to his, fever hot, scrambling his senses beyond reason.

He reached for her mound and dipped his finger

inside her.

Wet and hot, she cried in release and still he drove her higher. Her eyes fluttered shut.

"Let me see what I do to you, *Querida*."

"Now, Milo."

She bowed up, shivering with desire. He thrust inside her, hard and deep.

Gasping, her fingers gripped his muscled shoulders. Quaking shook her to her core. The seismic strength of their passion shuddered toward her heart as they rode each other.

In the aftershocks, they lay facing each other. He brushed his lips over her shoulder.

Sex had been basic—an uncomplicated release. This casual intimacy shook her. Her heart tripped. She wasn't ready to know what it meant.

"Rubina, I'm sorry. I don't know what to say."

"You're . . . sorry?" Her heart dropped. She covered herself with a sheet. "I think it's time for you to go." She managed over the lump of tears threatening to choke her, refusing to let him see his effect on her.

"As you wish. You must know . . . I've never lost control like that."

She studied him. "What, exactly, are you apologizing for?"

"I didn't treat you with the proper care." He raised his hand to brush her cheek, lowered it and his head. I was practically—"

"A sex maniac?"

He sat and held his head in his hands.

"Who's the prude now?"

"I have the blood of Diego Ramirez coursing through my veins. You can't know what that means, Rubina. I should have told you."

"I think I have a good idea. But why don't you tell me?"

"He's more beast than man. I've prided myself on being nothing like him. And I've succeeded—until tonight." He held her gaze as sadness crested into sorrow. "I failed you, Rubina."

She let out a long sigh. "I'm no good at this, Milo. All I can think to tell you is that you're being awfully moronic for a genius."

"Excuse me." He lifted his head.

"Aren't you supposed to be a ladies' man? Honestly, Emilio. You send orgasms ripping through me. I'm ready to blast to Venus. We're talking cosmic-grade explosions, and then you apologize. Apologize." She emphasized.

"I didn't frighten you?"

"You're impressive, but I think I proved I could hold my own." She gave him a smug smile.

"I meant to make love with you, Rubina."

"I told you. Mission accomplished. We've rearranged the cosmos." She grinned, and her breath caught when she saw his tender look.

"No, *Querida*. Let me show you." He eased her back against the pillows and captured her mouth in kisses as delicate as butterfly wings. His hand traveled down her, molding her shape as an artist caresses clay. Slowly, he trailed his mouth down to her breast, tasting her, teasing her until she went wild at his tongue flicking her nipple, stoking a fire burning hot at her center.

"Milo." She whispered.

He gripped her ass with his strong hands and kneaded as he sent sparks shooting with his tongue. He traveled down, murmuring his musical language as she fell beyond reason, spellbound. His whispers warmed the trail down as his hand moved around to cup her center, flicking her higher and higher. She heard a feral cry, too swept away to recognize it as her own. She lost sight to pleasure so intense it shifted her senses. It robbed her of sight and heightened the sensation in every synapse, as every fiber of her nervous system enlivened at his touch.

"Again, *Querida*."

Her vision filled with him. She saw what she'd hoped for long ago in his dark, decadent eyes. Terrified and thrilled, she pulled him up and shifted her hips, cradling him. She cupped his face and nodded, readying herself to take the plunge. "Together, Milo."

He slid inside of her and filled her to bursting. She arched, vibrating, as he slid into her, over and over, tantalizing her with the delicious friction of their union. He emptied himself into her and captured her mouth in a lingering kiss. He kissed her temple and watched her.

A tear escaped from her eye. Shocked, she shifted to swipe it away but he beat her to it, gently sweeping it with his thumb. "What's this?"

"I have no idea. All I know is I can't move. You've electrified me. I'll die a happy woman. If that was heaven, I'll go back. All it was missing was donuts."

"You have a one-track mind."

"Two-track."

He lowered his head to her hair, breathing in her scent.

"Stay," she heard herself say, and realized she didn't want to retract the invite.

"It would take superhuman strength to leave you. I'm only a man, Rubina."

She ran her hand across his muscled back. "Yes, you certainly are." She peered into his face. "Though that could be the face of a Grecian god."

"You needn't talk me into bed. You've already had your way with me."

"Maybe my aim is to do so again." She laughed, and caught her breath as he drew her close and trailed kisses along her neck. "Milo?"

He lifted his head and grinned at her. "Yes, *Querida*?"

"What are we doing?"

"We're having a romance."

"I was afraid you'd say that. Are you sure it can't just be sex?" she asked hopefully.

"Is that what you want? Casual sex between consenting adults? No strings, leaving me free to chase one of those heiresses you're so fond of tossing me in with?"

"Do you?" she asked, eyes narrowed.

"She would wrinkle her surgically-shaped nose and swoon over me. She'd be into the latest health food craze. That is, if she ate at all. She might subsist on smoothies and Botox."

"I could snap her like a twig. But if that's what you want, be my guest."

"No, I don't want casual. I much prefer a sugar-aholic, spitfire lawyer. A natural beauty with a slightly crooked nose."

She raised her hand to her face.

He moved it away. "I'm quite fond of it." He demonstrated by kissing the tip of her nose, both cheeks, and then moved over her lips before pulling back. "And I'm not comfortable with this either, Rubina. If that makes you feel any better."

"Actually, it does. Not much, but a bit." She paused before continuing, "There hasn't been anyone else."

"It's too late for that now. You've already told me there have been others, and I've already envisioned bloodying them."

"No, I mean it's never been like this, for me, with anyone else." She searched for the words, and dropped her hand to his chest, helpless. "I'm not good at this. This mushy stuff."

"*Querida*, I wouldn't want you any other way." He gave her a feathery kiss. "There's been no one else for me. Not like this." He held her close, delighted with her. "Let me show you."

"Again? You are a sex maniac."

"No, not that . . . not yet anyway." He sprang to his feet, grabbed his pants from the floor and produced a scrap.

She took it gingerly and gasped. "That's—"

"Yes, it's yours."

"You said you'd get rid of it." She eyed him warily. "Are you a hoarder?"

"No, I said I'd take care of it. It seems you started to matter to me before I realized it."

"I, I don't know . . . it's all so fast."

"You needn't say a thing."

She kept her eyes on his as she pulled him back to the bed.

Their bodies communicated what neither was ready to say.

Later, when they lay tangled together in sleep, Tara returned to Ruby in her dreams.

"You didn't keep me safe. You won't keep her safe."

"Who?" Ruby stepped forward.

"Me." Tara's hair lightened. Amber eyes turned hazel. Toffee skin paled to wraithlike white. Susan stared at Ruby, eyes pleading. "He's coming for me."

"Who?" Ruby turned to see tousled brown hair and a cocky grin.

"She's mine." He spread his lips in a snarling smile.

"No, she never was, you bastard. You'll never be free again. You're going to rot in Mardova."

As he shook his head, his hair thickened into a mane as black as the heart of darkness. Piercing blue turned to steel. He grew until he filled the room. "I'm too clever for that. Mardova or dead. And I'll kill anyone that stands in my way. She's mine. Stand aside."

"No. I won't let you have her."

He lifted a kitchen knife and walked slowly toward her. "Your death will be slow and painful. Like the woman's."

Ruby looked back toward the closet. In its place stood a twin bed. On it laid a woman with dark blonde hair and hazel, unseeing eyes.

"You're too late."

"Susan! No!"

Ruby thrashed against strong arms.

"You're safe. It's me, Emilio. I have you. You're safe."

She pushed up on her elbow and leaned forward, filling her lungs as he stroked her back.

"You can go back to sleep. It's early."

"No. Not while he's still out there."

"Nobody will hurt you. I'll make sure of it."

"I believe you. But you can't protect me from my own nightmares."

"If only I could, *Querida*."

She kissed him gently. "You can go back to sleep."

"No, I'll make coffee." He rose.

"The coffeemaker can be touchy."

"Rubina, really?"

"Sorry, I forgot for a minute. You sure don't look like an e-man." She passed her gaze over him.

"And I'm the sex maniac?"

She eased back and stared at the ceiling, willing herself to settle.

Emilio returned with steaming mugs.

"You're drinking coffee now?"

"Yes. Even I cannot make tea from thin air."

"Right. I guess I haven't gotten around to stocking anything except necessities."

"Yes, sugar is crucial to one's survival." He waited for her to gulp half her coffee before asking, "Where did a lawyer learn to fight like that? Even in sleep, you're formidable. Do they teach martial arts in law school?"

"No, I've been training since I was sixteen."

"Why?"

Ruby closed her eyes and considered how to navigate this new territory. Looking him in the eye, she began, "When I was sixteen, I had a crush on a boy at my school."

"What were you like at sixteen?"

"Innocent, naïve. I wore frilly skirts and my hair long. I took everything I did seriously—student council, schoolwork, softball."

"Surprising. You're so cavalier toward your engagements now."

She half smiled, at him and her younger self. "I

thought I knew everything."

"Also far different than now."

Ruby chucked a pillow at him. "Hey, do you want to hear my story or not?"

He propped himself on the pillow. "You have my undivided attention."

"And now that I do, I don't know how to continue."

He reached out and took her hand. "You don't have to."

"No, I want you to know." She gazed at her bright orange wall and saw her past. "He was a rule breaker. That he seemed slightly dangerous was part of his appeal. I know, it's cliché. Good girl attracted to a bad boy. But there it is." She braced herself against the headboard for the next part. "It was a small school. He knew about my crush." She clasped a pillow to her chest. "On a Saturday in June, he came for me. My parents were hit or miss on the alarm. They missed. And he wasn't alone. He brought in a buddy. Three others waited in his car. They had me restrained and drugged before I was fully awake. It wasn't long before the drug took hold and I was out again. They took me into the woods a few miles from my house. I came to while they were raping me. I couldn't do anything to stop them." She shut her eyes against the stabbing pain of remembering.

Emilio eased her from the headboard and held her close. "You're safe. I have you."

"After that night, I heard them in every sound. I'd

jump out of bed screaming. Amy helped me figure out how to take my power back. I vowed to never be helpless again. Instead of vulnerable, my body became a weapon. I could fight back. No longer exploited and violated, no longer a victim—I became strong. I trusted my body again." She pulled back and searched his face. "I can only imagine what you must be thinking."

"Some of us are born or thrust into unimaginable situations. It takes immeasurable strength and courage to rise above them. And more to help others through theirs as you do for your clients. I couldn't admire you more."

"I, I didn't expect that." Spent by the telling, she relaxed into the warm acceptance of his embrace.

He eased her onto her side and kept his arm around her—tight.

Soon, she slipped into a dreamless sleep.

Upon waking, Ruby stretched and wondered when she'd last had this feeling. Rested. Smiling, she replayed the night before, and frowned as she reached the end. *I blubbered in his arms like a fool*, she thought. She looked at his side of the bed, empty, with disappointment. I*'m not surprised. I'd run from my past too if I could. Hell, I've tried.* She grabbed a pillow and covered her face.

"Ah, she's moved."

She yanked the pillow away and found herself

beaming at the sight of him. *I'm hopeless*, she thought. She went for casual. "You're still here."

"I am. How do you feel about it?" He asked.

Responding to the uncertainty in his eyes, she said, "I'm glad," she admitted.

He smiled and swooped down for a lavish kiss.

"And I'm hungry." Hope bloomed in her eyes. "Could you rig me a FastFare for cinnamon rolls?"

"Not even I could transform your paltry stock into sustenance. I have a better idea. Hurry and we'll make it."

"But—"

"Yes, I'm well aware we have dragons to slay. It's not yet time for it. And you won't need it where we're going, though some consider it a castle." His eyes danced.

"Gabriella Center. Is your mom cooking?"

"She says breakfast is her best meal."

"Is she right?"

"It's comparing a sunset to a waterfall."

"I had to fall for a romantic." She nudged him, humor lively in her eyes.

"Did you?" He trailed his hand along her side.

Unable to say the words, she shrugged. "It's a figure of speech."

He studied her. "Very well, Rubina. Lead the charge."

She stopped in the doorway to the bathroom. "I'm not very good at this. The morning after. You're the first I've had here." She raised her hands, grasping to convey these newly stirred sentiments.

He moved to her and took her hands. "It's new for me as well. We'll figure it out together."

"You know, I haven't had my coffee yet. I could use a pick-me-up. Care to join me?"

"Yes, I do. But real food awaits us. We don't have time for both."

"Your priorities mystify me."

"You brought me here for stick pastry and hot chocolate?" Ruby asked.

"I had a feeling you'd find the menu palatable," Emilio said.

"What are those?" She pointed to a scalloped platter filled with small rolls.

"Those are savory, not sweet. They're filled with ham, cheese, and sausage."

"I'll have another sugar stick. What's it called?"

"A churro." He passed the platter with a grin.

"Wait a minute, you're not grimacing. What's the deal?"

"I came by my nutrient-dense creations honestly. Family recipes, you could say."

"The cinnamon rolls. And now these churros. It's the Martín conspiracy." She chewed and contemplated. "I suppose the same rules can apply. The trickery ends at my taste buds, understood?" She gestured with her churro.

He mustered a serious expression. "Yes, I'd never

dream of crossing you. I have no doubt you'd wield that weapon expertly. Death by sugar stick, as you call it."

"A delicious end." She finished off her breakfast and brushed sugar from her hands.

Gabriella appeared and hugged Ruby with her free arm. "Have you had enough to eat?"

"Yes. It was delicious. I wish we could stay, but we have to get to the office."

"*Café cortado* to go?"

"I caught coffee. I never refuse it."

"*Sin leche, por favor,*" Emilio added. "It's a Spanish espresso. I asked for yours without milk."

"Would you come with me?" Gabriella asked. "I could use a hand."

Emilio started to stand.

Gabriella pushed him down with an affectionate tug to his ear. "Give us a minute, *Mijo*."

"*Vale*."

Out of earshot, Gabriella asked, "I could ask you what your intentions are for my son."

"Gabi, I—"

"But I believe they're clearer to me than they are to you. It's the province of being an old woman. I can read the eyes of the young."

"You're not old, Gabi."

"My work keeps me young."

"He's not at all what I expected."

"I brought him into this world, and he still surprises me. I've seen many after him for devious reasons."

Ruby started to speak, "Gabi—"

"No, *Cariña*, you don't need to tell me. I know enough about you, your work. Your intentions are pure. I think, like my son, you are unaware of the brilliance of your own light. Maybe you'll discover it together."

"Gabi, I'm not sure what to think of . . . us, I guess. He's starting to matter, you know? I'm not ready for this."

"When I found out I was pregnant with him, I was so afraid. I wasn't ready. I didn't have a good example for a mother. How could I be a good one? Sometimes what we're not ready to enter into our lives becomes one of the best parts."

"I can see where Emilio gets his persistence."

"Take your *café* and be off. You've a big day ahead. *Ten cuidado*. Stay safe."

"Thanks."

"Wait, there's always time for *besos*." Gabriella embraced Ruby, kissed her cheeks, and waved her into the dining room.

Ruby handed Emilio a travel cup as he fell into step beside her. "Here, your mom says it's your favorite. And she gave me enough kisses for both of us."

"What's your mother like?"

"Imagine the opposite of Gabi."

"Sounds dreadful."

"She kept me clothed, fed, and sent me to good

schools. Others have it much worse." She looked up and saw that her description pained him. "Gabi's wonderful. What does *Mijo* mean?"

"It means son. *Mi hijo.* My son."

"That's sweet." She turned and grinned. "Yes, Milo was a good nickname for you. More apt than I'd realized."

"Is it?"

"*Mi Emilio*. Milo." She stood on her tiptoes and kissed him.

"Yes, it's a good one." He clasped her hand. "Yet another endearing quirk." He said.

"What?"

"Your proclivity to nickname."

CHAPTER 18

"Audio?" Ruby asked.

"Check," Justin said.

"Visual?"

"Crystal," Emilio said.

"All right. Send me in."

They watched on-screen as Ruby appeared, walking toward the waiting area. Another screen showed Stuart Johnston leaving the elevator.

"That bag is too big for case files," Emilio said.

"A travel-sized kill kit. Handy. He's turned pro," Justin said.

"Focus," Ruby said. "We have one crack at this."

The suite door opened as Johnston approached. "Ms. Miller."

"Let's not waste time." She motioned him into the conference room. "Please, take the head. It's not every day I receive such an important visitor."

"You have a reputation for flouting authority."

"I can acknowledge when I've overstepped. Your commitment in this case has been admirable."

"It's in service to my community, and my dear friend."

"Yes, and out of respect to you, I wanted to show you the results of my investigation. Your cooperation and speedy delivery of discovery didn't go unappreciated." Ruby signaled the screen. "We found tire tracks consistent with the vehicles of Susan and Jerald Combes at the cabin."

"Of course. It's as I said. She followed him."

"And tracks for your vehicle."

"Obviously, I found Jerry." He walked to the window and bowed his head.

"And the fourth vehicle—" Ruby broke off as Stuart whirled.

"Fourth vehicle?"

"Yes. This one." Ruby brought up a photo of the rattletrap parked near Susan's barn. "We had a hard time locating it." She waited. When he said nothing, she went on, "Don't you want to know where it's parked?"

"Yes, yes. Where?"

"On an old farm property about twenty miles from here."

"It must belong to an accomplice."

"An accomplice?"

"Jerry suspected Susan was sleeping around. When he confronted her, she admitted she had a lover. She rubbed his face in it."

"A lover," Ruby repeated. "This is news."

"Yes, I should have realized before that Susan had an accomplice. You've done good work, Ms. Miller. Who else have you presented this evidence to?"

"Nobody else. Let's work together, Stu. Let's follow the evidence. You and I, together, will get justice for Jerry. We'll know what really happened."

"Yes, I believe we would. It's only a matter of time, and you'll have it all figured out. You're smarter than I expected."

"Thank you, but there's more. Why do you think Susan would cheat on Jerald?"

"She said he was a disappointment in the sack."

"That's interesting. I talked to Deanna Connelly—his neighbor. She seemed pretty pleased with Jerry's sexual performance."

Stuart's brow lowered.

"I hope you don't mind, while we're here, if I bring up another client charged by your office. I know you allow leniency for helpful information. You're determined to find the head of the new coke ring that's been the bane of your existence. You've adamantly told the media so on countless occasions."

"Why yes, it's a special interest. You know any information is welcome. Please, do tell me what you uncovered. I have officers primed to act on any credible information."

"The ringleader is . . . Stuart Johnston, Kaye County Attorney."

He kept his back to her and his face blank.

"I'm sorry, Stu. Do you prefer a different title? Kingpin, perhaps? Drug Lord? King Cokehead? I'm unfamiliar with the terminology. I predict you'll lose your legal title, so let's make sure they address you properly."

"What gave me away?"

"You told the citizenry you'd take drugs off the streets, ramp up punishments, and crack down on crime. But your conviction rate is atrocious. At first, I thought you were ineffective—another overpromising and under-delivering politician. Do you fuel addictions and direct the shadow dwellers? Who would miss them—these purveyors of illicit substances? It turns out they're sons, daughters, friends. People are more complicated than you realized, and have relationships you cannot understand. And they're smarter. A low-level dealer, dispensable in your eyes, helped to bring your entire organization crumbling down around you. A federal task force is tracking down your cokehead buddies because of the records she kept."

Ruby cued the next image as Stuart spun and trained a handgun on her. The silencer at the end hung menacingly between them.

Raising her hands, she asked, "Do you recognize that man?"

"No, I've never seen him before."

"Do you have a twin, Stu?"

"No."

"Then who is this guy patting the stranger on the

back? He looks a lot like you, right down to the mega-grin. Why did you do it, Stu? Why did you kill your best friend?"

He laughed, deep and long. "You're looking right at my best friend."

"Of course I am. It turned out your new best friend was your old best friend. What if I told you the plastic surgeon figured out a way to get you from the grave? He concealed data within the hairline of your buddy Jerry."

"You're bluffing."

"Am I? It's quite clever. You told him it would be his last job for you. The truth, as it turned out. You and Jerry had everything planned so well, down to the last minute. You executed your plan perfectly. But you made one grave mistake. You didn't factor in the human element. Dr. Abrams didn't play along. Neither did I."

"Sit down. It's my turn to have the floor."

Ruby sat and splayed her hands in front of her.

He scrubbed his face. "So you've figured it out, have you? I should have eliminated you when I had the chance. I underestimated you. You did good work. It's a shame no one will see it."

"And no one will know about your greedy, corrupt little hobby. Why, Stu? It's the one part I couldn't figure out. Why did you do it? Were you always after capitalizing on cokeheads? Did you find your calling when you made your first kill?"

Stuart rushed toward her.

On instinct, she covered her head to defend against the anticipated blow. When it didn't fall, she looked up.

Stuart stood staring at the screen. "I was idealistic once, like you. Fresh from law school and assigned to the Community Prosecution Division. I thought I'd make a difference. Help clean up the streets. Make the community safer. All that crap they force-feed you in law school to make you think you'll stand for something. That your work will matter."

"What happened?"

"The years went by. I worked harder than anyone. I'd come in first, leave last. Like you—you were a joke. The intern who lived at the office. You took your work so seriously. So did I. But I woke up."

"How so?"

"I sat in my pathetic excuse for an office. I took out my stash, needing a hit to deal with the miserable affair of being a cog in a wheel. Drug cases stacked in front of me. All that money flowing in an industry we demonize that has no victims—only those self-medicating by choice. Like me. You see? What about the others like me? Like Jerald? How would we get our medication? That fucking federal bust. I called my supplier. He was lying low. What was I supposed to do?"

"Ever heard of cold turkey? Narcotics anonymous? You're nothing special. Just another cokehead. Just another corrupt politician."

"No, don't you see? I got smart. I stopped being a

pauper for a meaningless cause to become rich. Haven't you yearned to be somebody, to make something of yourself? You have a fine mind. I could put it to use and make you richer than your wildest dreams. You'd be an asset to my organization. What you do now means nothing. Your case files today will close and new faces will replace the old. Friendship? This is friendship!" He lifted his hand to the picture, and laid his palm on Jerald's new face. "I went to great lengths for my friend—to help him, to protect him. Are we so different, Ruby?"

"Not in all ways, but in the most important one. You stand for nothing. Let's talk about friends. Mine are cleverer and better equipped. You didn't think I'd walk in here without my team, did you? A sniper has you in her sights. I assure you that her bullets will slide through this glass like coconut spread. Drop your weapon, Stu."

"I'll never surrender to a stupid bitch like you."

"I'm disappointed at your lack of creativity."

He fired three shots at her, blasting the wall behind her.

She clutched her chest, and dropped to a knee.

He lowered his weapon, and walked toward her.

Reaching out her free hand, she sent out an electrical burst.

Stunned, he fell onto his side.

Ruby disappeared, and entered through the door to stand over Stuart's paralyzed form.

Federal agents streamed into the conference room,

led by a stocky man with a wide smile on his square face.

"Let us finish our chat, Agent Mitzu. Then he's all yours."

"How? How'd you?" Stuart mumbled.

"Hologram, not yet available on the market. And there was something about rigging doors and synchronizing projectors. Very realistic, don't you think? Boggles my mind, too, how it manages to deliver that jolt. Agent Mitzu, kindly add attempted murder to the litany of charges against Mr. Johnston. You'll have my full cooperation."

"But, but you weren't here. It wasn't real."

"You didn't know that, did you? You intended to kill me, and took a substantial act toward that end. An issue of first impression, I suspect—attempted murder of a hologram. It'll be a fun trial. Of course, it won't really impact your sentence. You'll get a lifetime for the first-degree murder of Anthony Priestley. Another, I suspect, for Patrick Abrams, and yet another for a guy known to you cokeheads as Cheeze. Save us some time and tell us where they are."

"You're too late."

"No, you're too late. You had your chance to wear the white hat, and you blew it. Get comfortable on Mardova. Don't worry. Your best buddy will be there, too. In a separate section, of course, but you're smart enough to figure out how to pass notes across a super-max, right?" Ruby knelt down. "You'll see my pretty face at trial. I have a feeling you won't forget it anytime soon."

"You're dead, do you hear me?"

"You already tried that and failed. Yes, I'd say we're markedly different, Johnston, in all the ways that matter." A glint caught her eye. "Nice ring. Priestley would like it back. Agent? Your call."

He beckoned an officer over. "Hawke, photograph and document this item, and give it to Miller. She's collected enough evidence to lock him away without the ring."

"Thanks, Mitzu."

"Thank you. If you ever need any assistance from my office, you know where to find me."

"He gets a one-way to Mardova, and we're square. Oh, and Stu? As a parting gift, I'll ensure you make the news—as soon as your buddy joins you in lockup. I know how you love the limelight."

"Please, remain sitting, Susan," Ruby said. "We have much to cover and most of it will shock you." Ruby passed the threshold into the cramped holding area with Jasmine by her side.

"We've had a busy weekend," Jasmine said, and sat next to Susan, giving her a small smile.

"How's your wrist, Susan?" Ruby asked.

"It's better than it's been in a while. Thanks. I don't know what you said, but whatever it was, they had a medic back as soon as I got to my quarters."

"Good. Susan, we figured out what happened to Jerry."

She raised her hand to her mouth. "I've been going over it. I can't figure it out. Who would want him dead? I didn't want him dead. I just wanted him to stop hurting me. I wanted to go back to being happy. He was so different when we were first married."

"Marriage is a common change point for batterers."

"He wasn't a bad man. He could be so charming."

"Susan, I know he could be charming. You may rethink that first part after you hear what we have to tell you." Ruby handed her PSC to Jasmine.

She propped it up for Susan.

"Jerry rigged surveillance equipment in your house —the kitchen and master bedroom."

"Why would he do that?"

"To monitor your movements."

"I don't understand."

"Susan, it's going to take a long time for this all to sink in, and for it to make sense."

"We'll get you through this, Susan." Jasmine said.

"Do you want me to continue?" Ruby asked.

"Yes. I need to know the truth."

"Good. Let's walk through your birthday. You didn't misplace your car keys. Jerry took them from the bowl."

Jasmine played a video clip. "See, he's caught red-handed."

"You put it there, as you thought. He took it, and twisted reality."

"Why? Why would he take my keys?"

"To drive your car to the cabin."

"I don't understand."

"You noticed his zippy new car?"

"Yes, the red sports car."

"He didn't get a promotion at work. He's had an illegal business with Johnston. Remember your inheritance?"

"Yes, Jerry said he'd take care of it. He'd sell it for our nest egg."

"He lied," Ruby said simply. "That property is still in your name. We sent out a drone to survey. He cleared out the farm equipment and created a private coke lab."

"Coke? Why would Jerry be involved with cocaine?"

Jasmine pulled up a photograph.

"Who is that?" Susan asked.

"Jerald Combes."

"No, no. It couldn't be. My husband is dead. They told me he's dead."

"No, the man in the morgue is Anthony Priestley. Anthony took orders from Johnston. He hadn't met Jerald. When Anthony wanted a fresh start, Johnston said he'd reward his loyalty, and help him get a new identity. He paid a plastic surgeon to give Priestley what he thought was a new face. Turns out someone already had that face." Ruby waited for it to sink in.

"Oh my God. Jerry."

"Yes. What Jerald and Stuart have done is horrifying. Do you want to take a minute?"

"No, no. I have to know it all."

"Once Priestley had Jerald's face and his fingerprints, Johnston told him to meet at the cabin. Anthony thought he'd have a week to put his affairs in order before starting a new life."

"They . . . Oh my, they, they killed him."

"Yes, and they laid a trail pointing to you."

"Why? Why would Jerry do that?"

"He's an abusive and controlling man. His objective was to ruin your life. Once you were shipped to Mardova, Johnston would inherit and liquidate Jerry's assets. They'd add it to their drug money and take off."

"I, I thought I was going crazy. What am I going to do? What's going to happen? Oh my God." She looked up. Fear ran wild in her eyes. "He's going to come after me. He'll kill me."

"No, Susan," Ruby said forcefully. "We're ahead of him. He's never going to touch you again. I promise you. Have I done everything I told you I'd do?"

"Yes."

"Then trust your own judgment on whether I'm a woman of my word."

Calmer, she nodded. "What happens now?"

"You'll get released this morning, possibly with a tracking device. Johnston was taken into custody by federal agents this morning. He's out of the picture.

Jerry doesn't know. Your safety is my top priority, do you understand?"

"Yes, yes. It's just that he's—"

"Violent? Devious? I know what he's really like, Susan. I've taken that into account. I've assigned my investigator as your protection detail. His name is Justin Kottke. He's an ex-cop with a heart of gold. He'd be embarrassed if he knew that I told you that. He's one of the good ones, Susan. He's helped piece this together."

"I, I can't go home."

"We don't want you to."

"Where will I go?"

"To Ramirez Ranch. It's about thirty-five miles north of the city. A dear friend of mine owns it. Arianna would love to have you. She's one of the bravest women I know. You'll like her."

"I wonder what she'll think of me, for staying with Jerry. A coward, I bet."

"She'll understand better than you can imagine. Ask her about the work she does." Ruby placed her hand on Susan's, and squeezed. "You're not at all to blame for what Jerald has done. And he's not going to do anything about cleaning up the mess he's made. We are. Is that arrangement okay with you?"

When Susan hesitated, Jasmine said, "You wouldn't go alone. I'll go with you and get you settled in at Arianna's. What do you say?"

"Yes, I'd like that."

"Would you like me to stay in here with you? We

can go into the courtroom together," Jasmine offered.

"That sounds good. Thank you both. I don't know what I would have done without you."

"You're very welcome, Susan." Ruby rubbed her hands together and grabbed her PSC. "I'll go meet with the prosecutor and judge. See you in court."

"She looked excited. She really likes her job, doesn't she?" Susan smiled.

"Yes, she loves it."

Susan's smile drooped as dark thoughts crept in.

"Have you ever been around a horse?" Jasmine asked to distract her.

"Not for years. I've always loved horses. I used to ride all the time. After I married Jerry, he told me I was too clumsy. I'd go and break my neck. Not wanting to worry him, I stopped riding."

"It's time to get back on the horse."

CHAPTER 19

"Ms. Miller," the gangly man greeted her. He straightened his red tie, and brushed the sleeve of his crisp black suit.

"Mr. Stark," Ruby acknowledged, and strode to the clerk's desk. "Hi, Nancy. Sorry to not have time to catch up."

"Next time, Ruby."

"I'm here for Susan Combes. Mr. Stark and I have important matters to discuss with the judge. May we head back to chambers?"

The clerk checked the judge's availability on her screen. "She just finished a conference. You may head back."

Ruby turned. "Coming, Counselor?"

"One minute." He stood and scanned the gallery.

Ruby caught his gaze. "I'll wait." She joined him at counsel table, and said, "Congratulations on your promotion, Stark. Manager of the Community

Prosecution Division—that's a lot of responsibility. Johnston must have great confidence in your abilities. And your first murder case. Welcome to the big leagues." She thumped him on the back, and grabbed his arm as he toppled forward.

"Thank you." He tugged at his collar.

"New suit for your new promotion, Stark?"

"Why yes."

"Looks expensive. Too bad you won't have the chance to break it in at trial—not in this case anyway."

He sniffed. "I presume your client will not be entering a guilty plea at today's hearing?"

"Since the complaint charges an offense punishable by life imprisonment, under eight-point-oh-two, subdivision two, my client cannot enter a plea. You're familiar with the rule? If the rules permitted it, she'd enter a plea of innocence."

He cleared his throat, and rearranged his reference books. "Let's discuss the course of this case."

"Yes, let's." She picked up a book. "What a wonderful relic. You tabbed it and everything. I'd highly recommend LegalSeek. Its search capabilities are astounding. Far more efficient, if you don't mind me saying, than flipping through that small forest."

"It's hemp paper, environmentally friendly."

"And still inefficient. I had this debate with a family lawyer before she went virtual. She'll never go back to hemp. It's important to recognize when there's a better way, Stark."

He snagged his book with a huff, and reordered it.

"Let's talk about your killer client," he said.

"Here? I'm astonished you want to address evidence that reflects so poorly on your boss in open court."

"What evidence?"

"The evidence my paralegal transmitted to your office this morning. That was hours ago. Well, I've waited long enough. I'm ready to discuss this matter with the judge. Shall we?"

"But . . ."

"This is open-and-shut, right? Didn't you say that my client is a killer? Well, what I have to say is confidential—and fascinating. You won't want to miss this. Are you coming?" she asked again.

"Yes, yes. I'll be right along." He fumbled with his stack of books, and scanned the courtroom. He stared at the heavy oak entry.

"Are you willing it to open? If you're waiting for Stu, he's unable to make it."

"How could you possibly know that?"

"Come on back," Ruby said simply. "Besides, as a material witness, he wouldn't have been allowed in chambers with us. But you already knew that, didn't you?"

"Yes, of course."

"Johnston chose you to lead. Take charge, Stark."

His knuckles turned white as he death-gripped his briefcase. His face soon matched.

"Are you all right? Would you like to send someone else from your office down?"

"No, I'll proceed."

"Very well, then." She motioned him ahead.

They pushed past the heavy divider and filed through a discreet door.

"I appreciated the state's timely disclosure of its discovery," Ruby said. "Do you have anything further for me?"

"No, the state has disclosed its discovery."

"You've had nothing new all weekend?"

"No."

"That's odd. Fortunately, my team conducted its own investigation and recovered that footage. You know which footage I mean, right? We'd hate to see a miscarriage of justice, wouldn't we?"

He shifted. "I'd have to review it again to determine if it's all that you say."

"I could re-send the discovery if you can't locate it on your office's server."

He pulled his cell from his pocket, and checked. "Yes, well. It does appear my office received your discovery."

"I'm aware. Your legal secretary sent written confirmation to my office, as requested by my capable paralegal."

"I, I was running behind this morning."

"May I ask why?"

"Traffic."

"When did you make it in?"

"At nine."

"It's one o'clock, Stark."

"Yes. You can hardly—"

"Expect you to make the defense's disclosure in a first-degree murder case a top priority? Were you in court on another case?"

"No, I, I was preparing for this hearing."

"By not reviewing the defense's disclosure? What could have possibly taken precedence?"

"I had notes to review."

"Instructions from Stuart Johnston?"

"Well, yes. If you must know."

"I bet he was rather detailed on how to pin the murder he committed on an innocent woman."

"That's preposterous! How dare you defame the county attorney! He'll have your bar card for such an unfounded and heinous accusation. Where's your proof?"

"In the discovery file I sent over."

Stark stood still, jaw open.

"I know of two others that followed Stu's instructions. One is dead. The other is missing. And they followed his orders perfectly."

"No, it's . . ."

"It's what?"

"It's all set. The grand jury is scheduled. It's open-and-shut."

"Do what's right. This isn't about you, Stark. It's about a woman who did nothing wrong. She deserves to go home."

He stared back at the door—lost, silent.

"See you in chambers. I trust you know the way?"

She breezed down the hall, and into reception. "Hi, Regina. I'm here on the Susan Combes matter."

When Stark entered, the Regina asked, "Who's this?"

"This is Eugene Stark. He's lead counsel for the state."

Regina raised an eyebrow at Ruby.

"An assignment made by the county attorney himself."

"I see. Go ahead."

Without waiting for Stark, Ruby strode into chambers. "Good morning, Judge Penwick."

"Please, have a seat, Ms. Miller." Not one to waste movement or time, she gave a curt nod, and asked, "Which matter?"

"Susan Combes. Fourteen-eleven-seventy-one," Ruby recited from memory.

The judge pulled the file and perused it. "Where's the prosecuting attorney—a Eugene Stark?"

"He's still in with Regina."

"What's he doing there?"

"I believe he's composing himself, Your Honor."

"Is he new?"

"New to his current position, yes."

"Is he qualified for a first-degree murder case?"

"The county attorney made the assignment."

"Then who are we to question it?"

"Precisely."

Stark emerged—pale and slouched. He focused on a chair and made a beeline for it, head down. He dropped his briefcase to his right and looked up. Somewhere along the way, he'd lost his books.

"Shall we begin?" Judge Penwick asked.

"The defense is ready to proceed."

"Go ahead, Ms. Miller."

"This morning, the defense submitted its discovery to the state."

"Have you had the opportunity to review it?"

"No," Stark squeaked.

"That's not entirely accurate, is it, Mr. Stark?"

He sank in his chair.

"What do you mean, Ms. Miller?"

"For safety reasons, I had to wait to disclose discovery until Johnston's arrest, which occurred at —" Ruby checked her PSC. "Eight-fifty-two."

"On what grounds?" the judge asked, eyebrows raised.

"Stuart Johnston is in federal custody on charges related to first-degree murder for the benefit of a drug enterprise."

Stark did a boneless slide halfway off his chair before his elbow caught in an armrest.

"I see."

"Shortly after his arrest, my paralegal sent discovery to Mr. Stark via his legal secretary. It included investigatory reports, photographs, forensic results, an expert profile by Dr. Amy Larson, and footage from surveillance equipment surreptitiously installed in my client's home by Jerald Combes."

"The victim?"

"No, Your Honor. You see, the murder for which Stuart Johnston is held is of an Anthony Priestley. He hired a plastic surgeon to give Priestley the face and prints of Combes. The surgeon is now missing."

"You cannot blindside me with this! It's not fair!"

"You arrived in the office today at nine. The discovery file was transmitted by then. You accessed the discovery file sent by my office. True?"

"Yes, but—"

"You haven't reviewed discovery?" Judge Penwick asked.

"No, Your Honor." He squirmed in his seat, and pulled at his tie.

"The most compelling piece is footage showing my client cleaning up her kitchen and heading to bed at the time of the murder."

"In light of the new evidence, will the state dismiss its case against Susan Combes?"

"I'll have to ask—"

"Stuart Johnston?" Ruby interrupted. "You can see how that'd be inappropriate, as he's held in a federal facility for the murder your office has pinned on my client. You're lead counsel, Mr. Stark. The decision is yours."

"Well, I, I won't dismiss at this time."

"Very well, then. If the state submits the evidence collected with Johnston's involvement, and excludes the aforementioned exculpatory evidence, the state may bamboozle the grand jury into returning an indictment. In which case, the defense would request an Omnibus Hearing. The issue would be probable cause. In consideration of the extenuating circumstances in this case, it's appropriate to release Susan Combes on her own recognizance until the defense may be heard on the issue of probable cause. If not an RPR, then any public safety concern would be assuaged by requiring Ms. Combes to wear a Trak bracelet. I'd request that her restrictions include movement about her home, the Ramirez Ranch for domestic-violence survivor therapy, and her place of employment."

"Domestic-violence survivor therapy?"

"Yes, Your Honor. Her husband installed surveillance equipment in her house, and a spy application on her phone. Footage from the home shows Jerald Combes fracturing her wrist. The obvious conclusion is the correct one." Ruby held up her hands. "A Trak under the requested conditions would be amenable to my client pending further proceedings."

"It was open and shut!" Stark blurted.

"If that's all the state has to add, I'll grant the defense's request."

Stark placed his hands on the armrests and looked ready to flee.

"The state will be present to go on the record in open court?"

"Yes, Your Honor."

Ruby rose, and offered her hand. "Thank you, Your Honor."

"Thank you, Ms. Miller."

Ruby returned to the courtroom, located Emilio and Colin, and motioned for them to follow her out.

"We're on track. Let's take a page from Jerry's playbook, shall we?"

"The spoofing application is activated. Stuart Johnston's number is entered. What should I send? Susan is out? She goes home today?"

"No way, this is Stuart talking," Ruby said. "Hand it over. Let's see." She typed, and said, "Your woman is out on house arrest. That should do it." She handed the PSC back to Colin. It beeped. "Well?" she prompted.

"The bitch dies tonight," Colin recited.

"He expects his biggest thrill yet," Emilio said.

"It just might be."

Arianna descended the steps and approached Susan slowly, as she did for each newcomer to her ranch, whether human or horse. Maintaining eye contact, she smiled and held out her hand, waiting for Susan to come to her. When she did, Arianna smiled. "I'm Arianna Ramirez. You can call me Anna. Welcome to my ranch. It's not big enough to get lost on, but it's the perfect size for my work. We'll take care of your bags, and get you settled."

"I don't have any—"

"Sure you do, Susan. Ruby had your things sent over. She doesn't miss a trick," Jasmine said, and started to unload.

"Justin, would you help Jasmine? I've set Susan up in the Virginia Room."

"Sure thing."

"What would you like to do, Susan?"

"I, I don't know."

"Would you like to take a walk with me? Get some fresh air after being in a stale space?"

"Yes, that sounds nice."

"I love this time of day. It's still early enough that it could turn into anything. Full of potential. What's your favorite time of day?"

"The hour before dinner."

"Why's that?"

"I'm home from work, and have the house to myself."

"You have as much time and space to yourself here as you'd like. Feel free to wander the property. It's all fenced in. You'll know when you run out of land. Would you like to meet my staff?"

"I'm, I'm not really dressed to meet anyone."

"You're dressed perfectly." Arianna led her into the stables. "They pay attention to how you act, not how you look."

A great white head poked out. "That's Willow. She's the most curious, always first to see what's going on."

As if in response, Willow shook her head and whinnied.

"It won't be long now before Trenton takes a

look."

Two stalls down, a black head appeared, shaking his mane.

"He likes to look good for company. I was going to take him into the exercise ring. Would you like to join us?" Arianna asked.

"Sure."

Arianna expertly haltered Trenton, and held the rope out to Susan. "Would you like to lead him? He's an excellent follower."

"I, I wouldn't know what to do," Susan said, and kept her free hand at her side.

"You'd take the lead rope a foot from the head collar with your right hand, and you'd hold the rest of the lead looped up in your left hand." Arianna demonstrated. "You'd face this way, bring your hand slightly forward and click your tongue. Then you'd start walking. Would you like to try?"

"What if he runs? He'd pull at my wrist." She held up her cast, and wiggled her fingers.

"I know him. He won't run. I could stand to your left and hold the looped portion. What do you think?"

"I think you should lead him. I'm no good at that sort of thing."

"You may be better than you think. Do whatever seems right. Feel free to walk alongside us. It's enough that you're with us, Susan."

Susan stayed at Arianna's side, and gazed over at Trenton. Pace matched to Arianna's, he gazed forward

—the equine silent treatment.

Tuned into him, Arianna said, "I know, Trent. You'll have your freedom soon."

When they approached a round pen, Arianna said, "You may join us or stay outside. Once you've chosen your spot, close the gate." Arianna led Trenton past the gate, and said, "Whoa."

Trenton stopped and lowered his head.

Arianna removed the lead rope, patted his neck twice, and settled on the fence next to where Susan stood—inside.

"What do we do now?" Susan asked.

"I'm going to sit right here. You can do whatever you'd like."

Susan stepped toward Trenton, and then back to the fence. She started pacing. "I, I feel like I'm supposed to do something."

"What?"

Susan held up her hand toward Trenton.

He stood still.

Susan started to cry. "I don't know. I don't know what to do."

"Where else in your life do you feel that way?"

"Everywhere."

"Horses are empathetic creatures. They pick up on cues. Trenton doesn't know what you want from him, because you don't know yourself. He's as confused as you are. You've lost touch with what you want. Your world became what Jerry wanted. It's your life, Susan. You get to choose."

"You're a horse whisperer," Susan said, awe-struck.

"That's what Ruby likes to say. We humans are not the only conscious beings to converse with one another. Horses have a native language. I've taken the time to learn it."

"You make it sound so easy." She eyed Trenton warily. "You said I'd see your staff."

"Yes, and you have. Trenton and Willow are my best therapists. My ranch is a retreat center for survivors of abuse—like you, and like me."

Susan studied her and cast her eyes down. "I had no idea. You're nothing like me. You're so sure of yourself."

"I think we're more alike than you realize. My abuser never cleaned up the mess he made. Neither will yours. He's trashed your front yard for years, and left you to clean it up. You don't have to do it alone."

"I don't know where to start."

"We're going to spend the day working through where you've been. You need to understand you weren't responsible for any of it. By the time the sun rises tomorrow, it will be over. He won't be able to hurt you anymore. And you'll have these beautiful possibilities spreading before you for your life. It's yours. It was never his. I'm going to help you figure out what to do with it, if you'd like."

"Yes, I'd like that."

"See, you've made a choice already. Well done, Susan. And look." She pointed.

Trenton ambled toward Susan.

"Hold out your hand again. This time, bow your head, and hold still."

Susan did so.

Trenton nuzzled Susan's hand.

She laughed, and stroked his nose with her free hand.

Trenton moved forward.

Susan stepped back.

Trenton stepped back.

"You're okay, Susan. You're safe. If you'd like him to move closer, hold your hand out again and bow your head."

Eyes on Trenton, she gave a heavy sigh. She extended her hand and lowered her head.

Trenton nosed in and nuzzled her hand.

"If it feels right to you, reciprocate however you'd like."

Susan walked to Trenton's shoulder and leaned her forehead against it.

Turning his head, he enfolded Susan between the barrel of his torso and his solid trunk of a neck.

"Horse hug. Trent loves giving them. He'll hold you as long as you'd like."

After a while, Susan pulled back, and stayed near him, stroking his neck. "That was . . ."

"The best thing ever?"

She broke into a grin. "Yeah, it felt amazing."

"Would you like to sit?"

"Yeah, I would." Susan joined Arianna on the fence, and watched Trenton break into a trot.

CHAPTER 20

Ruby and Emilio carried groceries into the kitchen and put them away, knowing if they put them in the wrong place Jerald wouldn't notice.

Jerald perked up and moved closer to the screen. *Look at that worthless woman*, he thought. *She needs another idiot to help her unload groceries.*

"I have no idea how you talked me into an e-geek as backup."

"I demonstrated my affinity for rigorous exercise. I can hold my own." He watched her toss ingredients haphazardly on the counter and dig through cookware, selecting a jumbo pot and perching it on the stove with a look of triumph.

Stupid woman, fumbling around.

Holding up a lemon, Emilio said, "Your cooking skills leave something to be desired."

Ruby laughed. "True, although you won't be able to say that for long. Gabi is determined to make a chef of me yet."

"Yes, she is. Until the transformation is complete, allow me to cook you dinner. My stomach and I insist."

She raised her hands and stepped away from the stove. "Go for it, Chef Milo."

He swooped down for a quick kiss.

"Enough sap. I'm hungry."

"Your romantic bent is irresistible. We must make this realistic for our audience."

"How so?" Ruby peered over his shoulder as he sliced a lemon.

That bitch isn't even replacing me with a real man.

Emilio pivoted and covered her mouth with his. He held her emerald gaze with his smoky eyes before turning back to their dinner. "Now you can attest to my agility."

Whoring herself in my house. Jerry chucked his glass at the screen, and swore when both shattered. *She deserves everything that's coming to her for all she's put me through.*

"This pert nose I'm sporting for the evening is pretty cute," Ruby said.

He tapped her nose. "I prefer slightly crooked." He turned to the cutting board to hide his smile. "Although I have a weakness for brunettes. Perhaps you'd consider a change?"

"Careful, I have very good aim. And it'd blow our cover to have me chuck this plate at your head."

"I'm relieved you've fallen as soundly under my

spell as I have under yours, *Querida*."

Ruby grinned. "And I do not have a crooked nose. It healed quite nicely."

"From?"

"From when a girl kicked me in the face during a karate tournament. We were thirteen. She was sick of second place. I left a nice bloody handprint on the back of her white karate uniform when the match was over. Good sportswomanship is important."

"That's only fair."

"I thought so. My mother was mortified."

"By your injury?"

"Yes. She feared no boy would have me. I'd be dateless and scorned at homecoming. Mother refused to let Clubfoot Cassie dash her dream—to have a daughter perfect in appearance and manner."

"Clubfoot Cassie?"

"Mother coined the nickname. She loathed that girl, and demanded that I undergo repairs."

"Why didn't you?"

"I had no interest in being a pretty, pretty princess."

"What did you want to be?"

"An international spy. Mother refused to let me study languages I insisted I'd need for my future profession."

"Such as?"

"Sanskrit, Farsi."

"You never put your differences in aesthetics aside?"

"The older I got, the more different we became. She'd tell you that her hard work amounted to nothing. I'm in an abominable profession, the sewer of the legal profession—nothing prestigious or fancy enough to tell her country-club friends about over tea."

"Your work matters."

"I know."

"You're here tonight catching a batterer, a stalker, a drug kingpin, a murderer. Nobody would have seen his sinister side if not for you. You uncovered the truth."

"It was a team effort."

"And you're humble. I keep seeing new sides to you, each appealing in its own way." He encircled her in his arms.

"I don't know how to do this. Us. I know how to take down this bastard. Let's focus on that and figure this out later. Deal?"

He released her with a quick kiss. "As you wish. Let's have a simple evening, then, of capturing a murderer. Tell me how you met our dear mutual friend."

Her smile added warmth to her eyes. "His shop was between my law school and my job at the county attorney's office. I'd pop in to look at antiques. It took my mind off the law. Alfred delighted in telling me each piece's story. He took more care with his antiques than some parents do with their children." Pain cooled her eyes.

"Rubina, I—"

"No, it's fine." Her hardened gaze said otherwise. "It's fact. Anyway, I liked that about him. How did you meet him?"

"When my mother and I came over from Spain, we had very little. What we had, we sold. I started making money as a teen, and went to Alfred to find a gift for my mother. He'd secreted away everything. He said he knew I'd be back someday for them—these pieces of our family history."

"That sounds like something he'd do. I wonder what he did with my Sherlock Holmes set."

"How did you come upon it?" he asked.

"It's all my grandmother left me. She'd read to me from it, and tell me to never mind my mother. I was destined to do great work, important work. I'm sure Alfred found a good home for it."

"Was this set leather-bound with gold inscriptions?"

"Yes, why do you ask?"

"I admired it in Alfred's shop, and made him a generous offer."

"You have it?"

"No, he refused to sell."

Ruby gave a hearty laugh. "I love Alfred."

"Well, you've given your heart to a worthy gentleman." He turned to drizzle olive oil on thick fillets of pink salmon before topping them with garlic and lemon slices.

"I have, Milo." She finished the place settings, and

peered over at him. "And he's insane if he thinks I'm eating that. I thought you were making us real food."

"Try one bite. If you're not hooked, then move onto dessert."

"What's for dessert?"

"Flan. It's a decadent custard topped with soft caramel."

"Is it a Gabi recipe?"

"Yes."

"I suppose one bite won't kill me. Want a hand?"

"There's wine in that bag." He gestured with his head, and slid their entrée into the oven.

"That I can manage."

Kottke's voice came over the two-way audio bugs planted around the kitchen. "Target spotted, heading north toward the front entrance."

"Yeah, lovebirds," Colin said. "We've enjoyed the show. I'm sure Jerry did, too. We'll listen and record on this end as soon as Jerry crosses the threshold."

"Dinner will have to wait." Emilio turned off the oven.

"Disarm only. Think you can handle that?"

He shot her an impatient glance.

"Hey, brain and brawn don't always co-exist."

"I can handle myself."

She reached up and stroked his hair. "Good. I don't want any injuries." She gave him a wicked grin. "It'd put a damper on my sex life." Turning serious, she said, "I get the take down."

"I could disable him with one jolt."

"No, nothing fancy this time. He wanted Susan to do everything the old-fashioned way. Her stand-in is going to kick his ass, no-tech."

"As you wish."

"Target is gaining access," Justin said.

With a last look, Emilio moved into the shadows of the living room.

"Not that it'll prevent you from standing at the ready armed with God-knows-what gadgets," she muttered at his back.

I knew the dumb bitch wouldn't change the locks. He smiled as he stepped into the darkness. Facing the lit dining area, he reached into his leather bag to decide how the fun would begin. He didn't see the shadows take shape. His legs flew out from underneath him, and he landed flat on his back. When he shoved to his feet, he saw his woman standing across the room, smiling. The brainless brute stood at her side, holding Jerald's black bag.

Thinking fast, Jerald said, "It's me, Susan. Don't be alarmed by my appearance. I'll explain everything."

"Oh my God, Jerry! It's you! I thought it was an intruder. I thought you were dead!" Ruby gestured to the bag. "That my birthday present?"

"Yes, it's for you, Susan. Don't open it yet." He turned to Emilio. "Did she tell you she's married? She's my wife. Mine. Get the fuck out of my house."

"He's right, Antonio. You heard him. Get your sexy Spanish ass out of here," Ruby said, enjoying herself. "We had our fun. The real man of the house is home now. Leave us alone so I can welcome my husband home properly."

"That's more like it. You heard the woman. Get out of my house."

"And set my gift on the table on your way out. No hard feelings, Antonio." She waited for Emilio to slam the garage door.

She strode across the living room, smile in place. "Now things can go back to the way they were, Jerry. I know you didn't mean for me to end up in that terrible place. Everything's going to go back to normal now. We'll be happy. Won't we, Jerry?"

He waited until she was within arm's length before grabbing her and spinning her into a chokehold.

Ruby gripped his arm with both hands and struggled to pull it far enough away to breathe.

"You were supposed to go to Mardova. But I have a new plan. I'll get my things back sooner than I thought, and I'll never have to worry about you wrecking my plans again. You're done being a pain in my ass, woman."

"Not quite yet, Jerry." She yanked his arm away from her neck. Dropping her hips and sinking her base, she tripped and flipped Jerald to the side. She jammed her knee into his throat and produced a gleaming knife. "Recognize this? I take care of what's mine. It's nice and sharp. I want you out of my life, Jerry. I mean it. It's over. I'm not yours. I never was."

"You have no idea, you stupid bitch. No idea what's been going on under your nose."

"What? Are you a drug addict? Is that it? Maybe if we get you into treatment, we can go back to being happy. Maybe you didn't know what you were doing." Ruby pressed, taking away his defenses one by one.

"I knew exactly what I was doing. I'm a fucking chemist. The best Tycon has ever seen. I knew I could make the best. I deserve the best, like the women I've been fucking. Not like you, you fat cow. Real women. Your nosey bitch of a lawyer should've let you get shipped to Mardova where you belong. You're nothing without me."

Ruby patted her hair as she dug the knife tip into Jerald's neck. "I forgot to ask if you like my new look. It's okay if you don't. It's not permanent." She peeled off her face clay. "Not like yours. Now that's a real pro job. The key, though, is what lies in here." She tapped his hairline. "Time to clean up," she called out.

Agent Mitzu barreled through the front door followed by his team.

"Who the hell are you?" Jerald asked Mitzu when he appeared in his line of sight.

Ruby answered. "What? One minute you're a brilliant chemist and the next you're illiterate? Says right on his vest—federal agent. I called in the big guns for you, Jer-Bear."

"Allow me to introduce myself. I'm the man who's not going to rest until you're locked away on Mardova. Ruby's made my job a whole lot easier."

"I can't take all the credit. Wait until you see what Jerry's surgeon left us. He'll have to undergo another procedure."

"You can't do that," Jerald said.

"No, I can't, but Agent Mitzu here has the power of the federal government behind him. They'll find everybody that you made disappear. Mardova or dead —right, Jerry? I can see the appeal. If you weren't going to a manmade hell, I'd be tempted to send you to the real deal myself."

Eyes wild, he said, "I, I didn't know what I was doing."

"It's too late for that, Jerry. On behalf of Susan, thanks for that generous birthday present. You made all of this possible."

"Need anything from me before I take him in?" Agent Mitzu asked.

"Did he drive a rattletrap here?"

"You could call it that."

"Perfect. I believe it's Anthony Priestley's car. If there's a green package in it, I'd like it when possible. Yes, it's evidence, and a good link to Priestley. You'll have better evidence once you extract that chip. It's a necklace meant for Priestley's mother. After delivering the tragic news, I want to give her something good."

"Consider it done." He gave the orders to a nearby agent. She disappeared out the front door. "You know, it'd make my job a whole lot easier if every defense lawyer was like you."

"Mine too, although I'd have to work harder to get business." She watched Agent Mitzu haul Jerald out the door.

Emilio saw Ruby's shoulders droop as adrenaline dissipated and exhaustion took hold, and went to her. Wrapping his arms around her, he held her tight, and said, "It's over, *Querida*."

She closed her eyes and sank into his strength. "We have to get these electronics out of here. I want Susan to have a home."

He kissed her head. "I'll take care of it."

"God, if she would've been here."

"She wasn't, because you discovered the truth. She's safe, and will remain so. He's not Eric, and she's not Tara. Susan will return here, when she's ready. You've given her a home."

"It was a team effort. I need to check in with the others."

"I've already sent them home. They've had a very long weekend."

"You dismissed my team?"

"Yes."

"Remind me to tell you why that's unacceptable when I've had some fuel."

"I suggest we swing by the Castle."

"I'm not up to a crowd."

"I've called ahead. We'll have Spanish food to-go."

"Yes, and let's toss out that fish," she said. "Stinky seafood would be a terrible welcome home present."

He laughed. "That worked out well for you."

"Do I still get caramel custard?"

"Yes, you can still have your flan, *Querida*."

Ruby didn't rouse until the sun had been up for hours. When she did, she looked at her clock in alarm, and at Emilio in outrage.

"You rat! You drugged my flan, didn't you? I should call Agent Mitzu to arrest you."

"I gave you a mild herbal sleep aid. It worked so well because you were exhausted." He went into the kitchen, and emerged with a tray piled high with waffles and steaming mugs. He handed her one and took the other. "You can say it." His eyes danced.

"What?" She feigned obliviousness.

"You're glad I stayed."

"Of course I am."

"Now that's progress."

"You brought me this spread. Who wouldn't want you around?"

He groaned.

"And you're an exceptional view." She said, and dug into the waffles.

Lines creased his brow.

"It makes me realize something."

"What? You'd like me to program an automaton to bring you breakfast each morning?"

"No, but you'd do that for me, wouldn't you?" She took a generous bite and made a happy hum. "I realized I could get used to this."

"Which part?" he asked, suspicious.

"The you-and-me part. The waking-up-to-you

part. To you slipping me health food disguised as waffles." She dipped her next bite in syrup, and stopped. "Not that I'd object to the breakfast-in-bed part." She chewed with a sated smile.

"Yes, we're figuring this out, aren't we?" He smiled at her.

She took in his appearance. "I'm not going to ask how you got those fancy duds to my apartment. But don't let me keep you. You've spent much more time at my office than yours lately. Go be a global tycoon, whatever that involves. I'm fine, Milo. I have a busy day ahead, too." She scooted out from under her tray and wrapped her arms around his neck, pushing him back to the door as she gave him an enthusiastic kiss. "Thanks for breakfast," she said when she broke the contact. She opened the door and gave him a playful swat. "Now scoot."

He scanned her face. Color bloomed in her cheeks, and her eyes sparkled. "Very well. I've done all I can here. Unless . . ."

She laughed. "Later, Milo."

He left, satisfied he'd distracted her from her hard day ahead.

She sang her way into her shower in an off-key soprano.

Ruby parked in front of a rambling house. The porch engulfed the exterior as far as the eye could see. An old chair rocked itself in the breeze. The seasons had given it character.

She got out and leaned against her car, eyes closed to enhance her other senses. As the sun warmed her face, her smile bloomed and she gave into the urge to reach up in a luxurious stretch. Bringing her arms down, she inhaled the familiar mix of scents—wildflowers, hay, and summer. When she eased open her eyes, she laughed.

A stream of chestnut and bright yellow dashed to embrace her.

"Hey, Ari."

"Hey yourself. You look pretty damn good for having been through the ringer. A certain Spaniard didn't have anything to do with it, did he?"

"It's not over yet, Ari. And yeah, I may have had waffles in bed."

"Is that code?"

"No."

"He knows the way to your heart. Come in, let's get you coffee. I made it strong, knowing you'd turn up at some point."

"How's she doing?"

"She's in rough shape, but I've seen worse. We began yesterday afternoon. She's as skittish as a foal. Trenton didn't know what to make of her, at first, and neither did she."

"It's a start."

"Yes, it's a start. A good one. He ended by giving her a horse hug, and prancing around for her."

"Ever the showoff."

Arianna held her by the shoulders, and took a good look at her. Satisfied by what she saw, she said, "I'm so happy you're here. You missed a delicious breakfast. Justin has been spoiling us rotten."

"Isn't he supposed to be on protection duty?"

Arianna beamed.

"You look happy."

"I am happy."

"I see you, and have hope for Susan."

"You should. She's a survivor, and stronger than she knows."

"You're the expert. Any chance there are leftovers?"

"Didn't you say Emilio fed you?"

"Yes."

"You're a bottomless pit. Ask Justin."

"I think I'd have better luck if you asked him."

"Ruby, stop."

"Are you blushing? What went on with you two last night? Did you two have waffles in bed?"

"Stop it!" She nudged Ruby with her shoulder. "Your turn. What about the e-hunk?" She bent to pick a daisy, and held it to her nose.

"I can't get enough of his waffles."

Arianna swatted her with the flower. "You know what I mean."

"I can't figure him out."

"I bet that drives you crazy."

"He's full of surprises." She caught Arianna's look, and asked, "What?"

"You've fallen for him." She grabbed Ruby, and squeezed.

"Stop bouncing me around. I'm not happy about this."

"Oh, but I am. You're a walking contradiction, Roo."

"Real supportive, Ari. How's that helpful?"

"In your professional life, you relish investigating —brainstorming the novel, testing the uncertain. There's no guarantee of success, and it doesn't stop you from committing to a path. You go with your gut, because it's worth the attempt, even if you're wrong."

"And you think he's Mr. Right?"

"Let's see, brilliant, handsome, rich—he's the most eligible bachelor for good reasons. But that's not why he could be right for you. I'm saying it's worth finding out. Go for it in your personal life."

"Those must have been damn good espresso beans. He really won you over, didn't he?

"I really like him, Roo."

"What if—"

"Get out of your own head. I know how to distract you."

"How?"

"Cinnamon rolls. Gooey frosting."

"Lead the way."

She linked arms with Ruby, and led her up the steps and into the kitchen.

"Look what I found, wasting away in the front yard." Arianna walked over to Kottke, and gave him a long kiss.

"Okay, this is too weird without nourishment. Maybe even with. Don't get me wrong, I'm happy for you guys, but hold off for a minute. Set me up with the goods, and I'll be on my way."

Justin pulled rolls from the oven. "I knew it was only a matter of time before you showed up." He filled a plate, and poured coffee. "Now scram." He served her, and waved her away, grinning.

"You don't have to tell me twice. Where's Susan?"

"In the stables or out for a walk. She hasn't been going far."

Ruby sat in the mudroom, a safe distance from whatever sounds might come from the kitchen. She devoured her rolls, and washed them down with coffee. Fortified, she rose and went out the back door empty-handed, feeling lighter than she had in days. The ranch had spun its magic around and through her.

She walked down the path, and waved when Susan sighted her.

Susan ran to wrap Ruby in an embrace. "Thank you, thank you. I can't say it enough. I don't know what else to say."

Ruby patted her back, fingers sticking to fabric. "You're very welcome, Susan. How are you doing here?"

"I love it. There's so much space. And Justin and Arianna have been wonderful."

"You're welcome to stay here longer. I'm sure

Arianna has told you about her program. It's your choice to enter it, or you can go back home."

Susan's eyes flashed with fear.

"Susan, it's safe there now. We swept it. Nobody is watching you. Nobody is there to tell you what to do or how to do it. Jerry is locked up. He's not getting out. It's a process. It'll take a while to feel like home. But it's yours."

"I'd like to stay here a while, if that's all right."

"Arianna is thrilled to have you. If you think Kottke's cooking was good, wait until you try Ari's. You're in exceptional hands."

"I am. I do feel safe here."

"Good."

She hugged herself. "I'd almost forgotten what that felt like."

"Do you mind walking me to my car?"

"No, not at all."

When they reached the car, Ruby pulled a blue box with delicate white ribbon from the passenger seat and handed it to Susan.

"This is beautiful."

"I can't take credit for the wrapping job."

Susan pulled the ribbon, and slowly opened the box.

"The suspense is killing me, and I know what's in it."

Susan pulled her hand back as if slapped. "I'm sorry. You're nice enough to give me a present and here I am futzing. I'm always doing that."

"No, I'm sorry, Susan. I was kidding. Take your time. You're doing it perfectly."

Susan lifted the top and pulled back the tissue. She raised her hands to her face as tears spilled. "How did you—"

"It's not the same one. The pieces of yours are back under your bed. This was hand-painted by the same artist. Do you like it?"

"I, I don't even know what to say."

"You don't have to say anything. I brought it here figuring you might stay. It might make it feel more like home."

"Thank you," she managed as she sobbed, clutching the vase to her chest. She wiped her eyes, and examined it. "It's beautiful."

"So are you. You'll find that out more and more the longer you stay here."

"I'll go put it on my nightstand. Arianna said I can pick flowers, and do whatever I please."

"That sounds wonderful. You'll want to make a lot of noise on your way in."

Susan laughed. "They're great together. Justin has treated me so well."

"There are a lot of great guys out there, Susan."

"That reminds me. Emilio called today, and told me about the Gabriella Center. He invited me there for dinner on Thursday."

"You're in for a treat."

"They do food prep the old-fashioned way. Emilio said they could use my help. I think I'd like that."

"I'm so happy for you, Susan."

"I'm happy, too. I realized it as I was taking my walk. I didn't recognize it right away—it's been so long since I've felt this way. I used to dance and laugh and host parties."

"You'll do so again. Let Arianna know when you'd like to throw a party. She's always up for an excuse to salsa."

CHAPTER 21

Ruby charged into her office. "Where's Cass?"

"She beat you in by hours, Ruby. You're buying lunch tomorrow."

"We'll see about that."

"She didn't agree to a rule change, did she?"

"No, I have something else that might work, though."

"What do you have in mind?"

"Is Cass in her office?"

"No, she's in court. She'll be back around five."

"What's her schedule for the rest of the week?"

"Meetings, a mediation."

"Could they be moved?"

"Yes. Are you going to tell me why?"

"I will if you give me a hand with a little surprise for Cass."

"Does it involve heavy lifting?"

"It might. But I promise there's a reward in it for

you that you're really going to like."

"Better than Belgium chocolate?"

"Yes, better than chocolate."

"Better than sex?"

"It's right up there."

"I'm in."

"Clear Cassie's schedule, and meet me in her office."

Ruby and Colin stood back and admired their work.

Checking the time, Ruby said, "We'd better take our positions, or she'll suspect something's up."

Minutes later, Cassie stalked in, dressed to impress for court and hopping mad. She smiled at Colin before glaring at Ruby. "You're unbelievable!"

"What?" Ruby raised an eyebrow at Colin who shook his head.

"Two words, Rubina Miller. Two words. Emilio Martín. I'm out of the office for three days, and you manage to get a legend as a consultant. Do you have a stash of gold bars I don't know about?"

"No, he's a friend of Alfred."

"No way." She shook her head in disbelief. "Alfred never ceases to amaze me. Well then, I'd like his number. I require our new e-man's services." She wiggled her eyebrows, and leaned on Colin's desk.

"No, you don't." Ruby glowered.

"Come on, Ruby, we have in our midst the most

eligible man on the planet, and I'm not even exaggerating—"

"That's refreshing," Ruby interjected.

"You can't tell me you haven't noticed his hunkiness factor. Introduce me."

"Weren't you saying last week that your thing with that corporate attorney is turning into something?"

"That was before I had a shot with the prime bachelor. Unless, of course, you want dibs. After all, you did see him first."

"Dibs?" Ruby echoed, amused.

"Not that either of us are his type. Too brainy, no man-made enhancements. He takes the leggy, ultra-curvy type to his fancy functions."

"I hate to break it to you, Cass. But he's taken."

"No! Who is she? Model? Starlet?"

"Criminal-defense lawyer."

"Wait, I should have known. I know exactly what's going on here. This is a prank, isn't it? You've been gearing up for this, laying the groundwork. I'm not going to fall for this. I'm going to put my briefcase in my office, and then come back here and get a full confession to this farce."

"You do that, Cass."

She stalked off.

"Wait for it," Colin said. "Five, four, three, two—"

"Rubina Miller!"

"I think it's time to head home and pack your bags, Colin."

"Pinch me."

Ruby obliged.

"Not that hard." He rubbed his upper arm, and then beamed. "We're on vacation."

"Enjoy yourself, Colin. You've earned it."

"You're the best boss."

"Can I tell Cass?"

"Yes. Give me a five minute head start."

"Will do," Ruby said, and went down the hall. When she stepped into Cassandra's office, she did a wide circle. She pointed to the ceiling where she and Colin had mounted Cassandra's furniture, mirroring its prior placement. "Love your new décor, Cass. Very forward thinking." She pulled out her PSC. "Smile for the camera, Cass. Be a good sport." She moved to the threshold and left Cassandra in the middle of the room. "It's only fair. You made a vid of me wading through a paper flood in my office."

"Why the hell not?" Cassandra threw out a hip, and gave a sassy smile. She got into it, and held up her arms as if holding the scales of justice.

"The camera loves you."

"Let me see."

"In a second." Ruby tapped her PSC, and looked up, satisfied. "PSC, display on-screen."

The wall screen blinked on and showed Cassandra, arms up, furniture above. She saw the slogan, and read, "'When your world is turned upside down . . . Wait, Ruby, is this?" She clapped her hands over her mouth.

Ruby nodded, and said, "'Trust Cassandra Dayton

to set it right.' It's your new billboard. I negotiated for a two-for-one. By the way, we're on vacation. By the time we get back, your billboard will be up."

Cassandra started laughing so hard she bent double. When she recovered, she swiped a tear from her eye, and said, "Rubina Miller, I have to hand it to you. This is extreme pranking, even for you. There's no way in hell you're giving me a billboard, dating the world's most eligible, and going on vacation. This is all part of the gag, right?"

"None of it is." Ruby left Cassandra gaping in her wake. She popped her head back into Cassandra's office. "By the way, your plaque is crooked. And no, I'm not helping you get your furniture down. I have a hot date."

She found his outer office unstaffed, and his door wide open. Ruby stepped to it, and watched him. He sat at his gleaming desk, concentration on his chiseled face while he studied his wall screens. He fits here, surrounded by streaming numbers and an ambience of power and prestige. She wondered at a man who could be as at ease in a resurrected graveyard of tech discards as in the sleek and streamlined.

She believed he could do anything from here, high above the city. And yet he'd thought to build a castle for his mother, to find a job for a survivor, to open his properties to a widow and her daughter. He hadn't captured her with his looks, his wealth. He'd won her with his choices.

She knocked lightly at the doorjamb.

His eyes warmed at the sight of her. "Rubina."

And he'd chosen her. The wonder of it stole her breath.

"What brings you here?"

She held up bulging bags and moved toward a small table.

Joining her, he asked, "What's that delicious smell?"

"You missed Thai night at the Castle because of me. I figured it's the least I could do." She set the bags on the table, and turned. "There, now I can say hello." She gave him an enthusiastic kiss and broke free. "I'm starving. You know, this mushy stuff isn't as hard as I thought it would be. It certainly has its perks. Makes me hungry though."

"What doesn't?" He produced place settings from a discreet compartment.

Table set, he scooped up generous portions of noodles and ladled out miso soup. "Two lockups and one release—it's a lot of action for a single case. Are your cases usually this lively?"

"Yes. But doing it all in three days is a new firm record." She put her hand on his. "It was a nice thing you did for Karen and Claire Abrams."

"I wanted to help his family find joy in living. Losing a father is never easy, regardless of the circumstances."

She caught the spasm in his jaw. "And Susan is

thrilled about the Gabriella Center. It's a wonderful idea. She'll love it there."

He shrugged.

"You're a softy."

"It's nothing. You remind me incessantly I'm a gazillionaire."

"You thought to do it. You made it happen. You're a softy."

"Yes, I suppose so. I have no desire to be macho and unaffected. That was my father, not me. I've no inclination to fight bulls, or be surrounded by a gaggle of women. And I'm not the only softy in this relationship."

"You aren't?"

"No, Alfred told me about the vase."

"He did, did he? No confidentiality—what kind of a shop is he running?"

"Susan loved it, I presume."

"Yeah."

"It's those moments that make this all worth it for you, isn't it?"

"Yeah, I guess so."

"Softy." He gripped her hand before he continued. "Colin told me that Eric Longhorn transferred to Mardova today."

"His shuttle took off at three."

"Colin was surprised that you didn't visit Longhorn before his transfer to give him a piece of your mind."

"I thought about it—a lot. What I'd say. How I'd

say it. I'd tell the bastard Tara was never his."

"Why didn't you?"

"My time was better spent elsewhere, on women who have bright futures. I had enough closure for one day."

"Is that what this is? A farewell dinner?" He pushed back his plate.

"If you want it to be."

"And if I don't?"

"I'm not due back in the office until Monday."

"The infamous Ruby Miller takes a vacation? Unprecedented."

"I figured since you own half the planet you might know of a few good vacation spots."

"What are you after?"

"Secluded. No reception."

"We can find secluded. Satellites make unreachable impossible. Fortunately, your PSC has an off setting."

"Wow, this gadget does have everything."

He pushed back from the table, and moved to his desk. "I have something for you, Rubina." Pulling a velvet box from his desk drawer, he approached her, held it out, and opened it.

She sat motionless, hand at her throat, as she stared at the gleaming turquoise gems and black pearls.

"When it catches the light, its colors transform. They're stunning in all their dimensions."

"Is, is this from Alfred's?"

"No, it's from my personal collection."

"From Spain?"

"Yes."

"Why did your mother leave Spain, Milo?"

"E-skills are in my blood, but not making an honest living from them. You see, my father was *un fantasma*."

"A phantom?"

"No, trust me. He was flesh, bone, and deadly. It's a Spanish saying. Literally, yes, it means ghost. It's used to describe someone who's not what they appear."

"Like Jerald Combes."

"Yes, similar to Combes. My father seemed to be a handsome bullfighter, a family man. He loved the attention. And on the side he was an e-man. That's where he made his real money. He was one of the best, until Interpol caught up with him. It came to light he dispensed with anyone who got in his way."

"Where is he?"

"Mardova."

"Was it hard to see him go?"

"Most of me was glad to be free of him. I didn't get the chance to grow big enough to fight him off until he was already in prison. If I had, I might have killed him for what he did to my mother."

"Why didn't your mother stay in Spain after he was in prison? Didn't she have family there?"

"He'd isolated her from them. When I told you I understood the dynamics of domestic violence, I meant firsthand. But you already put that together at the Castle."

"Yes, we don't have to talk about it tonight."

"You need only look at my mother to know she's in a happy chapter of her life. And Susan will be, too. Thanks to you."

"It was a team effort. It always is." She toyed with a gem. "I'm not comfortable accepting this. It's beautiful, truly."

"I'm not comfortable I wanted so much to give it to you. It would seem we are even."

"And Gabi is okay with this? With me wearing it?"

"With you having it. It's yours—no strings, no expectations. She's thrilled. She cried when I told her. That's yet another aspect I'm uncomfortable with."

"Gazillionaire thrown off his game by a lady lawyer. I am making headlines. And yes, I accept." Her eyes met his as he clasped the bracelet on her wrist. "I still haven't decided what to do about you."

"Bringing me Thai food was a wonderful idea. May I suggest dessert?" He grinned at Ruby.

"I, I don't think—"

"The new face of criminal defense blushes?" He teased. "My FastFare is slightly better stocked than yours. What would you like?"

"Surprise me."

He typed a command into his PSC, and said, "I know why Arianna does her work. You've guessed at why my mother does hers. Why do you, Rubina?"

"You already know I didn't get to be sweet sixteen. Sixteen was the hardest year of my life. My mother was mortified what her friends would think. The scandal. My father was happy to sweep it under the rug. Nobody stood for me. Nobody told my story. And I was too hurt, too afraid, to speak for myself. I was drowning in my own shame when I met Amy. She tugged me to shore. She helped me find my voice."

"And that's why you stand for your clients." He brought her a piece of cake.

She stabbed at it without picking it up. "Seems like an awful lot of fruit. What is it?"

"Pineapple-mango upside-down cake, smothered in caramel. It's made Thai-style with coconut milk as an appropriate end to your themed meal. The tropical fruit will give you a taste of vacation."

She put down her fork. "You put that much thought into picking out my dessert?"

"Why wouldn't I?"

"Milo . . ."

"Yes, Rubina?"

"It was you. It was this." She gestured. "This is what I was waiting for at sixteen. I'd stuffed it down, I guess. You made it happen for me. I don't want to mess this up. I'm not any good—"

"Oh no, you don't. Not after a speech like that. You're not getting off that easy. It's my turn to reciprocate."

She took a deep breath.

"I love you, Rubina."

"Well, then. It's a good thing I love you back." She

sighed—relieved at how easily the words had flowed and the sense of rightness they triggered. Forking up cake, she asked, "How's Chiang Mai for secluded?"

ABOUT J. R. RASK

A strong champion for equality and empowerment, Activist **Rita Johansen** writes romantic suspense novels under the pen name **J. R. Rask**. An attorney with a background in criminal law, she's quick to say her fiction works are true flights of fancy. Criminal cases do not unfold this way in real life. Intended as a fun frolic, she hopes that you enjoyed your adventures with Ruby Miller and her eclectic team.

Visit her websites:

www.jrrask.com
www.ritajohansen.com

HEARTFELT MESSAGE

Thank you, dear Reader, for making time to read my story. The best part for me, as an author, is to hear from my readers! Your feedback, insights, and stories matter to me. And I love to hear your ideas and hopes for these colorful characters I created. Who knows, maybe your input will impact a future book as Ruby's adventures continue to take shape.

I invite you to:

- Review my book on Amazon, Goodreads, or another reader-community website;
- Email me at rita@ritajohansen.com, or at author@jrrask.com;
- Visit my website, www.ritajohansen.com, to discover more about me and my work to empower women;
- Visit my website, www.jrrask.com, for fun extras, and for the latest on my romantic-suspense works;
- Tweet me, @TrueRita, #DefendingtheHunted.

I wish all my fiction-loving friends out there many more delightful adventures immersed in the pages of a good read. And may you, with each passing moment, create the kind of life story you will someday review and say, "Wow!"

With great appreciation,
Rita Johansen

ALSO AVAILABLE FROM RITA JOHANSEN:

TRUE TO YOU
A REVOLUTIONARY WAY TO GROW YOUR PROFESSIONAL PRACTICE

In business, we have countless opportunities to stay true to, or betray, who we are. We can do what everyone else is doing, and moan and wail that we're surviving, not thriving. Or we can dare to do business differently for extraordinary outcomes. When Rita Johansen launched her solo practice, she shattered the Mr. Defender Model for a criminal-defense lawyer. Using her own experiences, Johansen guides us through the True to You Approach™ to use the greatness within you to transform your professional practice. You'll learn how to claim your rightful place, magnetize your right-fit clients, cultivate meaningful relationships, and set and exceed expectations to satisfy clients.

35487600R00201

Made in the USA
Charleston, SC
10 November 2014